Dear Reader,

In one of his books—the first, I think—Robert Fulghum included a storyteller's creed, a powerful piece containing many sentiments with which I heartily agree.

Those of us who write romance live in a special place. Daily, we have the opportunity to look hard at a world that seems to embrace ugliness and violence and search there for the beautiful and the good.

If I had a creed for my vocation it might be this: that I believe in the power of love and the tenacity of human courage. I see that heroism exists in real people and that humans can forgive even the unforgivable. I know that love begins before life and lives on after death and that life's strongest bonds are not first of blood but of love. I accept that truth is told in fiction and that, as my father is fond of saying, a novel should be first and foremost a good read.

I hope you enjoy *Waiting for You*, its landscapes and escapes, and especially its people, Christopher and Dulcinea, who, with courage and compassion, rescue and protect each other and reaffirm a love that once seemed as though it wasn't meant to be.

Please write to me at P.O. Box 611, Montrose, CO 81402-0611. Your letters help *me* believe.

Sincerely,

Margot Early

Margot Early
WAITING FOR YOU

Harlequin Books

TORONTO • NEW YORK • LONDON
AMSTERDAM • PARIS • SYDNEY • HAMBURG
STOCKHOLM • ATHENS • TOKYO • MILAN
MADRID • WARSAW • BUDAPEST • AUCKLAND

For my mother and father,
who gave me life,
who first showed me love,
and who have always taught me to look for
the best in people...
because it is there.

ISBN 0-373-70694-4

WAITING FOR YOU

ACKNOWLEDGMENTS

I am indebted to the following people for help with this book:

My heartfelt gratitude to Mary Miller, for anwering my questions about Dopplers, for letting me share the experience of an ultrasound and vicariously enjoy her pregnancy, and, especially, for letting me hold the baby.

Many thanks also to Goddards' Peruvian Paso Horses. The Goddards supplied me with invaluable information about this fascinating and spectacular breed and invited me to ride their splendid Paso stallion, Rayo del Sol, a creature of gentleness, grace and *brio*.

Additionally, I'm very grateful to D'Ann Linscott-Dunham, for sharing her love and knowledge of horses, and to the Linscott family, for providing some of my best experiences with these animals.

Most of all, I would like to thank my father, James M. Early, who knows more about technology than I ever will, for all his assistance with this project. He and my mother have encouraged my hopes and dreams in ways too numerous to mention here.

All technical errors in this fictional work are mine.

...the Princess said, "Take off your cap. It is not proper for you to wear it before me."
He answered again, "I may not take it off because I have a wound on my head."
But she took hold of the cap and pulled it off, and all his golden hair tumbled over his shoulders in a shower. It was quite a sight....

—"Iron Hans," the Brothers Grimm

Grimms' Fairy Tales
by the Brothers Grimm
translated by Mrs. E. V. Lucas,
Lucy Crane and Marian Edwarde
(1945. Grossett & Dunlap)

CHAPTER ONE

Sneffels, Colorado

THE CLINIC WAS HOUSED in a two-story Victorian building on Silver Street. The sidewalk in front was sloped, like the snow-packed gravel streets that made the whole town of Sneffels seem pitched at angles. On each side of the narrow valley, the peaks rose so steeply that in many places the snow wouldn't hold to the faces, leaving bare rocks in colors such as Dulcinea had never seen. Burgundy red. Gold. Powdery white cascaded down chutes between them; perhaps that explained the distant rumbling she had heard periodically since she'd stepped off the van from the airport. Avalanche blasting.

As she heard another far-off explosion, she stared through her steaming breath at the words on the window of the clinic, the same words hanging on a shingle over the sidewalk.

SNEFFELS FAMILY PRACTICE
Christopher Choqueneira, M.D.

Cristobal, thought Dulcinea.

She had found him. He was really here, alive and well in the United States. He was more than an address on the torn-off corner of an envelope she'd found among Barnabas's belongings. He was here in Sneffels, Colorado, U.S.A.

Summoning courage, Dulcinea reached for the handle, pulled open the door and stepped up into the clinic. She paused just inside the doorway, taking in the Victorian furniture that looked as though it had never been re-upholstered, the magazines strewn over an incongruous varnished table made from a tree stump, a basket of children's toys in the corner between a tattered love seat and a long couch.

On the walls hung a poster about a recall on infant car seats, a rack of brochures on subjects from alcoholism to breast cancer, a framed botanical print, signs in English and Spanish about the hazards of smoking and the benefits of breast-feeding, and posters issuing warnings about back-country travel: lightning, hypothermia, frostbite, avalanche and other wilderness dangers.

No one was in sight. Even the room behind the reception window was deserted. A row of scarred wooden filing cabinets faced her, and over them hung more posters and signs, which she began to suspect covered tears in the ancient wallpaper. A waist-high partition at a ninety-degree angle to the front counter divided the office area from a hallway that must lead back to the examining rooms.

There was no sign of Christopher Choqueneira, M.D.

Her brother-in-law, who had once been something else to her. Who had once been something more.

Nausea passed through her in waves, and Dulcinea's hand dropped to her abdomen, over the pile sweater she'd picked up in the "free box" on the street, where citizens of Sneffels left discards for whoever might take them. As she stood fingering the barely worn pile, thinking of what lay beneath, inside her, she heard a door open down the hallway, and voices.

One—elderly, female, with a quiet melodious drawl—said, "Well, I'm sorry for going on and on so. I know your time is valuable."

"What you told me is valuable," answered her companion. "I love hearing stories about the Politician Mine. That's family history."

Dulcinea's heart shook in her chest. She knew *that* voice. Low. Resonant. With a unique warmth and depth. A voice that could laugh and flirt or drop to gentle and tender tones. A voice Dulcinea would have recognized just as easily had its owner been speaking Spanish or Quechua or Aymara.

She edged along the reception window toward the hallway. Her stomach felt as though insects were swarming inside it, but she crept forward, clutching the front counter and peering past the partition at the visible section of corridor. Each step felt like a mile, and all she could think was that he was so close, the man she had traveled from another continent to find. Everything depended on Christopher Choqueneira.

It was a bitter acknowledgment. God, that she had to *see* him after all he'd cost her. But everything she had was invested in coming to ask his aid. And she was at the mercy of the man who'd abandoned her six years earlier and disappeared without a word or a trace. A man who had cost her everything that ever mattered to her. Who had ruined her life.

A man she hated.

He was still talking, asking the woman if she'd had her back porch repaired yet, and Dulcinea followed the sound of his voice until she stared down the hall and saw him, not ten feet away. He spoke with a small silver-haired woman dressed in white slacks and a navy cashmere coat, leaning on a cane.

Six years had passed, but Dulcinea knew him at once.

He stood with casual grace, listening attentively as his patient said, "Well, I appreciate your advice about not lifting groceries. It's just so hard when I'm alone."

"I'll tell you what. Why don't you write a list for me, and I'll pick up your groceries when I go into Ridgway? You'll save money that way, too. The prices are better there."

"Oh, I couldn't ask you to..."

Dulcinea barely heard. Her eyes ate up the man in the hallway—the worn denim clinging to his hips and his long legs, the black fleece pullover hugging his broad shoulders.

His hair.

He still wore it long, shoulder-length. Straight, thick, mussed. It was carelessly bound in a ponytail, windswept as though he'd just returned from snowshoeing in the woods, and to her eyes it still shone bright as the sun, almost supernaturally bright, beautifully at odds with his darker skin.

As Dulcinea stared, her heart in her throat, he glanced down the hall and saw her. An unconscious sexual reaction stirred just below her rib cage. *No,* she thought. Not still.

He said, "I'll be with you in a moment." Giving her a brief, polite smile, he turned back to the older woman, but only an instant passed before he looked toward Dulcinea again. A double take.

He paled. "Dulcinea?"

Her pulse seemed rapid and weak as she felt the impact of his eyes. Brown, almost black, irises were rimmed by whites that seemed startlingly clear against his light golden tan. His gaze swept over the sweater she'd picked up in the free box, the dark red pile cardigan with its navy zipper and pockets and trim, and she had the unsettling feeling that he knew where she'd gotten it.

The thought embarrassed her. Her cheap khaki trousers showed twenty-four hours of travel in the bed of a supply truck—a *camión*—and on one of those decades-old Bolivian planes that looked as though they'd been purchased secondhand from another Third World country. Travel conditions had improved once she reached the United States, but she had no change of clothing. All she carried was the oversize leather purse Barnabas had brought her from Brazil, and it contained little of value— to anyone but her. She felt tawdry, gauche, unfeminine. And she was miserable to have to appear before Christopher Choqueneira thus arrayed.

She loathed having to see him at all, and being in his presence after six years seemed like a hallucination brought on by hunger and fatigue.

But it was Christopher. There was no mistaking his hair, nor his face, with the slight signs of beard and mustache, as though he shaved sporadically. The blend of features inherited from his American mother and from his father, a Kallawaya Indian of Bolivia. The Kallawaya were the famous herbalists of the Andes. Healers.

Christopher was a healer, too.

It was really him.

Dulcinea swayed on her feet.

He moved fast. Closing the space between them in a few strides, he gripped her forearm, and Dulcinea stared down at his fingers, which seemed harder and less polished than she had expected the hand of an American small-town doctor to look. Trembling, she lifted her eyes to his face. It was her first close view of him in the better part of a decade. He seemed altered in ways she lacked the strength or presence of mind to pinpoint. But it was him.

And, God, he was still so handsome, so eerily like his brother and yet entirely different. They were fraternal twins—unlike. It had been her mistake to think one could take the place of the other. But their similarities had haunted her for six years.

Before her flew the past weeks of indecision, the fear, the solitude, the shame of the steps she'd been forced to take to afford the trip to Colorado. The reality that she had gambled everything on this moment.

As she met Christopher's eyes, a wave of sickness swept over her again, and she thought she might faint.

He steered her into the office area behind the reception counter, yanked a stenographer's chair across the floor and propelled her into it. She sat.

From the hallway, the elderly woman peered into the office. "Is something wrong? Can I help?"

Christopher considered. The best thing would be to finish with Mrs. Prosper and see her out. The sidewalks were icy; he should help her to her car. But Dulcinea was so pale he didn't dare leave her until he learned the problem.

He told Mrs. Prosper, "No, thank you, but if you take a seat in the waiting room, I'll see you out in a moment."

She sighed. "Oh, Christopher. You don't need to help me to my car."

"I'm happy to. I'll just be a minute." Christopher turned away, closing the subject, and he heard her continue toward the waiting room.

Crouching beside Dulcinea, his eyes taking in everything, Christopher bit down a dozen questions. The staggering thing was that she was here in Sneffels. The bizarre touch was that she was wearing the pile cardigan he'd just left in the free box. *Dulcinea de la Torra rooting through the free box?*

What in hell was going on?

He found her dark eyes in her white face and waited until they met his. Then he asked, "Are you all right?"

She nodded, but her face was damp with perspiration.

Christopher stood up and strode across the hall to the bathroom. Swiftly, he filled a paper cup with water, returned to the office. He handed the cup to Dulcinea and watched her bring it to her mouth. Abruptly, she handed it back to him and put her head down between her knees.

His hand moved instinctively toward her hair, then stopped before he could touch her. Instead, he opened a cabinet and removed a plastic dish.

Realizing he thought she was going to be sick—and that she might be—Dulcinea was mortified. She made herself lift her head, even as saliva filled her mouth and heat enclosed her like a sauna. "I'm fine."

Christopher couldn't hear her, though he had seen her mouth move and knew she had spoken. Irritated, he automatically recited the words he resented, the words he uttered at least once a day. "I'm sorry. I didn't catch that. I'm deaf in my right ear. It helps if you look at me when you speak."

She looked, her eyes too big and dark. She seemed malnourished, anemic, and her taking a sweater from the free box assumed new meaning.

"What happened to your ear?"

Christopher stared at her, astonished that she could still be so naive. Had it slipped her mind what had happened to him after they'd parted? After her father had discovered them together?

On the verge of a bitter retort, he saw her white face and changed his mind. "*No importa.* Put your head down if you feel sick."

"I don't." Shaking, she took the cup of water from Christopher's hand and clumsily brought it to her mouth. But she knew food was what she needed. She hadn't eaten since a bag of peanuts on the flight from Denver, and now her stomach felt airy as a drum.

She tried not to think about it. She had no food, nor means to buy any. The ground transportation to Sneffels from the airport had taken her last dollars. In fact, she'd been short.

"Let me finish with this patient, all right?" Christopher tilted his head in the direction of the waiting room.

"Then we can..." Without finishing, he stood up and walked away.

Dulcinea heard the old woman saying, "How much do I owe you?"

"I'll bill you," answered Christopher. "That lady is my sister-in-law, and she's not well. I should see to her."

The front door opened, blasting cold inside. A moment later, it closed with the faint ring of a bell as they went out.

Dulcinea closed her eyes, then opened them and stared dully at the reception desk. A cumbersome botanical text lay open behind the counter, as though perhaps someone had been studying it while manning the desk. Even more than seeing him, the book seemed evidence that the clinic doctor really was Christopher Choqueneira. It was an evidence that hurt, because his knowledge of plants and herbalism represented a side of him she had admired. It reminded her that once she had loved him, but that he'd found her lacking.

It reminded her that he had left.

She reached over to the counter to set down the paper cup, then sank against the back of the chair, her hand on her stomach. The world around her was spinning. Her emotions tumbled against one another, pieces of her life falling in a heap.

Bleakness of day after day living with grief. Old heartache beyond anything she could ever have imagined six years ago. And now, the reality of being in the same room with the source of that heartache. She had expected to feel only loathing when she finally saw him again.

Instead, she felt an anguish that made anger and hatred stop cold in their tracks. Seeing his brown eyes had made her remember that once they had lain in each other's arms and loved each other—and that together their bodies had created something precious, something now gone forever. Something that could never be replicated or replaced.

Desolate, she shut her eyes, trying not to cry. Why did it still feel as though it had happened only yesterday? Would it ever stop hurting?

Uninvited, an old question came to her. *Does Christopher know?*

Had anyone told him what he'd left behind when he fled from her father six years ago?

With the last of her faith in the Christopher she'd once loved, Dulcinea told herself again that he didn't know—*couldn't* know. If he'd ever been told, he would have written to her, come to her, done something. Wouldn't he?

But she remembered again that he had deserted her, and she realized he was capable of anything—capable of refusing to help her now.

CHRISTOPHER RETURNED to the office five minutes later, after helping Kitty Prosper into her car and listening to her lengthy expression of concern for his "sister-in-law," a label Christopher had supplied but found absurd in its inadequacy—and reality. Dulcinea still sat in the chair behind the reception counter. She was resting her head in her arms on the desk, but when she heard the bell on the door she sat up and looked at him.

Christopher closed the door, shutting out the cold.

They were alone.

He came through the waiting area and around the reception counter to join her. As she stood up, he noticed again the zip-up pile jacket she wore—his castoff. Again, the sight unsettled him, but he made himself meet her eyes. A moment later, his gaze was sweeping over her features, examining her in a way he hadn't intended.

She was still snow-white under her tan. Once her skin had been like flawless ivory, and she'd been proud of it, proud as her father was of her pure Spanish blood—although she would never have admitted that pride, definitely not to a man who was part Indian, like Christopher Choqueneira.

But for the past six years Dulcinea had been living as a *campesina* at 13,000 feet above sea level in the Kallawaya village of Chulina, and it showed on her skin. How old was she now? Twenty-four? Twenty-five? Her eyes seemed older. Ancient.

Your brother's wife, coached a voice inside him. *Remember?*

He remembered . . . more.

Trying to sound like a friendly brother-in-law, rather than a man who had more than once envisioned murdering both Barnabas and Dulcinea, he asked, only a little coolly, "So, what brings you here? Did Barnabas come?"

Dulcinea stared at him, the question echoing through her. *Did Barnabas come? Did Barnabas come?*

She said, "Didn't you get my letter?"

"No." *What letter?*

Dulcinea's pulse pounded in her throat, and she forgot she hated him, forgot why. Gazing up into his eyes, she groped instinctively for one of his hands and wrapped both of hers around it. "Cristobal, your brother is dead."

The doorbell jangled. Cold air swept in, but neither looked up.

Christopher stared at her, feeling her small hands holding his. *Your brother is dead.*

Her hands slipped away.

He didn't know what to say or do or feel. His mind seemed paralyzed.

There was movement in the waiting room, a flash of red hair, someone taking off a coat and hanging it on the wobbly coat tree. Sissy, his nurse, had returned from lunch. He glanced at her, barely registering the curious look she shot him and Dulcinea.

Joining him, her freckled face betraying as much concern as twenty-two untroubled years could muster, Sissy asked, "What's up?"

Dulcinea seemed to be staring at the nurse without seeing. Quietly, Christopher told Sissy, "This is my sister-in-law, and my brother is dead."

Sissy's face changed, falling to lines of sorrow and compassion. "Oh, Chris."

"See if you can reschedule my appointments for this afternoon and tomorrow. If there's anything urgent, call Dr. Wayne in Ridgway. I'm going to take..." He made a gesture toward Dulcinea. "We're leaving. Call my pager if you have a problem."

Sissy nodded, and Christopher thanked her. He looked at Dulcinea, meeting her eyes for only an instant. "Let me get my coat, and we'll go."

As THEY STEPPED outside, Christopher watched Dulcinea huddle deeper into his cast-off pile sweater.

Outside, the day hung between snow and sunshine. Shining or not, the sun had already dropped out of sight behind Whitehouse Mountain. The Uncompahgre River gorge ran north-south, and the valley usually lay in shadow during the winter.

Avalanche blasting echoed in the distance, from up on Red Mountain Pass. Buildings, including his office, hid the southern mountains from view, but Christopher's mind was up on the pass. He was thinking about avalanches. It had snowed for two days, clearing long enough that morning for helicopters to drop charges and bulldozers to begin clearing the scenic and treacherous Million Dollar Highway that wound through the mountains from Sneffels to Silverton. But it was the season for tragedy.

As his breath plumed near Dulcinea's, Christopher asked, "Do you want to get something to eat?"

She lifted her eyes. Did he mean at a restaurant? She remembered seeing cars parked outside a diner at the corner of Main and Silver streets. On the doors of other businesses, signs read, Closed for the Season. Everywhere were decorations left over from the recent Christmas holiday, but the only activity Dulcinea had noticed on her way into town was at the big hot-springs pool at the north end of Sneffels and at several hotels that advertised their own mineral springs.

"I..." Etiquette seemed like an algorithm she'd learned in high school and forgotten. *Something to eat.* "Yes, please. I..." Her carefully prepared story came back to her then, and she made herself recite the lie. "The airline lost my luggage. I was...so stupid. Most of my money's inside. I'm afraid I'm broke."

It even *sounded* like a lie. She looked down at the pavement.

Christopher said, "Don't worry. You'll get it back. I'll—" He stopped. He'd almost said that he'd take care of her. *He* couldn't take care of her. "I'll buy lunch."

"Thank you," she said. "I'm starving." She was hungry enough to swallow her pride.

"Great. Great," answered Christopher absently. His mind echoed the haunting words she'd spoken minutes earlier. *Your brother is dead.* But his mouth pursued a topic that didn't matter. "Things are slow here in the winter. We have no ski resort. Summer is the tourist season." His eyes drifted toward hers. "How did you get here?"

"I flew into Grand Junction. The airport shuttle brought me."

Christopher nodded. They'd reached the corner, and he turned to the right and led Dulcinea to the door of a Victorian building much like the one that housed his office. There were several vehicles, mostly trucks, parked diagonally to the curb in front, near old-fashioned gaslight-style street lamps. The arched sign over the restaurant door read

Yellowjacket Café. Christopher stopped at the entrance and crouched to pet a collie-husky mutt sleeping there.

As he held the door, Dulcinea stepped inside and was immediately assaulted by noise and scent. Low talking, dishes clinking. Hamburgers, the yeasty scent of bread. Onions, garlic. American food—like her school days. Her mouth watered, and her nausea intensified.

Even the warmth of the building seemed stifling. Fans whispered near the pressed-tin ceilings, their slowly revolving blades circulating the heat from a wood stove against the north wall.

At a pine table near the stove sat four old men, their faces as lined as the mountains, drinking coffee and munching on burgers and fries. A young, athletic-looking couple in flashy outdoor togs sat near the tall front windows. They were peering up at golden rock showing through the face of a precipice to the east, and as the man spoke to the woman, Dulcinea recognized the language as German. Apparently, Sneffels had some tourists even in the off-season—probably for the hot springs.

Christopher scanned the room, looking toward a doorway on the south wall, with shadowy darkness beyond.

On her way to take the European couple their bill, a saffron-haired waitress with big hips tossed over her shoulder, "If you want to sit in the bar, I'll serve you there, Doc."

"Thanks, Marcia." At lunchtime, Christopher preferred the bar, which was usually deserted. If he ate in the restaurant, people approached him every few minutes to talk. But for some reason, the few drinkers occasionally inhabiting the bar at noon seemed to sense that he wanted to be alone. Christopher led Dulcinea to the darkened doorway. He glanced inside first and was glad to see the bar was empty. Nonetheless, he chose a corner table near the back. He pulled out a chair for Dulcinea; when they were both seated, Marcia appeared with menus.

The voluptuous, fortyish waitress smiled at Dulcinea. "I always serve the doc in here, so I can keep him to myself."

Christopher answered her saucy wink with a smile that felt unnatural. His mind was on Barnabas. His brother. His twin.

Dead.

Marcia asked, "What can I get y'all? Something to drink?"

Christopher looked at Dulcinea.

She shook her head.

"A glass of Madeira, please." After brief consultation with Dulcinea, he ordered a vegetarian pizza. Marcia slipped behind the bar to pour him a glass of wine, and he studied Dulcinea. She was still pale, still seemed exhausted. He shouldn't question her now. But he needed to, and it was easy to cast aside consideration for her when he remembered his months of torment, of holding her memory in his heart until he emerged from one hell to enter another—when he learned she had married his brother.

Aware of the waitress across the empty room, he leaned closer into the table, closer to Dulcinea. "Tell me what happened." To Barnabas. To my brother.

Your husband.

He watched her slow breaths. She seemed to lack even the energy to open her eyes, but Christopher felt no guilt.

"Two months ago. He left in his plane for Trinidad."

Christopher knew she meant the Bolivian city of Trinidad on the Rio Ibara. The violent river town had been a favorite haunt of his brother's.

"He never got there," said Dulcinea. "He went down in the forest."

"Where?"

"In the upper Yungas." She closed her mouth tightly.

The Yungas. The heavily forested area to the north and east of Cochobamba and La Paz. There, the Andes fell steeply to the Amazon Basin. One of the most beautiful areas of Bolivia. Well populated in some areas. In others, inaccessible. "Where?"

Dulcinea shook her head. "I don't know." She wouldn't meet his eyes.

She did know, thought Christopher. She knew something.

"Your uncle tried to find out."

Tomás. His father's half brother, who was by Kallawaya tradition also Christopher's "father." A Kallawaya could have many "fathers," and Tomás, in some ways, had been more father than his own. Christopher and Barnabas had been born in Sneffels, but after their mother's death, Roderigo Choqueneira had brought them home to Bolivia. While Roderigo immersed himself in academic life as a university professor in La Paz, Christopher and Barnabas had stayed with Tomás in the country village of Chulina, attending school a few miles away. Each year, their grandparents had sent plane tickets to bring them to Colorado, and they had gone for two months. That annual trip, Christopher often reflected, had been one steady force in an otherwise chaotic existence. Tomás had been another. With Christopher, Tomás had shared his knowledge of herbalism through an eight-year apprenticeship.

A long time ago, Christopher thought. He didn't ask Dulcinea how Tomás was. He didn't wonder. He had stopped wondering many things. And now he was more interested in Barnabas. He felt relief. Missing wasn't dead.

Dulcinea said, "Your uncle searched for him. He checked the prisons—"

Christopher's pulse quickened.

"—and he went to Chojlla and Chulumani and Chirca. In Huajtata, someone had seen a plane like Barnabas's fly over. The engine was smoking, but the pilot didn't attempt to land. They think he must have crashed in La Boca del Diablo."

The mouth of the devil, Christopher translated. Magic and spiritual beliefs were a way of life in the Andes—the soul of the people. It wasn't surprising that the humid treacherous area known as La Boca del Diablo had a reputation like that of the Bermuda Triangle. Disappeared planes. Disappeared hikers. Disappeared scientists. It was inhospitable country. Steep terrain alternating with sweltering, snake-infested ravines. Exposed slopes where temperatures could drop below freezing with a change in the wind. Frequent landslides.

People did go in.

Few came out.

Dulcinea said, "Your uncle can't go in there. He's an old man. He wouldn't, anyway. No one will."

"If no one's found the plane, how do you know he's dead?" He couldn't attach his brother's name to that most final word.

"I know, Cristobal. I just know."

He sat back in his chair, skeptical but doing his best to hide it. She was exhausted.

Marcia brought Christopher's drink from the bar and, moments later, a basket of bread sticks from the kitchen. When the waitress had left, Dulcinea looked across the table questioningly.

"Go ahead." Christopher sipped his drink.

She reached for a bread stick and didn't bother to dip it in the red sauce before bringing it to her mouth. Nothing had ever tasted so good. The salt and garlic melted against her tongue. She gnawed hungrily, silently, until it was gone, a work of seconds, and then realized what she'd done, how swiftly she'd devoured it. She picked up a paper napkin and wiped her mouth. "I'm sorry," she said. "Airplane food. You know."

Another lie, designed to hide the real reason behind her ravenous hunger. At the thought of that reason, her spirits sank. She had been through it all before. The hunger, the fatigue, the weeks of nausea, the months of waiting. The love. She had taken every care with herself and with the other entrusted to her. She had tried to do everything perfectly, and it hadn't mattered.... The old wound was still an open sore. It would never heal. The worst thing that could happen had happened to her.

And it could happen again.

The thought dulled her appetite, but she ate, anyway, for the nourishment she needed. Christopher seemed uninterested in either food or conversation, so while he sat sipping his drink she helped herself to more bread sticks until the basket was empty but for an oil-stained paper napkin. She ate even the crumbs. Dulcinea saw him watching her, his gaze sober and steady.

He smiled faintly. "You *were* hungry."

"Yes." She looked toward the door to the kitchen, so she wouldn't have to meet his eyes.

Marcia brought the pizza, and Christopher ordered another drink. Between bites of pizza, Dulcinea nodded at his glass. "Do you do that often?"

"No." He had a good idea why she'd asked how often he drank, but he didn't want to talk about it. Discussing Barnabas's habits with Dulcinea— No. "Why are you here, Dulcinea?"

She was eating her third slice of pizza, but she put it down, and he could see her carefully choosing words. "I— I wondered if Barnabas has any property here. I thought there might be something I should do."

She shifted in her seat and said something he couldn't hear, and he turned his head slightly, frustrated. "What did you say?"

She flushed, eyes darting at his, obviously recalling what he'd told her about his ear. "I'm sorry. I forgot. I said Barnabas might have business here I should attend to. His estate."

Christopher watched her warily. At one time Dulcinea had been a woman of wealth, of privilege. Now she had spent six years living in a poor Kallawaya village, and she wanted to know if, in death, her husband would give her more than he had in life.

His mind wandered back four years. Months after Christopher's return to the States, after he'd been freed from the nightmare into which his relationship with Dulcinea had cast him, a friend from college had gone to Bolivia, visiting ruins. Anxious to learn what was happening in his brother's house, Christopher had entrusted his friend with a package of antibiotics and other pharmaceuticals for his uncle in Chulina. Unfortunately, Christopher hadn't been able to find out everything he'd wanted to know—about Barnabas or about *her*. He had learned that Dulcinea was living in the house he and his twin had once shared. She was building solar gardens, tending a very few llamas and reading from a small personal library. Barnabas was gone frequently in his airplane, and Dulcinea was closemouthed about her personal affairs.

They had no children.

Christopher thought of all this as he pondered her explanation for returning to the States. *Was Barnabas really dead?* Cautiously, as though testing a sore tooth, he probed the unseen with his thoughts and feelings, reaching out to his twin through a haze of unnameable emotions.

Nothing there.

As he'd expected. He and Barnabas were fraternal twins and had never shared the psychic connections common to identical twins but only the intense relationship of brothers who'd grown up in the isolation of parental neglect.

Now Barnabas was dead.

At last he said, "Barnabas does have property. But there's a problem."

Dulcinea continued chewing on a piece of pizza, almost as though thinking of something else.

"You'll need a death certificate if you hope to get his estate settled. It won't be easy to convince the executors that he's dead." *I'm* not convinced, he thought. Is this denial?

He hadn't spoken to his brother for six years. He had written him once, from the States, but Barnabas had never written back, and when Christopher recalled his own angry letter, he could understand why. Though the letter had been preferable to the likely alternative. Even now, he felt his twin's betrayal. Still, he wished he could meet him on the street so that he could punch him. Kick him. Kill him.

Embrace him.

The worst part was that sometimes he missed him.

They ate silently, Christopher numbed by the possibility of Barnabas's death. His mind spun between his brother and his brother's wife—and into painful reminiscence.

Twenty minutes later, while he counted bills onto the table and Dulcinea visited the ladies' room, he allowed himself a mental side trip to realms he seldom explored. Not the chain of events he and Dulcinea had inadvertently set in motion. Those grisly memories recurred daily without his consent.

Instead, he remembered what they had done that had led to such grief. A love affair that was never meant to be....

CHAPTER TWO

THE SUMMER he met Dulcinea, Christopher had just finished an accelerated medical program in Chicago. Before starting his internship in an inner-city emergency room, he had returned to Bolivia to continue practicing herbalism with his uncle Tomás.

He had arrived to learn that his uncle had broken a leg and could not ride to neighboring villages to see patients. So Christopher, who had completed not only medical school but his apprenticeship as a Kallawaya herbalist, had assumed his place, bringing herbs, as well as antibiotics and serums for inoculations, to Andean villagers. He had been accepted as both Kallawaya healer and *doctor,* and all classes of people sought his help.

One day he had been called to the Department of La Cumbre to heal a sick man. A very rich sick man . . . with a beautiful eighteen-year-old daughter.

During those few months—that Andean winter— Christopher had retained a measure of sanity. Esteban de la Torra was a former tin merchant, of the uppermost echelon of Bolivian society, and his daughter, Dulcinea, was off-limits. Even though she'd been educated in the United States and had been shaped by American values, Dulcinea was a direct descendant of the *conquistadores,* the only daughter of a wealthy, very traditional Latin American man.

Christopher had healed Esteban de la Torra, and Esteban, who bred Peruvian Paso horses for a pastime, had given him a dun gelding as payment. Pasos could cover long distances—forty miles or more—in a single day. Guapo, the gelding, was a valuable resource for a traveling healer in the Andes. When Christopher returned to the U.S., he would leave the horse for Tomás.

But he'd been surprised when Esteban de la Torra had begun to take a personal interest in him and to cultivate his friendship, asking Christopher to make the hacienda his home whenever he visited the Department of La Cumbre. Intrigued, Christopher had accepted the invitation. He and Esteban had discussed books and medicine and mining— which had been Esteban's livelihood and was the source of Christopher's mother's family wealth in Colorado. Often Dulcinea was present when he visited her father. Christopher had found her bright, interesting—and deliciously attractive, as only something one could never have could be.

But in August, Dulcinea told him which college she'd decided to attend that fall—a Catholic women's college in Wisconsin, within hours of Chicago.

Her announcement had made Christopher queasy with foreboding. In her eyes, he'd seen the truth. Dulcinea had chosen the school because it was near him. Heady thought.

But it changed nothing.

Christopher knew Esteban de la Torra. A Kallawaya healer was an interesting friend for the father—but an unthinkable suitor for the daughter. That he was also an American citizen, a doctor, and that in two years he would come into an inheritance from his mother's family, could make no difference to Esteban. Christopher had grown up among the Kallawaya, who lived in mud houses and worshiped ancestors and mountain deities, who fed earth shrines and guarded themselves against evil spirits. When he visited Bolivia, he always stayed in Chulina, moving easily from his life in the States back into that traditional culture. To be perceived as "white" in Esteban's eyes would require him to forsake that part of his identity, to set himself apart from his father's family and pretend intellectual superiority to them and disdain for their beliefs. But even then, Esteban would not accept him for a son-in-law. In the eyes of most Bolivians, a wealthy Indian could be considered "white" if he dressed in European clothes and lived in the city.

Esteban was not that color blind.

Nonetheless, when Christopher bade farewell to the Hacienda de la Torra that August night, saying he'd be returning to the States later in the week to start his internship, Esteban had suggested he check up on Dulcinea periodically during the school year—as a favor to him, her father. Riding back to Kallawaya country under the starlight, Christopher had felt physically ill—nauseous and light-headed.

The sickness had abated with his return to the States, only to reappear one night in November when the phone in his apartment had rung and he'd heard Esteban, calling from Bolivia, saying that Dulcinea had fallen riding at school and broken her arm. Could Christopher trouble himself to drive to Wisconsin and see that she was receiving good care?

Christopher had made an excuse about work. Esteban had said, *But surely you have a day off? I don't like to impose, but...*

He had driven up that night. And months later, when his carefully chaste friendship with Dulcinea had exploded into more, both had said they'd known then, from the moment he'd walked into her hospital room with a stuffed animal in his arms—a vain attempt to establish her as a little sister, himself as a friend of her father's.

No such luck. He was twenty-four.

She was irresistible. Sweet. Smart.

A virgin.

As he finished his wine, Christopher turned his thoughts from the preciousness of those days—the friendship deepening to love—to the chaos afterward. The end of her school year. Separation.

My father says I must go to the university in La Paz next year. Come back to Bolivia, Cristobal. Please...

He had resisted. Then gone.

It was the worst move of his life, and it had led to a day neither of them would ever forget.

Six years past—Bolivia

IT WAS JUNE TWENTY-SECOND, the winter solstice, the time of Inti Raymi, the Inca Festival of the Sun. Throughout the Andes, people were celebrating the feast. They had flocked to the cities for dancing and pageantry, and no one ventured near the ruined moon temple at the earthquake-buried village of Aiquile, just two kilometers from the compound of the Hacienda de la Torra. Who wanted to be out on the inhospitable *puna* on a day when breath looked like the mist encircling the mountains?

Even inside the walls of the deserted ruin, a thin cold numbed the senses. But still Christopher could smell the dust on the floor and the animals who had once lived there, and the other scent, the scent of love. Sex.

Christopher prayed no one at the Hacienda de la Torra would detect that scent on Dulcinea when she returned.

Her fingers were in his hair, exploring the pale locks mingling with her own blue-black tresses because their heads lay so close. He moved her hands as he sat up. "We should go, *querida*. Someone will notice the horses outside." Christopher realized how edgy he sounded and regretted it. He wanted things to be as they'd been when he and Dulcinea were in the Midwest together. But there was no chance of that. Here, Esteban de la Torra made the rules.

Christopher lifted the edge of Dulcinea's vicuña riding poncho and draped it over her body, against her white skin. "If we lie here much longer you'll catch a cold. Or tuberculosis."

"I never get sick," she answered matter-of-factly. "But if I did, it wouldn't be all bad. My father would call his favorite Kallawaya healer to divine my condition and make me well."

Christopher didn't smile. The prospect of her flirting with him in front of Esteban was not amusing. Especially not after the warnings her father had dropped when Christopher arrived at the hacienda the previous day. Mention of a Peruvian diplomat who would make a suitable husband for Dulcinea. Talk of a temperamental Paso colt Esteban was planning to geld if he continued to misbehave. The colt really wasn't fit for breeding, anyway, Esteban had added with a smile.

Christopher turned from Dulcinea to look for his clothes. "Don't underestimate your father, Dulce. He didn't become one of the richest men in Bolivia by weakness or stupidity." Or kindness. Christopher had once believed he knew Esteban. Lately, he'd begun to see that he didn't. "If he had any idea that his only daughter was lying on the floor of a pre-Columbian ruin with an Indian—"

"You're not an Indian." She jerked upright, responding to the term, which was considered an insult and which had been made illegal by Agrarian Reform. "Not that it would bother me even if you were a *campesino.*" Dulcinea intentionally used the more respectful word. "But good grief, Christopher, your mother's family is rich. You're an American citizen, and you're a *doctor*. My father likes you. He says you have a good mind. He called you a gentleman."

"I'm sure he'd change his opinion on both counts if he could see us now." Christopher reached for his pants. The thick stone walls of the ancient structure felt tomblike, and the cold of the *altiplano* had seeped inside. He and Dulcinea had spent most of their lives in the highlands and were used to bitter frosts, but now he was freezing. Standing to dress, he gazed down at Dulcinea half lying on his alpaca blanket on the stone floor, her perfect ivory skin and paintbrush eyebrows at odds with the earthy wool, her emerald ring winking in the shadows.

Dulcinea de la Torra. Refined. Aristocratic. Cherished and protected daughter of a very powerful man.

He should never have made love to her even once. And what they felt for each other now could lead only to disaster—and not just because of Esteban de la Torra.

But Dulcinea would never understand the other reason.

Shivering, he shrugged into a faded red canvas shirt. It was too cold to talk, but he did. "Dulcinea, your father suspects us, and he has warned me—which is generous. In his eyes, I'm an *indio*. I live in a Kallawaya house in a Kallawaya village among other Kallawaya—to whom I'm related. Your father never lets anyone forget that your family was descended from the *conquistadores*. It hasn't slipped his mind that I'm descended on my father's side from a tribe of Andean sorcerers."

"Sorcerers! You and your 'sorcery' saved his life! He appreciates that."

"And he gave me a horse to show his appreciation. He didn't give me you." Though some of Esteban's behavior *had* been ambiguous. *Perhaps you could check on Dulcinea....*

Christopher zipped his pants, then scooped up Dulcinea's clothes, the satin bra and panties and the cashmere sweater and fine wool riding pants, all purchased in the United States. Kneeling beside her on the blanket, Christopher set her clothing on her lap.

Dulcinea's eyes rose to his, and he saw trepidation in them. She knew it was the last time. Her father was serious. Christopher sat down and put his arms and legs around her, pulling her close, wrapping her against his body. At eighteen, she was tall and surprisingly strong for one so slender. And smart enough to do anything she wanted. If she was allowed.

Sick at heart, he remembered Esteban's hints of an arranged marriage.

And there was nothing Christopher could do about it.

How had he ever gotten into this? Her father's prejudice and position weren't the only obstacles between them, nor the largest. The largest was himself, his birthright, his private curse—the enormous duty that had been born to him with that other anomaly, his blond hair.

It was his greatest grief.

It was the fault of an ancestor, almost two centuries dead, whom he would never forgive.

And it was something he could never explain to Dulcinea. He had to hurt her—and himself—instead.

"I can't marry you, Dulce."

She pulled back from him, and again he saw her fear, the fear of losing him. "Cristobal, I know what you're thinking. That we're from different worlds. It doesn't matter. We can live like *campesinos* for all I care."

Oh, God, thought Christopher. She didn't know what she was saying. By Andean standards, the Kallawaya were rich, Chulina a wealthy village and the house he shared with his brother considered very good. But the cheap linoleum that covered the floor was cracked, absent in places, the bed frames were rusted, and the windowpanes had been broken by hailstones and never replaced.

What could Dulcinea know of that? Dulcinea, who'd been taught that carrying her own shopping bags was manual work, beneath her station. Dulcinea, who never left home unchaperoned unless secretly, to roam the *altiplano* on one of her father's champion Pasos. Dulcinea who lived in a hacienda whose borders were those of a compound.

Dulcinea of the tower.

He said, "That's not the problem. You know your father. You know his *compadres*. And if you stop and think for a minute, you'll realize what he would do to me if he knew what I've done to you."

He saw her reaction—the slight shudder of denial. "My father's not like that, Christopher."

"And his friend Captain Mayorga?"

She said nothing. The atrocities committed by the local police captain were too numerous, appalling and well documented to deny. And Esteban had Bartola Mayorga under his thumb.

Christopher clamped his mouth shut. It was over. Even if Esteban hadn't objected, Christopher's own destiny was an impassable chasm between them. Dulcinea couldn't be expected to understand or accept his secret, the identity he longed to shed like an uncomfortable costume. It separated him from Dulcinea as it had separated him from every person he had ever known. All but his brother, who knew the truth. Barnabas, his twin, who by chance and genetic odds—dark hair, instead of blond—was free. Would always be free.

Abruptly, Dulcinea spoke. "Yes, Christopher, my father will be angry if he learns that we've made love. But he'll forgive us both and he'll accept you. He admires your intelligence and what you've made of yourself."

"And from such inferior stock, no less."

"That's not what I meant!"

He let it drop. "Look, Dulce, there are other problems—things I don't want to talk about." But after a moment he tried to explain. "We could never have children." As soon as he said it, Christopher knew it wouldn't make sense to her. Hadn't he been the one to insist on birth control?

He groped for words and at last the truth came out. Not the whole truth, not the part he must hide, but the facts that were common knowledge among the people with whom he lived. "The women in my family die in childbirth. Or the babies die. It's—" He stopped.

"What?" She looked pale.

His lips felt parched. "It's a curse. From Occlo, the moon."

Silence fell between them, potent and dark. He watched her black-coffee eyes and saw the hurt creep into them—and something else. Fear? Worry? Whatever it was, she kept it to herself. With a dignity he admired, she said, "I'm not stupid, Christopher. Please pay me the compliment of being honest with me, instead of making up some ridiculous story."

"It's not a story. There's a curse." He wondered what she would do if he said more. *I'm supposed to break it. I'm the blond one, the Son-With-Hair-Like-Inti. My family has waited two hundred years for me to come and undo Mariano Choqueneira's crime. . . .*

The thought of telling Dulcinea was comforting.

But her reserved expression had turned to a glare. "I don't believe you. Why can't you just come out and say you don't feel like marrying me?"

His throat was choked, tight. Any thought of confiding in her vanished. Lying seemed easier—and smarter. "I don't want to marry you."

Christopher felt rather than saw her slight movement backward, as though he'd struck her. He stood up, so that he wouldn't touch her, wouldn't try to ease her hurt. Wouldn't tell her the truth. "Get dressed. We need to leave."

Dulcinea nodded but didn't move.

There was something she hadn't told him.

Christopher crouched beside her. "What is it, Dulce?" She shook her head. "Nothing."

She can't be pregnant, thought Christopher. He'd made sure of that. When the condoms he'd brought from the United States were gone, he'd made trips to La Paz for more. Third World rubbers were scarce as antibiotics and sound as sieves, and Barnabas, who viewed contraception as a woman's problem, had mocked his efforts. Health hazards aside, Christopher had always considered protecting his lovers from pregnancy to be far more important than anyone's sexual satisfaction—and for a reason that should have been imperative to his brother, too.

But Barnabas had never believed in the curse.

And neither did he.

Still, he wished he'd examined each of those condoms more carefully before relying on them. Esteban de la Torra would see his daughter pregnant by an Indian like he'd stand a nag with one of his priceless brood mares.

Christopher looked at her. "Dulcinea, are you pregnant?"

She was. As soon as he thought about it, he knew that had to be the answer, and his stomach plunged.

Hoofbeats sounded outside the stone walls, down the long, half-fallen corridor that led outside. Christopher didn't breathe as he listened to the horse's gait. It wasn't the clip-clop of a trotting horse, but a quiet rush of hoofbeats moving with power and elegance. The arriving horse was a Peruvian Paso, the smoothly gaited pride of the Hacienda de la Torra.

A rich man's horse.

Dulcinea had heard, too, and her eyes flickered in distraction as she heard the whinny of Encantador, her father's stallion, from outside where they'd left him with Christopher's gelding, Guapo. Dulcinea's own favorite mount, Piedro de Toque, had died of colic that spring in Wisconsin, and she'd been heartbroken. It had been a turning point in her relationship with Christopher.... But she'd told her father she wasn't ready to have another horse of her own. So Esteban had lent her his favorite.

Now, worry crossed her face, and she rose to her feet, listening. "We shouldn't have left Encantador out there," she said. "It's cold and someone could steal him. I'll bring him inside."

Immobilized, Christopher watched her yank on her pants and sweater and pull her vicuña riding poncho over her head. Then, barefoot, she ran down the corridor.

Christopher's throat was dry. He wanted to call out to her to wait, but his voice wouldn't work.

No one had come to steal her father's stallion. Whoever had arrived outside was well mounted. And, with the exception of Guapo, the only good horses for miles around belonged to Esteban de la Torra. If the rider was not Esteban himself, it was someone who worked for him— equally disastrous.

But Christopher was willing to bet it was Dulcinea's father. Probably he'd come looking for her and seen his champion stud outside the ruin with the other horse, the dun gelding that had been his gift to the Kallawaya healer who'd saved his life. Esteban would immediately perceive that his daughter was violating social propriety by meeting in a ruin with a man outside her family, an *indio* no less.

But more than propriety had been violated.

And Dulcinea, barefoot, her clothes donned in haste, was rushing out to greet her father, or one of his men. Any man could see that she was fresh from a lover's embrace.

Christopher held no illusions about Esteban's capacity for forgiveness. He'd been warned. If there was a chance for escape, this was it. But he hesitated. Dulcinea... regnant. It was cowardly to abandon her. He envisioned himself following her out of the ruin, facing up to his crime and asking for her hand. Esteban, angry at first, would eventually relent, and—

Never.

Esteban would never relent. He would send for his friend Bartola Mayorga, who would make sure Christopher Choqueneira lived only to regret that he'd ever been born.

Snatching up his sweater and his boots, Christopher ducked under a low doorway opposite the corridor Dulcinea had taken. He found another tunnel there, long and dark, and he ran down it blindly, moving deeper into the ruin and, he fervently hoped, out to the rainy mountain terraces beyond.

He was running for his life.

HE HAD RUN NEITHER FAST nor far enough. Too soon he'd stopped running from Esteban and begun hurrying to safeguard Dulcinea. He'd been nearly certain she was pregnant.

Wrong about that.

Right about her father.

As he sat in the Yellowjacket Café six years later, Christopher thought briefly of the hours and days and months following his parting with Dulcinea. He thought of what loving a beautiful woman had cost him. Laying aside the ghastly recollections, he considered what to do next. What to do with *her*.

Her missing luggage didn't explain why Dulcinea had taken his sweater from the free box. Though it was summer in the Southern Hemisphere, it was still cold in the Andes. And she should have taken better care with her money.

Christopher didn't mind lending her money—or giving it to her. He minded that now he had to decide whether to check her into a hotel or invite her out to the ranch—with him. He minded that she was his brother's wife and that she was alone without resources in a foreign country. He minded that he had to be near her, that he felt responsible for her.

He minded that she had come at all.

When he saw her emerge from the ladies' room, he stood, trying not to examine her too carefully, not to notice that she'd brushed her hair and that it shone, black and wavy.

But his chest felt as though it was caving in, and he searched hard for flaws in her nose and her cheekbones and her brown eyes and her ebony hair. He wanted to discover that her looks had faded or that he no longer found her physically attractive. Deliberately, he remembered what had brought her to him.

Barnabas.

Dead?

A smoking engine. La Boca del Diablo...

When he spoke he sounded tense. "You must need some things. Clothes. Toothbrush."

Dulcinea tried to summon the anger she'd felt during the plane trip, the anger she'd felt so many times over the past years.

She wasn't angry anymore. Not at the moment. He had bought her lunch, and he'd just learned of his brother's death. The well of hatred she had fed for more than five years had suddenly run dry.

But she wouldn't let him buy her clothes, especially when she had no means to repay him. Remembering to look at him and speak clearly, she said, "I'd like just a toothbrush. I'll make do with what I have otherwise."

He stared at her, and she was more than ever conscious of the shabbiness of her clothing—and thankful for the sweater she'd found in the free box.

At last he said, "Look, Dulce, the airline will take a couple of days with your bags. Let me buy you some stuff. Consider it a gift."

No. No gifts from him but the food she needed, the food she couldn't be too proud to accept. She shook her head. "I'll be fine."

"Look at me when you speak, or I can't hear you."

"I'll be fine."

Her eyes blazed at him, and Christopher wondered if she was angry and why. She had no reason to be angry. He was the one who should be angry—at her, for marrying his brother while...

His mind snapped back to the present, to the slender woman standing before him in wrinkled pants, his cast-off sweater and a pair of cheap loafers. He said, "I appreciate the niceties of your situation, but I think we'll both be more comfortable if you're not forced to wash your only set of clothes in the bathroom sink every night."

We'll both be more comfortable... Dulcinea stole a glance at his left hand. Bare. He must live alone. She felt a moment's misgiving at the thought of accepting his hospitality. But what choice did she have? She couldn't very well ask him to put her up at a hotel.

"I know you're tired," said Christopher. "Let's just get you a few things, and then I'll take you out to the ranch."

Thistledown Ranch. Barnabas had seldom mentioned his grandparents' ranch, where he and his twin had spent so many summers. But even after six years, Dulcinea remembered what Christopher had told her about it. A thousand acres. A house that was a hundred years old, with walnut wainscoting and a fireplace in every room and wallpaper ordered from England to match the original.

He was probably right about her washing out her clothes. If he had servants, it would be embarrassing for him. And her. But she hadn't seen the inside of a clothing store in six years. Fighting volatile emotions, she said, "Okay. But you must let me repay you." Somehow.

"Dulcinea, please look at me when you talk."

They left the restaurant and stepped out onto the street. "Nothing's open except the stores at the hot-springs resort, but we should be able to find something for you there," said Christopher as he led her down the sidewalk. Though everything downtown was within walking distance, the Uncompahgre Spa was at the far north end of Sneffels—and on the way to Thistledown Ranch. They would drive.

As they walked to his truck, Dulcinea slipped on the icy sidewalk and grabbed his arm for support. Feeling him flinch slightly in response, she quickly released him, her face hot.

But Christopher said, in a casual voice that had nothing to do with his feelings, "It's okay. Hold on to me. It's icy."

Dulcinea was grateful but embarrassed. She hated her cheap tattered loafers; they were part of the reason she'd slipped. Christopher wore strong leather work boots with good soles that left a sharply defined imprint in the snow. His jeans were faded, the soft denim hugging his long legs beneath the hem of his mountaineering parka that was the bright red color of a cactus blossom. To Dulcinea, he seemed very rich. Her father had been so silly about Christopher years ago. Silly and ignorant and small.

But it didn't really matter. Christopher was the one who had left.

THE RIDE to the hot springs took only minutes, and neither of them spoke during the drive. Christopher parked his blue pickup with the camper shell outside a three-story brick Victorian building that towered above the steaming hot-springs pool. Beside it was a wide park and athletic field, now empty and blanketed in snow.

Dulcinea didn't wait for him to open her door, but got out herself, slipping on the ice again. Coming around the truck to join her, Christopher resisted touching her, but instead offered his arm. She took it, and he felt her warm hand on him as they walked up to the ornate glazed doors of the resort building.

Inside, beyond a palatial lobby, were shops specializing in all kinds of shoes and clothing, from sportswear to mountaineering apparel to swimsuits and lingerie. Steering her into an outdoor clothing store with the deceptively unpretentious name Mount Sneffels Dry Goods, Christopher led her directly to a wall display of everything from running shoes to cross-country ski boots. Soon a casually dressed young man emerged from the shop next door, which he was also minding, and asked, "Can I help you? Oh, hi, Chris."

"Hi, Brett." Christopher nodded to Dulcinea. "The lady needs some good all-weather hiking boots."

The clerk glanced curiously at Dulcinea, then moved toward the shoe racks and showed her three styles. He and Christopher both waited for her to respond, and at last she stepped forward and picked up one of the boots.

It was beautiful, the kind of thing worn by American tourists in Bolivia. Her eyes traced the leather uppers, the perfect stitching, the bright-colored laces. She turned it over and saw the price tag on the hard Vibram sole. One hundred and eighty dollars.

She blinked, reeling backward ever so slightly at the price. Christopher's body brushed hers as he took the boot from her hand and set it back on the shelf. "We'll try that. What size do you wear, Dulce?"

Twenty minutes later, she left the shop with the boots on her feet and a bag full of gorgeous clothing she hadn't known how to stop Christopher from buying. A bag of goods that had cost, with the boots, almost five hundred dollars. More money than she saw in a year in Bolivia. She felt dazed and sick, and as he paused outside the shop, she leaned near him and said softly, "Christopher, please, let's go to the ranch now. I don't want anything else."

She stood on his right side, and Christopher heard only a faint murmur of sound from his left ear. On his right—silence. Emptiness. A melted ruin of an eardrum that heard and felt nothing. Because she wouldn't meet his gaze, he turned and tilted her chin upward until their eyes met.

"Dulcinea, I realize you're having a hard time remembering this, but I cannot hear you when you stand on my right side and whisper. I am completely deaf in that ear. What are you trying to tell me?"

"I'll pay for the clothes."

The words sounded almost desperate, and Christopher said, "That's fine. Consider it a loan against your husband's estate." *If Barnabas is dead.* The specter of his brother's disappearance hovered over him, and he felt numb, hyperaware of everything around him.

Especially Dulcinea.

Wanting space, he said, "I'm going to find a phone and see how Sissy's making out at the clinic. Why don't you—" There was a boutique across from the Dry Goods. "You're probably going to need some other things. Underwear, whatever." He nodded toward the doorway. "You can get what you need in there. I'll join you as soon as I can."

Dulcinea followed his eyes and saw that he had indicated a lingerie store. A long satin negligee and a teddy made entirely of lace were visible through the glass, beside a display of soaps and bath salts. Luxuries. With embarrassment, Dulcinea thought of her cheap, ill-fitting panties and bras.

She absolutely could not let Christopher buy her underwear.

And what if he expected something in return for all he was buying?

Alarm rang through her, followed by a surge of the old hatred, hatred fueled by memories. The mirage of Christopher's love had given so much—that was cruelly taken away. She thought, *I hate you. I hate you. I will always hate you, Christopher Choqueneira.*

But he was already guiding her toward the lingerie shop. When she glanced up at him, he said, *"Hasta pronto,"* then turned and headed back toward the lobby, carrying the bag of clothes he had bought her.

Dulcinea stepped inside the lingerie store, into the scents of flowers and spice. Lace, satin and silk hung from every rack, and the shelves were lined with baskets of scented lotions and body powders, fat bath sponges and cactus brushes. Behind the counter sat a woman slightly older than herself; alerted by the doorbell she peered over the top of her paperback. "Can I help you?"

Dulcinea shook her head. "No, thank you." Being in the store, seeing the well-dressed woman behind the counter, made her ashamed of her poverty, and the prices didn't help. Several minutes later, when the bell chimed again and she looked up to see Christopher, she felt a flood of relief. She moved toward him, eager to leave.

"Did you find what you need?" He glanced toward the counter. "Hi, Danielle."

The woman lowered her book. As she set it on the counter, her gaze washed over Christopher's tall body. "Hi, Chris."

Dulcinea longed to flee. Cheeks flushed, she told Christopher, "I don't need anything."

She had forgotten and murmured again, but he made no comment. Instead, he took her elbow and led her toward the bras and panties at the back of the boutique. The saleswoman stood up and her voice trailed after them. "Can I help you find anything?"

Dulcinea's mouth watered as the nausea returned, beyond her control. As the clerk appeared beside a rack of teddies and merry widows, heat embraced her, and she feared she would be sick in the store. "Excuse me," she said and darted past the woman, knocking a bra off a rack as she rushed out into the hall. She hurried through the lobby, her eyes on the exit, and with relief stepped out into the cold.

She strode into the deserted park, where she swept the snow from a wood-and-iron bench, sank onto it and put her head between her knees, willing herself not to throw up.

As the cold air wisped over her, penetrating the pile sweater, evaporating the sweat on her body, the bench quivered slightly. Christopher sat down beside her, his foot near hers.

The nausea was overwhelming. If she threw up in front of him, she would die.

He said, "Are you sick?"

She lifted her head and drew a huge breath as she stared up at him through a blur of tears. "Oh, Christopher. I'm pregnant."

CHAPTER THREE

SHE MIGHT AS WELL have punched him. For a moment Christopher couldn't talk.

Pregnant?

With Barnabas's child. It was the last thing he'd expected.

Images filled his mind. Barnabas snoring drunkenly. Laughing with red eyes. Talking about women...

Dulcinea in his brother's arms. Naked skin.

God.

Obviously, they'd slept together right up until Barnabas left for the last time. It had been a real marriage, not what he'd imagined, what he could hardly admit to himself he'd envisioned for so long. Dulcinea keeping the home fires burning while Barnabas flew his questionable cargos all over the Andes. Barnabas gone virtually all the time, home too seldom to be interested in his wife. And when he was home, too drunk to...

Emotions clawed at him. Gouged him.

Dulcinea was carrying Barnabas's child.

Once, he had thought she was pregnant with his. And that suspicion, above all else, had led him on a course that had landed him in hell.

He looked at her, his expression ferocious, and she cowered, backing away on the bench. When he grabbed her, she shook in his grasp.

Christopher dropped her arm, realizing how he must appear to her—a madman, insane with jealousy because she was pregnant by his brother.

He *wasn't* jealous. Just surprised.

He moved farther away from her and folded his arms across his chest. He said nothing because he couldn't think of anything to say—except a question that would sound like the height of absurdity. *You actually slept with him?*

She'd been married to him. For six years.

Dulcinea touched the sleeve of his jacket. Tears glistened on her face, and her cheeks and nose were red with cold. "I lied about the airline, too, about losing my luggage. I don't have any, only my purse. I had a knapsack, but it was stolen on the *camión* on the way to the airport. And I don't have any money. I had to sell my mother's ring to get here." Turning from him, she leaned her head on her arm against the back of the bench and sobbed.

He stared at the cascade of black hair tumbling down her back and over her arms. This was a nightmare. Sitting in the park in Sneffels, his home, with Dulcinea, who had appeared like an angel of death to tell him about Barnabas. She was poor and half-starved and pregnant with his twin's child. There was nothing he could do but take care of her, and he wanted to grab her and shake her until her teeth rattled. He wanted to scream at her, *Why did you do it? Why did you marry him?*

But he remembered that *he* had said he wouldn't marry her.

Listening to her sob, a sound he could hear clearly since she sat on his left, he put his head in his hands and wished he could drop off the face of the earth.

"Let's please take back the clothes, Christopher. I'll pay you for the boots somehow."

He lifted his head. "Stop it. The clothes don't matter."

"They matter to me."

"Barnabas is rich, Dulcinea!" He didn't mean to shout at her, but the truth begged to be shouted. "Your husband is rich! He just never wanted to take what was his."

She stared. The color faded from her cheeks. For the second time that day, he thought she might faint.

Christopher's heart gave one long, hard, painful beat.

Her drawn face reached him through his own misery, and he remembered he was the caretaker, the healer. He remembered to be gentle.

He said softly, "Come on. Let's go home. I'll show you."

THE BLUE PICKUP navigated the winding road north out of town, between burgundy rock walls and mountainsides thick with evergreens and draped in snow. Dulcinea sat quietly, watching the view through the window as the valley broadened. A river ran beside the road. Ice and snow covered its surface in places; in others, the water rushed over rocks and fallen tree limbs.

Noticing the direction of her gaze, Christopher volunteered, "That's the Uncompahgre River. Uncompahgre means 'hot springs' in the language of the Ute Indians. There's an underground vapor cave and mineral springs at the ranch, too."

Dulcinea barely heard him. A thought was pounding in her head, a memory she tried each day to suppress. Sometimes for a few hours, sometimes whole days, the recollection would slip away and she would forget, but then she'd see something that would bring it all back as sharply as though it had just happened.

Now the memory seemed less acute. But it pricked her conscience. How could she accept his hospitality and keep such a secret? Christopher must be told.

No! she thought. There's nothing to tell him. He probably already knows, anyway.

But in her heart she didn't believe it.

Stealing a glance at Christopher, she thought, He has no right to know. He gave up that right and every other.

He gave up me.

For just a moment, her hatred returned, and she clasped it to her like security and focused on what had brought her to Colorado.

It had nothing to do with Barnabas's estate.

It had everything to do with Christopher, the Son-With-Hair-Like-Inti.

What if he rejected her plea?

Her morning sickness intensified, and she peered ahead down the road, wondering how far it was to the ranch. Just then, he flicked on the turn signal, and a moment later, steered the truck across the road and through an opened stockade gate with a sign that read Thistledown Ranch.

Dulcinea's eyes swept over snow-covered acres fenced by rails of pine, long meadows broken only by the occasional stand of aspen, evergreen, willow or oak. As the truck topped a low rise on the valley floor, the view opened up on another wide meadow with corrals and two huge gray barns. Near the edge of the valley, before the land began its steep ascent, stood a three-story brick Victorian with white porch poles and scrollwork. Smoke puffed from one chimney, blending into the gray sky. And in front of the house, steam rose from what appeared to be a stone-rimmed swimming pool. The mineral hot springs Christopher had mentioned? Noticing new metal roofs, Dulcinea recalled what he had told her in the park, that Barnabas was rich. What did he mean?

He stopped the truck near the corral fence, and three dogs bounded toward the cab, tails wagging, barking. Christopher rolled down a window and put his hand out to touch an animal that resembled a cross between a wolf-hound and a horse. The dog placed its paws on the window and looked into the cab at Dulcinea. Then it barked.

Christopher said, *"No más."*

The dog got down and sniffed around the tires of the pickup, then woofed at the other dogs.

Christopher looked at Dulcinea. "How are you feeling?"

"Okay."

"Do you mind if I let the horses out before we drive up to the house?"

Horses. Of course he would have horses, and probably good ones. Envious, Dulcinea shook her head. "Not at all."

He turned off the engine and opened the door. As he started to get out, he glanced back at her. "You can come if you want."

THE BARN SMELLED of hay and tack, and she could hear the breath of the horses. One of them whinnied, and her mind conjured up a picture of Piedro de Toque, her old stallion, long since dead. Piedro de Toque—nicknamed "Taita," chief—had died the spring she was at college in Wisconsin. Grief-stricken, she had called Christopher...

As one of the dogs trotted past, going to investigate something near the other door, Christopher opened the first stall and went inside to slip a halter on a bay quarterhorse mare with white stockings and a white blaze on her nose. Swinging wide the gate, he led her out and handed the lead shank to Dulcinea. "Hold her for me, will you? Her name's Tinkerbell."

Dulcinea touched the horse, feeling her warm nervous breath, as he went farther into the barn and disappeared into another stall.

Hoofs rustled. She heard Christopher's voice—low, soothing an animal—and a moment later he brought out a deep-bodied buckskin gelding with a long tangled mane that swept its shoulders.

Dulcinea's eyes widened. "That's a Paso."

Remembering a fateful phone call about a dead horse, Christopher avoided her gaze. "Yes."

The gelding was pretty. Dulcinea blotted out thoughts of the horse she'd loved, and she squelched memories of the comfort she'd found in Christopher's arms after Taita had died. She said, "Guapo died of colic."

Christopher only glanced at her, as though he didn't recall the Peruvian Paso her father had given him, the dun he had left behind at the ruin six years before. But he was thinking that Taita had died that way, too.

They took the horses out to the corral and let them loose. Noticing an ancient green one-ton pickup and a seven-horse trailer near the barn, Dulcinea asked, "Are there more?"

"A few. They went out this morning before it snowed."

He secured the gate and gestured with his head for her to follow him back to the truck. He opened the passenger door for her and closed it after she got in. Once he'd climbed in the other side and shut the door, she looked over at him.

"Christopher, what did you mean when you said that Barnabas is rich?"

He had reached for the ignition, but when she spoke his hand came away and clasped the steering wheel. He stared out the windshield.

How could he explain? She would want to know *why* Barnabas had never claimed his inheritance. Christopher didn't know why; he could only guess. At last he said, "Well, for instance, this land has been in our family for more than a hundred years. Today it's worth several million dollars." Tens of millions. "Half of it belongs to me. The rest is my brother's." He took a breath. "If you're right and he's dead . . . it's yours."

Dulcinea gaped at him. How could land be worth so much? And how could Barnabas— "Didn't he know?"

"He knew." Christopher started the engine.

"Why didn't—" It was senseless. They'd been so poor, and . . .

Christopher said, "The ranch was part of my grandmother's estate. She was the only daughter of a wealthy mine owner." Harry Wright, a local legend, had struck gold near Mount Sneffels and taken millions in ore from the fabulously rich Politician Mine—then sold the operation for even more. "After her death, my grandfather worried about keeping it in the family. Years ago he decided to give the property to me and Barnabas, put the deed in our names to avoid the estate taxes. We were the only grandchildren, his only heirs." After a moment he said, "He passed away last year." Things had been lonely since. Dr. Jonah Gore, his grandfather, had helped him when he most needed it and in the ways he most needed. Christopher owed him all he had—not least his life.

Dulcinea asked, "But why didn't Barnabas— Is there anything besides the land? Was it that he would have to sell the land?"

"He has a trust. We both have, all our lives. But neither of us could touch it till we turned twenty-five."

Her jaw dropped. She'd known their mother's family was rich. But Christopher had never wanted to talk about it, and Barnabas had always spoken of his American grandfather with animosity. "Why didn't he use that money? We were always *struggling*, Christopher." Almost choking on the words, she said, "We would have been fine if we'd stayed in Chulina. But Barnabas wanted to live in La Paz. To be near the airfield. He . . . we never had much."

Christopher stared blankly through the windshield. That was why she was so thin. The Kallawaya were a highly successful people—culturally and economically. Those who resided in the cities worked as doctors or lawyers or jewelers, and several of those with homes in the traditional Charazani region where Christopher had grown up owned businesses in La Paz as well. His uncle, a respected herbalist, also operated a small transportation outfit consisting of a *camión* and a twenty-five-year-old school bus. And the Kallawaya used agricultural methods that had worked since Inca times. In the Charazani region, their homeland, they lived in *ayllus*— social, geographic and economic communities built on three levels of elevation. In the highest areas they raised sheep and llamas, in the central areas *oca* and potatoes, and on the lower level corn, barley, peas. In addition, they traded with the people of the Yungas region for fruit and coffee and with merchants from the city for other goods. Living in *ayllu* Chulina, among the Kallawaya, Dulcinea would not have been hungry.

Living in La Paz with Barnabas, she shouldn't have been.

Unable to go on, Dulcinea glared at Christopher. "This beautiful place was his. Didn't anyone ever tell him?"

They had reached the house, and Christopher parked the truck and turned off the engine. He faced her. "Yes. My grandfather met with him in La Paz."

"When?" Dulcinea could hardly believe what she was hearing.

"Four and a half years ago." He thought of what had taken a seventy-two-year-old man to Bolivia. It wasn't to have a beer with Barnabas.

Dulcinea's mind reeled. Four and half years. Was that when—She tried to remember. She thought that was when the letter from Christopher had come. With frustration, she recalled the letter's arrival and all that had happened afterward.

Barnabas with the match burning his fingers and the ashes scattered on the tabletop. Accusing her. The recollection stung. But how could she have defended herself? She still remembered her own frustration warring with guilt—because she had so badly wanted to know what was in that letter.

She still wanted to know.

CARRYING HER SHOPPING BAG, Christopher led her through a side door and into a small entryway where a duster and a black cowboy hat hung on hooks, and muddy boots and snowshoes were jumbled in the corner against a row of cabinets. Two broken dog leads hung from a nail, and a pair of cross-country skis leaned in the corner beside them.

Along one whole wall of the room were shelves stocked with labeled glass jars containing everything from salsa to preserves to dried plant matter—roots and leaves. Christopher's herbal pharmacopeia, thought Dulcinea. He hadn't changed so much, although the Kallawaya healer had become an American physician in private practice. She felt a strange relief that the part of him that knew and collected medicinal plants was still alive.

His voice summoned her from her thoughts. "I leave my shoes here. You don't have to, but it saves the floors."

Dulcinea unlaced her boots, and he did the same, kicking his into a corner with the others. Then he opened the door that led into the rest of the house and held it so Dulcinea could precede him up the wooden steps and into the kitchen.

What daylight there was passed through tall double-hung windows, illuminating the pale yellow-and-white floral wallpaper and the refurbished hardwood cabinets and the wainscoting. The solid, sprawling kitchen table was maple and looked as though it had come with the house and been loved and refinished a dozen times. It suggested that a big family had sat around it eating breakfast before dawn, before going out to the cows.

But it seemed like a lonely table for one man.

Christopher did not pause in the kitchen. He'd been wondering on the way back to the ranch which room to offer her. There was really only one. After his grandfather's death, he had donated several Victorian beds that were unfit for sleeping to the museum, leaving only two rooms intact. His own and the one next door, which had been his mother's.

Christopher silenced his own misgivings as he led Dulcinea through the house.

There was wainscoting in the hall, too, dadoes with finely carved moldings, and photos hung against the floral wallpaper, but Dulcinea didn't have time to look as they hurried past several rooms and up a carpeted wooden staircase. Clutching the banister for support, she followed Christopher's long, blue-jeaned legs as he climbed the stairs ahead of her. He reached the sunny landing ahead of her and paused until she joined him.

Their eyes met and held for a moment, and Dulcinea quaked. He was too much like Barnabas. And too different. Barnabas had been the dark side of the moon. Christopher was the sun.

Long ago, he had been her lover. Then he'd become her enemy. And now her feelings seesawed from minute to minute. Ever since she'd walked into the clinic she'd met one surprise after another. Perhaps the biggest was that Christopher now knew she was pregnant but had not guessed the *real* reason for her traveling thousands of miles to see the Son-With-Hair-Like-Inti, the one person who could break the Choqueneira family curse.

Christopher asked, "How are you doing?"

"I'm fine." But she wasn't. What would he do when he found out why she had come? How could she persuade him? According to Barnabas, Christopher had never shown any inclination to fulfill his duty to his family. He had never cared about breaking the curse, no matter how many women and children died.

Even if one had been his own mother.

Would he care that another had been—

His voice broke into her thoughts like an echo. "You're going to stay in my mother's room."

Great omen.

Leading the way down the hall to the right, he said, "The view's nice. You can see the pool and the meadow from the windows. And the horses."

He wanted to tell her, *If you feel well enough, you can ride tomorrow.*

But he didn't.

Horses were part of her past with him, and he couldn't look at it yet. There were things he wanted to know—what had happened that last day, what her father had said—but he couldn't bring himself to ask.

Christopher's mouth felt paper-dry as he pushed open the door of the bedroom that had belonged to his mother, a woman he'd never known. Now the furniture was draped with white sheets.

Behind him, Dulcinea felt cold and suddenly depressed. White was a color she would always associate with death. She watched Christopher set her shopping bag on the floor, then purposefully strip the sheets away, one by one, and fling them past her to the hallway.

When the sheets were off the furniture, he moved toward the radiator to adjust the valves, then went to the corner cupboard to remove some bed linen.

Dulcinea looked at the bare mattress. "I can do it, Christopher."

He tossed one edge of a mattress pad toward her across the mattress specially fitted to the narrow mid-Victorian bed. Together they made the bed, covering it with a "grandmother's fan" quilt that had been hanging in the wardrobe.

When they were finished, Christopher glanced about the room, checking everything. His mother's picture was a permanent fixture on the bureau with the mirror he kept meaning to have resilvered. He didn't look at the picture. He had one just like it in his own room, and it made him feel nothing.

What made him feel was the woman behind him.

A pregnant woman.

Standing in his mother's room brought the realization home to him. *Dulcinea was carrying a Choqueneira baby.*

He was stunned that it hadn't occurred to him earlier and almost immediately went to work eradicating the thought. It didn't matter. The curse was nonsense....

Absentmindedly, he turned and found Dulcinea staring at the wallpaper and the dark molding near the ceiling and the tulip lamps and the fireplace and the rocking chair and the mid-Victorian bedroom set, ash with black walnut carvings and trim. Even in her rumpled clothes, even thin and worn and tired, she looked like royalty. A princess fallen on hard times.

He nodded at the door that led to the bathroom.

"Go ahead and make yourself at home. You'd probably like a bath. I'll get some towels for you." He couldn't think. It was his bathroom, too. Dulcinea in his bathroom, in his house. In his life.

But she was Barnabas's wife now. And she was pregnant.

As the thought nudged him again, he said, "Help yourself to whatever you need. I'll bring you a bathrobe."

Dulcinea's eyes dropped shut, her black lashes touching her white cheeks.

He suggested, "You should take a nap."

She nodded, and he saw her mouth tighten as though she was trying not to cry. He didn't want to see her cry for his brother, so he left.

DULCINEA DID NOT SLEEP.

Lying on her side on the firm mattress, she stared out

one of the tall windows at evergreen treetops and tried to make sense of everything that had happened since she'd found Christopher.

There was too much. *Barnabas had been rich.*

She spent a long time on that thought, playing it out in her mind, considering both the past and the future. She fought a deep depression sprung of anger and old futility and despair.

All this land . . . and more money than she could imagine. Dulcinea couldn't bear to contemplate that it had been her husband's and that he had denied it to both of them. It wasn't hers now. The thought of actually having money again, of not having to worry about it, could make her cry with relief if she lingered on it. But Christopher had said that she wouldn't see an inheritance until she could prove Barnabas was dead.

Dulcinea put that out of her mind. It wasn't why she'd come.

Remembering the reason, she sat up, reached for her purse on the bed beside her and opened it. From its depths, she withdrew a manila envelope, the envelope she'd found taped under the table in the house in La Paz. She'd been terrified the customs officials would confiscate it, though she didn't know why they would.

She opened the envelope and slid the contents from inside. Eight-by-ten photographs in four colors, unnatural colors in unnatural places. Despite the wrong hues, she knew they were aerial photos, and they had to be important, or Barnabas wouldn't have taped them under the table.

With anxious indecision, Dulcinea slipped the photos back into the envelope. She had brought them to show Christopher, hoping they would help. They *were* aerial photos. Didn't archaeologists use such photos to hunt for ruins? Her heart raced. The photos might also help locate Barnabas's plane by showing where he'd been flying.

But... Old fears closed on her. Why had Barnabas had those photos? What had he been doing?

She reclined on the bed, and her eyes flickered to the photograph of the pretty blonde on the dresser. Christopher's mother. Barnabas's mother. Who had borne the Son-With-Hair-Like-Inti—and died of complications five days later.

Dulcinea pushed up the bottom edge of the pile cardigan she still wore and pulled out the hem of the cheap blouse underneath. Then she rested her hand on the bare skin of her lower abdomen and closed her eyes.

Hi, there, she thought. *Everything's going to be okay. I promise.*

She was glad Barnabas couldn't see her. He would have known what she was thinking and mocked her for believing that the ten-week-old life inside her could know her thoughts or feel her love. After all, he had never believed she could feel a mother's emotions, even for the daughter she had carried to term.

Look, Dulcinea, it was never really a baby, okay? It was never alive outside you. Get over it, all right?

Get over it. *Right,* thought Dulcinea.

She would never get over it.

All she could do was everything in her power to see that it didn't happen again. She had lost one child to the Choqueneira family curse. She would not lose another.

She couldn't bear it if she did.

CHAPTER FOUR

CHRISTOPHER MADE *spanakopitas*—Greek turnovers with feta and spinach—for dinner and brewed red-raspberry-leaf tea for Dulcinea to ease her morning sickness. Because there were just the two of them, he set the table in the kitchen.

While he worked, he thought about his brother and the plane with the smoking engine. Barnabas was a skilled pilot. Flying had been his pride and his love—and his weakness. But surely, if he'd survived the landing, he would have returned to Dulcinea.

Nonetheless, Christopher clung to other possibilities. Barnabas was on the lam. He'd moved to Brazil.

He would turn up again.

Christopher eyed the big table set for two, instead of one.

Dulcinea, he thought. *Here. Pregnant.*

Doesn't matter. Doesn't have anything to do with me.

It had everything to do with him.

The curse...

While the *spanakopitas* baked, he did something he hadn't done for more than a year. He went through the dining room and parlor to the living room and removed a particular volume from the topmost shelf. He had bound the pages himself, after photocopying them from a two-hundred-year-old journal that was preserved in his safe-deposit box.

The language was Spanish, and as Christopher opened the cover while making his way back to the kitchen, he felt cast back in space and time to the eighteenth century. To his homeland.

From the diary of Mariano Choqueneira
Curva, Alto Peru—1783

I am going blind.

Once, I would have said there was no magic involved, no spirits, no deities. I would have said that all can be explained scientifically, by the fact that I spent too long staring at the eclipse and burned my eyes. I could not resist the wondrous sight of the moon taking a bite out of the sun. I could not make myself look away from something so spectacular and strange.

Now my eyes can scarcely see the words I write, but my family says it is not so much the brightness of the sun that blinded me as evil. The evil of the eclipse.

The evil, they say, led you to the shrine, made you a thief of the moon, brought misery upon your family. Mariano, your own wife died in childbirth before you got home! And you bring your infant son to Curva for your sister to nurse because she lost a baby that same night. Stillborn. So much death can only be retribution from Occlo, the moon, for what you stole from her.

It's evil, Mariano—not science.

I have begun to believe now. I believe because I dreamed of the sun warring with the shadow of the moon. Then the shadow moved, and the moon became a tall spectral woman in the window of my house, swooping down on a crying infant and snatching it up as though to save it from me, the infidel. After that, there were other babies, and she took them, too, and their mothers. The men she left sobbing.

That was the dream, two nights ago. I asked Emilio what it meant, and he said we should hold a séance. So he and I and my father prayed, and Emilio prepared a sacred mixture of plants. We held a ritual, and we all saw the same thing. Now, before my eyesight is gone completely, I must write it down and tell the story again and again, so that my son will know it, and his children will know it, and many years hence, when the blond one comes, the Son-With-Hair-Like-Inti, they will tell him who he is and what he must do. I do not envy him, because what we saw, Emilio and my father and I, was a road of agony and grief. That is the destiny of the one with hair like the sun.

Christopher heard Dulcinea's footsteps in the hallway and shut the book. He stuffed it into the phone-directory holder on the wall, reminding himself to move it later, and stood up to greet Dulcinea.

She had showered and dressed in some of the clothes they'd bought at the hot springs, a brightly patterned pile pullover, loose black cotton pants and wool socks. When he saw her, Christopher realized she had considered her pregnancy when she chose the clothes. The pants had a drawstring waist, and the sweater was oversize. She would be getting bigger, growing with the baby.

Christopher slid his feelings into a pocket deep inside him. It was a trick he had begun learning six years earlier, the day he fell into the hands of Bartola Mayorga. Now he did it automatically.

With his brother in the back of his mind, he asked, "Feeling better?"

"Yes."

"I made you some tea. Red raspberry leaf." He turned toward the counter. Removing the tea basket, he picked up the steaming mug and handed it to her. "It should help your morning sickness."

Dulcinea took the cup, smelling the tea. Irrational doubts came to her—that these herbs would poison her or make her miscarry. Christopher wouldn't do that. He had shown no sign that he even remembered the curse, let alone suspected that she'd come to Colorado to persuade him to do what he must to break it. Nonetheless, before lifting the mug to her lips, she asked, "It won't hurt the baby?"

Barnabas's baby. Christopher's stomach tightened. "I'm a doctor, Dulcinea. And an herbalist. Why would I give you something that would hurt your baby?"

His eyes were cold as an Andean glacier. So cold Dulcinea wanted to shiver. Embarrassed, she said, "I'm sorry. It was a silly question."

Her discomfort worked on his conscience. He shook his head. "It was sensible. Some herbs *can* make you miscarry." Before she could reply, he suggested, "Bring the tea with you. I'll show you the house."

Briefly, he took her through the dining room with its built-in china cabinet, the parlor with its Wilton carpet and striped Empire Revival sofa, the living room with paneled floor-to-ceiling bookcases made of cherry. Dulcinea found the house beautiful. There were exquisite antiques throughout, but they all seemed present for function, rather than mere display. They belonged. As Christopher showed her each room, Dulcinea remembered what he had said that afternoon. *If you're right and he's dead . . . it's yours.*

Hers and Christopher's.

He led her down the stairs on the east side of the house to a long rough-hewn stone hallway. "The vapor cave is in here. If you use it, you should tell me—and not stay long. It's warm, and you're pregnant. You don't want to get heat stroke."

Feeling the dampness in the air, Dulcinea peered curiously down the dark corridor, but Christopher was already turning to go back upstairs. "The mineral-springs pool outside is just ninety degrees—fine for you. Tell me if you want to go swimming and I'll keep an eye on you."

Dulcinea preceded him up the stairs. "I can't swim."

Somewhere in the back of his mind Christopher remembered that. He began to say that she should learn, then thought better of it. She wouldn't—*shouldn't*—be here that long. But if she left, where would she go?

Dinner was quiet. Christopher's thoughts were on his brother, on the missing plane. He'd have to hire someone to look for Barnabas.

After dinner, Dulcinea began clearing the table and washing the dishes, which Christopher dried and put away. They worked together silently, with a strange intimacy that Christopher found oddly comfortable. But the warm tension in his chest made him cautious.

She was his brother's wife.

When the dishes were washed and put away, Dulcinea said, "I think I'll go upstairs." Her pinched gaze reminded him why she was there. Death. His twin's. Christopher thought he saw concern in her eyes, a silent, *Are you all right?*

He nodded, a knot in his throat. He was all right. She was going upstairs. "Let me show you where things are in the kitchen. I want you to help yourself to whatever you need. I'll mix up something else for your morning sickness tonight." Peppermint and wild yam, a teaspoon in water three times daily. "Have you seen a doctor?"

She shook her head.

Christopher made mental notes to himself. She should have an appointment with Dr. Trace in Ridgway—prenatal vitamins . . .

Ignoring the needles of emotion that pricked him, he showed her where to find snacks in the kitchen. They said their good-nights, and he listened to her footsteps in the hall and on the stairs and in the upstairs hall, and he knew when she closed her bedroom door.

The house was quiet.

Barnabas was dead.

It brought up other deaths, unwelcome memories. It brought up the part of Christopher's past that he'd never shared with the brother who had once been his best friend. Never been able to share.

Because of Dulcinea de la Torra.

Knowing sleep would bring nightmares and remaining indoors would have him opening a bottle of wine, he put on a duster, hat and riding boots and went out. It was snowing, big white flakes coating the lodge-pole fence rails, blanketing the meadow. Ferdy, the hired man who lived in Sneffels, fed the horses and cleaned their stalls. But tonight Christopher brought them in from the corral. The barn was warm, the smells comforting.

He looked in on each of the horses, pausing at the stall of a three-year-old Paso. Sombra de la Luna was a blood bay filly Christopher had purchased from a breeder in Pitkin County. He had trained her himself, learning from the breeder's Peruvian trainer or *challon*. The results were satisfying.

Naturally gaited and born with *termino,* a spectacular and beautiful movement in which the forelegs roll toward the outside as the horse strides forward, Pasos were bred for manners and for *brio,* a quality of pride and spirit and heart contributing to their unusual endurance. Even the stallions were gentle enough to be ridden by children. But Sombra de la Luna was special. She had shaped into such a good horse that the breeder had asked Christopher to think of him first if he ever considered selling. He was not considering it. But the smoothly gaited young horse might make a good mount for a pregnant woman.

He wasn't sure Dulcinea would appreciate the gesture—or the horse. Piedro de Toque had been a once-in-a-lifetime companion. The Paso stallion had won championships in the Plaza de Acho bullring in Lima, and Christopher knew Dulcinea would never feel the same way about another animal. He'd seen her heartbreak firsthand when Taita died.

But at least Sombra was well mannered and full of *brio.* Christopher had trained her carefully, a long process using the time-honored methods Peruvians had developed over centuries.

He went to the tack room and collected *cabezada* and *reindas*—the bridle and reins—the *montura*—the finely tooled box saddle—and all the other Paso tack. Last was the exquisite saddle covering from which hung hundreds of tiny horsehair braids, a piece that would take a craftsman a year to make. Each item had been made in Peru; the artisans were men whose families had been tack makers for generations. The horse's headgear was crafted of finely braided pieces of goat hide, some only one-thirtieth of an inch thick. The tack had been created with the same patience that had gone into the breeding and training of the Peruvian Paso.

Christopher stepped into Sombra de la Luna's stall, speaking to her softly in Spanish and English. Minutes later, he led the horse out of the barn, mounted and set off through the snow at a perfect *paso llano,* a smooth walking gait. Christopher had spent his childhood visits to the ranch on quarter horses, and he loved them. But he could never ride any of his three Pasos without feeling something keen and sweet and older than himself. Their gaits had made them the mounts of kings, and the surefooted, unshod Pasos never stumbled on the steep narrow footpaths of the San Juan Mountains. They were strong and elegant animals with the greatest stamina of any horses he knew.

Sombra de la Luna was a princess.

The falling snow lessened and at last ceased, and the stars appeared, lighting his way down a path behind the property to a graded road that went up into the national forest. He had brought saddlebags packed with emergency provisions, and he knew he would be out for hours trying to still his mind, to forget.

But even the beat of the Paso's gait called up the past.

He remembered Dulcinea and the sweet thrill he'd tasted when they were young. He remembered the price he'd paid, a price that made itself felt in scars on his mind and body and an ear that couldn't hear the wind.

THE DIAL on the alarm clock glowed 3 a.m. Dulcinea's stomach yawned, and she slipped from the bed, remembering what Christopher had told her that night. *Make yourself at home. Be sure to get whatever you'd like to eat.* Last thing before she went upstairs, he'd shown her where the crackers were and suggested they might ease her morning sickness.

She had slept in the powder blue silk long underwear they'd bought at the Dry Goods. Over the silk she pulled on a navy blue flannel bathrobe Christopher had lent her. She crept to the door, opened it and went out into the hall.

Barefoot on the cool parquetry, she walked softly past the closed door of the bedroom Christopher had said was his. Electric replicas of old gaslight wall brackets on hinged arms cast a low light on the corridor, illuminating the way to the stairs.

The first floor lay in darkness, but by the starlight outside Dulcinea found her way to the kitchen. She flicked on the wall switch, and the chandelier with its cup-shaped glass bathed the walls in a soft golden glow. But as she moved toward the cabinet where the crackers were stored, she started at a noise from the pantry. The outer door opened, then banged shut, and Dulcinea froze. She heard a sound like boots being kicked into a corner.

Christopher? It was the middle of the night.

The pantry door opened and he came in, his golden hair loose and uncombed, snow dripping from the ends, eyes black and riveting. The air left Dulcinea's chest. He'd always had that effect on her—on most women, she imagined. All her girlfriends at college had liked Christopher when he came to visit. For months Dulcinea had told them he was "a friend of the family," nothing more. The women in her dorm had been open in their admiration of his rugged looks, his lanky masculine body, his manner that could be flirtatious or warm or...

The pain of rejection stung her again.

And the never-closed wound of loss.

I hate you, she thought.

Christopher shut the pantry door and regarded her in surprise. She was clinging to the back of a chair as though she might pick it up and hurl it. Her dark eyes dominated her face, and Christopher wasn't sure when he'd seen such an expression of loathing. But, as though remembering herself, she lowered her eyes, curtailing the glower.

Christopher asked, "Do we need to clear the air?"

Clear the air? Dulcinea reminded herself again that she needed him. No, they should not clear the air. She turned toward the cabinet to get the crackers. "I don't know what you mean."

He pulled off his black pile sweater. Beneath, his faded red long undershirt was damp against his skin. He had ridden for hours. Miles to go, Robert Frost style. He felt as though he would never sleep. *Barnabas... where are you?* "You looked angry a moment ago."

Her fingers were on the handle of the cabinet door. She couldn't *afford* to be angry. "On the contrary. I'm grateful for your kindness."

Of course, thought Christopher. Why would she be mad at him? Why would she think anything about him at all? She had married Barnabas.

While he . . .

Moving only inches to laze against the doorjamb, watching her, he choked down the things he wanted to say.

Dulcinea exclaimed, "What do *you* have to be angry about? You were my lover, and when my father found out, you ran away and never looked back."

Christopher forced himself to breathe. He *had* looked back. He had looked back. "Did *you* look back, Dulcinea? Did you look back when you were in bed with my brother?" His easy posture tensed. "Did you ever think about your old lover, screaming while Mayorga carried out your father's orders?" And issued a few of his own.

Dulcinea blinked, as though clearing a film from her eyes, trying to focus, trying to see something just out of sight.

She doesn't know.

Someplace inside him, the truth registered, but Christopher denied it. She *had* to have known.

Her skin was dead white, her lips dry.

"Cristobal," she whispered. Clutching the edge of the counter, she stared at him. "What are you talking about? Oh, God, I know what you're talking about." Suddenly she rushed to the kitchen sink and bent over it, gagging on her own breath.

Christopher stood frozen.

This wasn't the same Dulcinea de la Torra who had denied that her father was like Bartola Mayorga. This was a woman who had been living in the real world. Who knew exactly what happened to those who were "disappeared."

"Your ear... They did something...." Screams filled her mind, and she leaned over the sink, breathing deeply, trying not to be sick.

Uneasily, in starting and stopping motions, Christopher went to her. She leaned against the counter, shaking, and he reached for her, then withdrew his hand before he could touch her.

"How long?" She spoke on a dragging inhalation, like a person straining for breath at the top of a mountain pass.

"Eighteen months." He had counted the days and lost track with lost consciousness. Many times he'd awakened on the floor of the cell knowing nothing—until the nightmare returned.

Bending over the drain, she gasped, "I didn't know. I never knew. That day at the ruin...my father said never to come back to the hacienda. He said it was not my home anymore. I was not his daughter. He took the horse I was riding, Encantador. I didn't know where to go. I went to your brother in Chulina. I didn't know what to do...."

Christopher's hands itched to touch her. To try to mend something that had been broken too long before. But a thought exploded inside him.

She had married Barnabas. She was carrying his baby.

Barnabas was dead.

He reached past her to turn on the water. Taking a clean dishrag from a drawer beside him, he dampened it and tried to hand it to her, and as he stood against her back his groin responded to the feel of the softly curved bottom barely touching him. His lungs were expanding and contracting only by millimeters, and his blood was streaming downward, filling him, making him shake with the need to be inside a woman, any woman.

Except her.

Only her.

Still leaning against the sink, Dulcinea saw the dishrag in his sun-browned hand and she took it from him. She sensed rather than felt his erection, and her body responded in kind. Behind her was a tall, hard man who smelled like horses and wood smoke from stoking the fire in that beautiful parlor with the Wilton carpet. A man who had cried and bled in Bartola Mayorga's prison, who had been robbed of his hearing in one ear. Who had been tortured.

Because of what they had done together.

Because her father—

Nausea rolled over her again, and she put her head down.

Christopher touched her. It happened instinctively, and he saw a smoking airplane in his mind and told himself it was okay to do this; Barnabas was dead. Anyhow, this wasn't about sex or love but about a pregnant woman who had just had a shock. He didn't *want* her.

Dulcinea felt his hands on her shoulders, then on her head, smoothing her hair back. He whispered something in Spanish, a quiet thing he might say to a crying child. Her body felt wild, and she remembered what it had been like, how easy it had been. She had never felt such attraction for any other man, before or since, and the thought made her want to laugh. A miserable, warped laugh. Barnabas had never had a chance. Not with her.

Not with his whole life.

Because his twin had always been like the sun, and what could anyone be beside Christopher but shadow?

After a time, the waves of nausea passed, the earth settled. Stomach pressed against the sink ledge, she glimpsed Christopher's hand and forearm sliding past her to turn off the water. He took the dishrag of crocheted cotton from her. Straightening up, she let him bathe her face, afraid of how she was shaking, of how it felt to have someone tall and strong behind her, holding her. His hand moved the warm wet cloth over her eyelids and down her cheeks. He turned on the water again, washed her face again, his other arm around her back.

It was his touch that triggered recollection. Love and rare closeness. She had believed in it for months after he abandoned her. She had told herself he would come back. And even after she realized he would not, there had been that part of him she knew she would always have.

Remembering, Dulcinea was cast into blackness, a place where there was no light and no hope. *My baby,* she thought. *I want my baby.*

It was a long time before she remembered she was carrying a child again.

Barnabas's child.

She turned and blinked up at Christopher. His mouth was inches from her temple. She could see the small lines in his flushed lips, could examine his beard that was darker than his hair, could admire intimately the straight lines of his nose, his lightly flaring nostrils. She knew he'd been beaten in prison. Brutally. But it hadn't affected his features. He was still the most beautiful man she had ever seen.

And why not? He was special.

The Son-With-Hair-Like-Inti.

She blurted out the truth. "Christopher, I'm here because of the curse. I came to ask you to return the urn to the shrine."

Christopher jerked away from her, realizing only as he did so that she'd been in his arms, that his fingers had been spread over her back, her hip nestled against his groin.

The urn?

He felt as though she'd thrown cold water on him.

She had come because of the curse.

Dulcinea's eyes were keen and urgent, and something cold settled upon him. What had made her believe in the curse? She hadn't six years earlier.

And how did she know about the urn?

Christopher stared. "Who told you?"

Her fearful look answered his question. *Barnabas.* The curse was common knowledge, but the journal and the facts about the urn and the shrine had been handed down from father to son for two hundred years. Dangerous knowledge. His father had told him. Christopher had told Barnabas, his twin, the person closest to him since before birth...

And Barnabas had told Dulcinea.

So what? thought Christopher. Mayorga knew, too. Any secret like that had a life of its own. Gold and silver. Pizarro hadn't been the last man to kill for it.

Christopher said, "My grandfather traveled to Bolivia and spent sixty thousand dollars to get me out of that jail. I'm not going back. Anyhow, there is no curse."

"There *is,*" said Dulcinea. "I know."

Why did she look that way? "You've been spending too much time with my relatives." His uncle Tomás could catalog the history of the curse, of everyone whose death had been attributed to the curse for two hundred years.

Christopher's mother had been the last.

"The curse is real," Dulcinea repeated. "I know."

He rolled his eyes, trying to forget she was pregnant—and that Choqueneira births never went right. Someone always died. A mother. Or a child.

But there was no curse.

"I can't do what you're asking. Don't ask again." He backed against the trestle table, almost fell over it.

"I had a child," said Dulcinea, watching him with her arms locked about herself. "She died."

Christopher's heart stopped. Intuition jolted through him. *No.* But Dulcinea continued to stare at him, that haunting emptiness in her eyes. He moved toward her, grabbed her shoulders, looked at her hard.

Dulcinea shook.

All went black inside him. He couldn't speak, couldn't ask. Instead, he released her roughly, turned and strode to the pantry door. He threw it open and in the dark he found his boots. He yanked on his parka, went outside and slammed the door.

THE WAXING CRESCENT MOON had already set. Now, only starlight shone on the meadow, casting the faintest glow through the vapor rising from the hot-springs pool.

Christopher was glad not to see the moon.

He knew all about it. Circumference, diameter, mean radius, speed and orbit. Astronomy, like all the sciences, reassured him. His Bolivian relatives were superstitious. Though he could never ridicule their beliefs, though he could always find a context for them as useful allegories, those beliefs were unscientific, based on fiction rather than fact, emotion rather than logic. Christopher preferred fact and logic. He anchored himself in a reality that could be perceived by the human eye and reasoned with the mind through scientific theory and with the help of technology. Myths like that of Occlo, the Kallawaya moon goddess, were stories man had created to explain what he could not understand. The Choqueneira family could not understand why their births always went wrong, so they'd created a curse.

Christopher's breath floated before his eyes. Two of the dogs came trotting across the snow, snuffled around his feet. Sancho, the bloodhound cross. And Lake, the fluffy white Great Pyrenees. Christopher offered a hand to each, and then the dogs, independent, went chasing across the white meadow, stirring misty clouds of powder behind them in the night.

I had a child. She died.

He wanted to escape. He didn't want to think about Dulcinea or what she had said or what she wanted.

There was no curse! He knew because he had tried to break it. When he'd left her that day in the ruin, he had thought she was pregnant. And he had been young enough and idealistic enough ... He stood out in the cold, waiting for it to numb him, and the memories filled his mind.

He had tried to break the curse.

Bolivia, six years back
Trying to break the curse...

FLEEING THE RUIN and his old friend Esteban de la Torra, whom he had betrayed by making love to his daughter *while a guest under his roof,* Christopher walked for three days and on the fourth caught a ride on a *camión* headed for the Yungas.

His decision was made. He still did not believe in the curse, but part of him did believe in duty. His duty was to appease the family superstitions. And in so doing, if by some chance the curse was real, he might safeguard a pregnant woman—and his own child.

He had envisioned the journey many times. He had planned to be prepared with maps, compasses, multispectral aerial photographs of the terrain. In his pack would be his photocopy of Mariano Choqueneira's diary, the journal his father had entrusted to him years ago and which was now in a safe-deposit box in the U.S. He would carry antivenin against snakes, be encased in boots and impenetrable leggings. He would be heavily armed.

He was none of those things. His medical bag and the woven shoulder bag that contained his herbs and identified him as a Kallawaya healer had been left behind at the Hacienda de la Torra. He carried only a knapsack that had been a gift from a *campesina.* Inside the pack was some *charqui* made from the dried meat of a sheep, some coca leaves, a homemade machete and a few plants he'd hurriedly collected along the way: *ajenjo,* wormwood, for treating intestinal parasites; *jinchu riquiichy,* mouse's ear, for wounds and burns; quinine bark as a febrifuge; and half a dozen others. He wore the same clothes in which he'd left the ruin and which he'd washed only once, the previous day, under a waterfall.

He knew he was being followed.

Death was on his trail. Behind him were Bartola May-orga and the *policía*. Ahead lay a snake's den, from which he must collect a priceless pre-Incan artifact to return to its home in a jungle shrine whose location he didn't know.

On the seventh day of his journey, Christopher reached the pit near the Rio Coroico, where family legend held that Mariano Choqueneira had two hundred years earlier cached a treasure.

Shortly before his death, Christopher's father had taken him to the spot to retrieve the urn. Twelve years old and newly apprenticed to his uncle, the most respected healer of Chulina, Christopher had longed to explore the cornu-copia of plant life in the rain forest. But his father had been determined that he enter the cave where the infa-mous moon urn was supposed to be hidden. Healing, said Roderigo, was only a vocation; the urn was his destiny. Near the mouth of the cave, they had seen a bushmaster slithering through the foliage. The snakes were there, as they had been at the end of the eighteenth century, and Roderigo had seemed to regard them with satisfaction rather than fear. *Good. They have guarded the urn. Now go ahead, Cristobal. It is time for you to come into man-hood.*

Christopher still remembered the emotions. Trembling with fear, he had crept forward, looking for snakes. See-ing another, he had shuddered and jumped away. *Go!* said Roderigo. *You must do it. For two hundred years, this family has been waiting for you....* So he had turned and crouched on his hands and knees and begun to lower him-self into the cave. Halfway inside, flushed and petrified, he had hesitated, hanging on to the rim, silently begging his father to say he didn't have to do it.

Instead, Roderigo had stepped on his fingers.

Later, his father had blamed Christopher's cowardly hysteria, his refusal to go the rest of the way into the pit, on annual visits with his American grandparents, on disconnection from his culture. *No more trips to Colorado, Cristobal. You need to grow up....* Christopher had been returned to Chulina in disgrace, and Roderigo had departed for La Paz in silent disapproval. It was the last time they saw each other.

Twelve years after his first visit to the spot, Christopher stood above the vine-covered hole in the ground and thought deliberately not of Roderigo but of his family's faith—that after two hundred years the cache would still contain its treasure.

Would it really be there?

The humidity had made his hair limp, and it dragged against his sweat-soaked face. Staring down at the dark hole in the ground, he recalled words from Mariano's diary.

> ...With the poor vision of my burned eyes, I took the urn in its llama-hide sack and picked a path through the forest to a cave I'd discovered years earlier, a cave inhabited by so many snakes I hadn't dared venture inside. I approached that dark hole in the earth and hurled the sack inside, knowing only a fool would attempt to disturb it there. Only a fool or the young man of my family I had seen during the séance, the Son-With-Hair-Like-Inti. Like Inti, the Sun...

"Bastard," muttered Christopher, contemplating the snake hole.

It was winter. The bushmasters should be sleeping.

Until he woke them.

More than once, in curiosity, he had read about the effect of a bushmaster's bite, and his medically trained mind had a fair picture of the reaction of the human body. The breakdown of red blood cells, the liberation of hemoglobin. Hemorrhage, swelling, vomiting blood, the discoloration of the skin. Death from cardiovascular failure.

Antivenin should be given within minutes of the bite. In South America, Christopher knew, the more popular remedy involved neutralizing the venom through a shocking encounter with an automobile battery. But he had neither horse serum nor car.

Crouching over the pit, he thought of Bartola Mayorga and what the police captain would do to him if he caught him. He stared into the hole. It was deep.

I'm going to die, he thought.

Machete in one hand, he turned, put his hands on the damp earth outside the pit and lowered his legs inside. Like the first time.

Christopher's skin crawled. The soil beneath his feet was so soft it seemed like sand. As he dug the toes of his hiking boots into the earth and ducked lower in the cave, something dropped off one of the walls. Something alive.

His fingers slipped, then his feet, and he fell the remaining inches to the floor, crushing an obstacle beneath him.

When he could see, he realized he was standing on the collapsed rib cage of a human skeleton, clothed in Indian dress. The decayed fabric of the dead man's shirt undulated as something stirred inside, beside Christopher's foot. He leapt away and struck down with the machete, then froze, looking around him in the shadows. The floor of the pit was ankle-deep in balled-up snakes.

And a cloth bundle the size of a watermelon sat inches from his foot.

The sight made him light-headed. Ducking, banging his head and knocking debris from the roof, he grabbed at the object.

The covering fell apart at his touch, like dried leaves, and he saw the glint of gold. Without time for disbelief, he dropped his machete and grasped the metal lip of the urn. It was heavier than he had expected, and that terrified him. Twenty-four-karat gold. Ignoring the snakes, he lifted it, grunting, and saw that the lid had fallen off and was at the bottom of what was left of the bag. He set down the urn, then snatched at the lid and threw it up out of the cave, mindless of the softness of the gold.

That done, he heaved the urn into his arms and up toward the daylight. As he did so, a long, shiny coil of brown and pink tumbled out of the vase, spiraling down on top of him, toward his face, down over his arms. Shuddering off the snake, Christopher struggled to push the heavy urn over the edge of the cave mouth. Then, grabbing the moldy soil at the lip of the cave, he dug his toes into the wall and scrambled upward.

His heart pounded and his breath came hard as his head cleared the opening and he saw day and the glint of the golden urn.

And black boots.

Like a living memory, one came down on the fingers he'd wrapped around a tree root. Bone crunched, and he gasped involuntarily. He couldn't move, and he thought of the snakes at his heels as he stared up at khaki uniforms over his head. Afraid.

A face bent down to his, and Captain Bartola Mayorga said, *"¿Qué es?"* His fingers touched the gold vase that still lay on its side in the foliage.

Through glazed eyes, Christopher saw the shimmering gold and made out the squared-off lady's face and geometric body of Occlo, the moon.

Mayorga said, "An antiquities violation. Señor de la Torra will be interested. Perhaps even more interested than he was that his whore of a daughter spread her legs for you. You'll need a good spell now, *brujo.*" Witch.

The captain laughed, and the boot pressed down hard, grinding, then lifted from Christopher's hand. Christopher drew a shaking breath as he stared dazed at the bloody mass of his fingers. It was his dominant hand, his left.

Mayorga said, "Get up."

Christopher used his right hand and his arms and elbows to haul himself out of the pit. As foliage brushed his wet jaw, a boot slammed into his chin, tearing upward, smashing teeth and gums, filling his mouth with blood. Then it drove into his groin.

Retching, he closed his eyes and prayed.

STANDING IN THE MEADOW at Thistledown Ranch, Christopher did not allow himself to walk through the memories of what had followed. The worst was not what had been done to him, but seeing and hearing what had been done to others in Mayorga's jail. Men. Women.

The frosty night made his joints ache. He'd ridden for too long.

Christopher thought of Sombra de la Luna and of Piedro de Toque, Dulcinea's horse who had died so long ago. Dulcinea sobbing in his arms. He'd kissed her. Piedro de Toque, the touchstone, had lived up to his name. What was between him and Dulcinea had been golden.

I had a child....

Christopher stood in the snow for a long time, imagining his brother and Dulcinea in bed together.

Remembering himself with her.

"DULCINEA."

She jerked awake.

Christopher stood over her bed in the dark. He had come through the bathroom that adjoined their rooms. Shaking, Dulcinea recalled what had happened earlier, the meeting with him in the kitchen.

She remembered waking to the sight of his brother standing over their bed the same way, then pulling back the covers... But this was Christopher. In the faint light from the window, she saw his pale hair spilling to his shoulders. He still wore the long undershirt he'd been wearing earlier. The buttons at the throat were open, the tails hanging over the waistband of his jeans. He was like a ghost.

She said, "Don't touch me."

Christopher stared down at where she lay against the sheets and the pillow. He didn't care what she thought he planned to do to her, or what in his stance had brought that look of fear to her eyes. He said, "Was the child mine?"

Even dazed with sleep, she knew what he meant. She pulled the sheets tighter around her. "Yes."

His throat clenched, and Dulcinea wondered if he would grab her and strangle her.

"How? Tell me."

She didn't recognize her own voice in the darkness. "Stillborn. It was a girl. Isabel."

Christopher continued to stand over her, and she saw it all penetrating him, but she couldn't tell what he felt. He revealed nothing but only turned and exited through the bathroom, shutting the door behind him.

CHAPTER FIVE

FOR A MOMENT after Dulcinea opened her eyes the next morning, she lay still, adjusting to her surroundings, taking stock of her feelings. She remembered that Christopher had come to her room and that she had told him about Isabel. And she recalled what he had told her earlier.

Prison.

A dark dullness settled upon her. She lay quietly with her thoughts, her memories. Her father. Christopher. Barnabas.

Barnabas had known his twin was in jail. When he met with his grandfather in La Paz, he must have discovered it. And Christopher had written to him.

But Barnabas had kept it secret from her.

Huddling between the fine cotton sheets, Dulcinea puzzled through it, fighting the sadness that recollection inevitably brought.

It was thoughts of the baby inside her that stirred her to sit up and pull back the covers. A reason to get up. To force herself to plan, to renew her goal. Though Christopher had said he wouldn't take back the urn...

She'd never really expected anything different. Would knowing that his own child had died because of the curse persuade him? Remembering Barnabas's feelings about the stillbirth, she was afraid to hope.

But she couldn't ignore her pregnancy. In her heart, she whispered to the life inside her, *Good morning. Let's get some breakfast.*

As she got out of bed, a familiar loneliness, the impenetrable solitude of a mother's grief, surrounded her. Breathing through it, living through it, she turned her eyes toward the window, thankful for the novelty of a different day, a different setting than the house in La Paz. Thankful for the temporary escape from a terrible sameness. She had awakened in a beautiful place, and she felt unexpected pleasure in that.

Outside, the sun shone on snow-dappled trees, making the world bright. Dulcinea studied the view from her window as she dressed in the clothes she had worn the night before. She could see the steam from the stone-rimmed hot-springs pool curling into the cold day, and in the corral, the buckskin Paso gelding was shaking his mane, steam billowing from his nostrils. Beyond the pasture, she could see a few houses in Sneffels, rising with the mountains to the south.

Half of this belonged to Barnabas. Why hadn't he claimed it?

Sorry, Dulcie, I'm not rich. I'm not a doctor like my brother.

Determined not to let bitterness or shame spoil the morning, Dulcinea made the bed, then brushed her hair with her pink plastic brush that was missing half its bristles. Taking a last look to see that her room was straight, she went downstairs.

At the foot of the steps, Dulcinea paused to look into the living room. Light flooded through a mosaic of clear panes in the bay windows. An exotic Moorish arch formed the entrance to a bright solarium, and a bookcase of cherry burl lined one wall. The shelves were filled with volumes, and Dulcinea slipped into the room to peruse the titles. Classics, paperback mysteries, an encyclopedia set. In La

Paz, books were expensive. And in Chulina there had been few.

"If you'd like something to read, help yourself."

Christopher's voice startled her, and Dulcinea jumped. He stood behind her under the arch to the hallway. He wore a faded blue canvas shirt and heavy tan-colored canvas pants, and his hair was down loose, as it had been the night before. He had not shaved.

Dulcinea wondered if he'd slept.

She wondered if he would agree to break the curse. He knew about Isabel now. Would it matter to him?

To his offer of the books, she said, "Thank you." His appearance unsettled her nerves, triggering the nausea of morning sickness. She knew she should eat, but it seemed rude to excuse herself so abruptly.

It was Christopher who said, "You should have some breakfast."

There was nothing tender in his voice, and Dulcinea knew she shouldn't be surprised by the suggestion. He was a doctor; he knew about pregnancy. But she kept expecting him to behave like Barnabas, who thought of no one but himself. Who had always needed someone to take care of *him.*

Christopher had never been like his twin. Not really.

As she moved toward the arch, she tried to forget the night before in the kitchen, when he had held her. She tried to forget waking up with him standing over her bed. But she couldn't forget all that lay between them this morning. During the past twenty-four hours, he had learned of two deaths. His brother's. His child's.

Barnabas had said, *It was never really a baby.* He'd been gone in his plane when Isabel was stillborn. And when he came home, he'd seemed almost relieved by the news. Freedom from responsibility—and from the reminder that his wife and his twin had been lovers.

Was Christopher, too, glad that the child had not lived?

He'd seemed upset the night before—even angry. Angry was all right. Just as long as it mattered. If he didn't care about his own daughter's being stillborn, how much less would he care about his brother's baby? About her baby.

But he didn't care, she reflected. *Six years ago, he thought I was pregnant... and he ran away.*

She started down the hall to the kitchen, and he followed.

On the counter beside the stove sat a clean mug with a tea basket dangling from the lip. Christopher nodded to it. "Tea?"

Red raspberry leaf. He must have set it out for her earlier. "Thank you."

As he lit the burner on the stove and put the kettle on, he nodded toward a glass bottle on the counter. "That's a morning-sickness formula I prepared for you. You can take one teaspoon in a glass of water three times a day. When you get some prenatal vitamins, that will help, too." Without waiting for a reply, he added, "I made an appointment for you with an obstetrician in Ridgway. Also, we should open a checking account for you. You'll need money."

"I can't take money from you," said Dulcinea, in agony at his words.

Christopher stepped away from the stove and leaned back against the sink, his arms folded across his chest. "How are you going to eat? And I think we bought you— what?—one change of clothes yesterday?"

The night before, Dulcinea had rinsed her panties and bra in the bathroom sink and hung them over her radiator to dry. But she said, "I don't need clothes." She took a breath. "I need you to do what I asked last night." *Say you will. Please.*

"No," said Christopher. "What you need is nutritious food in your body, a sound roof over your head, peace and quiet, and real medical care. There is no curse."

Dulcinea felt cold. He was wrong. And in his words were implications. "It wasn't my fault, Christopher. I had plenty to eat."

"I know it wasn't your fault."

She blurted out, "It wasn't Barnabas's fault, either."

Christopher's eyes were so black they frightened her. He turned away.

Dulcinea took a box of crackers from the cupboard and began snacking to take the edge off her hunger. She remained moodily silent, frustrated. Noticing Christopher fill a copper-bottomed pot with water and light a burner on the stove, she said, "I can make my own breakfast."

He didn't look up, and it occurred to her that she was on his right side, that he hadn't heard her. His ear...

She cast her gaze out the window at the fields of snow glittering in the sunlight. Watching Christopher's white dog, as big as a wheelbarrow, chase through the powder, she asked loudly, "Is there no vase? Is that myth, too? No shrine?"

A six-year-old memory snapped in Christopher's mind like a slide projected on a screen. A golden object on the ground, among pairs of black boots. The woman's face on the urn. The moon.

"There is an urn."

Dulcinea turned.

He felt a tight throbbing in his throat. "But I don't know where it is."

"What do you mean?"

Tension twisted inside him. Why go into it? "Drop it, Dulcinea. Would you like some oatmeal for breakfast?"

She glanced at the pot he'd put on the stove. *Nutritious food in your body, a sound roof over your head...* Giving her those things was easier than finding a moon shrine that had remained hidden in the Andean jungle for two hundred years. Easier than carrying a priceless artifact back to that shrine.

Dulcinea studied his profile silently. He would not meet her eyes.

He believes in the curse, she thought. *That's why he won't look at me.* At some core level, Christopher believed in the curse but would not admit it. So how could she make him take back the urn?

I can't. Helplessly Dulcinea remembered Barnabas and her own pleas. She'd never been able to make Barnabas do anything, either.

Despondent, she answered Christopher. "I'd like some oatmeal, but you mustn't cook for me."

"I'm cooking for both of us." Turning to a cupboard behind him, he removed a gallon jar containing oatmeal. "I have a woman who comes once a week to clean. There isn't much else to do. Don't worry about anything. Just make yourself at home."

"Thank you."

He stole a glance at her. All night he'd thought about her—first about her reaction to learning he'd been in prison. Then about her baby who had died.

His baby.

She seemed tranquil now, but he had to risk shattering that mood and bringing up the emotions he least wanted to see—her feelings for his brother. Why had she married Barnabas? After he'd learned about the stillborn baby, he had guessed that her pregnancy by him was the reason. He didn't want to find out he was wrong.

But they had to talk about Barnabas—some.

"My friend Moth is coming here after lunch. His father used to be with the FBI and heads an international investigation agency. I've asked them to help us find Barnabas's body. I'd like you to join us when we talk." He avoided her eyes. "If it's not too much for you."

"No," said Dulcinea, understanding what he meant. Grief...

"Later this afternoon I'll take you downtown. We can do our banking."

Dulcinea shook her head. She couldn't take any more money from him.

He turned on her impatiently. "Dulcinea, is my brother really dead?"

She blinked, confused and oddly hurt. "Yes."

"If he's dead, you own what was his."

In Christopher's brown eyes, Dulcinea saw what lay behind his words. He didn't yet believe Barnabas was dead. It made her sorry for him. At first it had been hard for her to accept, too—without a body. And now, in his face, she saw the desperate hope of a child longing to be told that some dreadful truth is actually false.

Dulcinea kept her eyes on his. "He is dead."

Christopher closed his lips tightly, afraid he might ask the question forming there. Afraid she might answer.

Do you miss him, Dulcinea?

AFTER BREAKFAST, Dulcinea straightened the kitchen, then went into the living room. Despite what Christopher had said about the urn, she felt a glimmer of hope. Obviously he cared about the outcome of her pregnancy. Perhaps, given a little time, his conscience would force him to accept that so many deaths couldn't be natural. That there was a curse.

Remembering his offer of books, she examined the titles on the shelves. There were dozens of well-read hardbound classics and newer books, too, paperback novels and nonfiction on subjects from wine making to ecology. She pulled down a mystery and read the back-cover blurb, put it back and took down *The Firm*. No. As she replaced it, she noticed a red volume on the shelf above. The spine, bare of title or author, was protruding from the edge of the shelf, as though the book had been consulted briefly, then carelessly returned to its place.

Vaguely curious, Dulcinea slid it from the shelf and opened it. The pages were photocopied from a smeared and faded handwritten source. Spanish. Her interest grew. Skimming the writing on the first page, she realized what she had stumbled upon.

Mariano Choqueneira's journal.

Good grief. Did Christopher just keep it in his living room, where anyone could find it?

She started at a sound behind her and saw him emerging from the solarium. His eyes registered the book she was holding, but he made no comment. Instead, he tilted his head toward a nearby door. "Come in here. Let's look at some maps of the Yungas, so we're ready when Moth comes."

Wishing she could read it immediately, Dulcinea put back the journal, crossed the room and joined Christopher. The door led into his study. Like the living room, the study opened onto the solarium. Clearly, this was Christopher's sanctuary. Plants growing in the windows. Books lining two of the walls. A comfortable couch with worn green jacquard upholstery.

Set into the north wall, opposite the solarium, was a hearth edged by ceramic tile painted with botanical images. Surrounding the tile and rising above it were ornate walnut panels, which framed a rectangular mirror. On the wide mantel lay a *quena,* a traditional Andean reed flute. She remembered how Christopher had played it and how he had sung to her in Quechua. It all seemed distant, as though they had been two other people.

She supposed that was the case.

There was a map table at one end of his desk. As she watched, he began sliding out drawers, removing charts. Some were geological survey maps, others computer-generated. Still others were handmade. Many regions of the rain forest had never really been mapped—others only by individuals, working privately. Christopher must have gone to some trouble to obtain the maps he possessed. Because of the curse?

He believes, she thought again.

Christopher tried to focus on the maps, to think of all the things he should ask Dulcinea, but the lack of sleep was catching up with him. So were memories of Barnabas.

He wished he could mourn. Wished it would all begin to seem real. If he could just see Barnabas's remains, he would surely feel something. But he knew how unlikely that was. In a hot, humid climate like the Yungas, there would be nothing but a skeleton. If the searchers were lucky. And if the plane had not exploded.

Couldn't be dead. Hadn't seen him in so long. Was my best friend, thought Christopher numbly.

Once.

I would have killed him over her.

Had Barnabas loved her the same way? It was easy to imagine. She was that kind of woman. All or nothing. With him, it had been all.

Aware of Dulcinea near him, he thought again of the revelation of the night. The stillborn baby. It seemed like a nightmare. Ghostly. Less real even than Dulcinea's appearing in Sneffels, saying Barnabas was dead.

Isabel.

Named her. People did that. In medical school, he'd been told it was good for the parents to hold the child. He would never see her.

Christopher stood lost in thought, forgetting Dulcinea was there. Almost two minutes passed before he gazed down at the open drawer of the map table and remembered what he was doing. Finding Barnabas.

He gestured to Dulcinea and she moved a step closer, near enough that he remembered holding her the night before. "So," he said, finding speech an effort, "what day did he leave? What was he flying?"

"He flew a plane like the one he had when you—when you lived together," replied Dulcinea with difficulty. *God,* she thought. *What did I do?* Only as a nineteen-year-old could she have made such an insane choice, to marry the brother of the man she loved. She made herself talk. "It wasn't the same plane, but the same kind. He bought it from a Brazilian rock band and painted a mural on the side. Mountains and a green meadow with wildflowers and a stream running through." It had been pretty, and she'd been surprised—by his skill but even more by the subject he'd chosen.

"I'd like you to draw a picture before Moth comes. Can you do that?"

Dulcinea nodded.

He watched her, waiting for more.

"He left La Paz for Trinidad on November first. That's all I know."

"What was he carrying?"

"I don't know."

"I'm not the police."

Was that a taunt? She withdrew inside herself. "He never told me." *I didn't want to know.* Especially the last year or so. He'd been involved in something dangerous. She knew it. He'd been so excited. And secretive. Resentful of questions.

She'd been terrified.

Christopher measured her words and her expression. Barnabas generally had not discussed his cargos. But on cold nights when hail pounded the tin roof and muddied the streets, he had been unable to resist bragging. How good the money was going to be. Sometimes it was, and he'd bought cases of rum, a leather bomber jacket . . .

Had he not told his secrets to his wife in bed?

Christopher's throat knotted.

Dulcinea was saying, "He didn't come back. Usually he wouldn't be gone more than two weeks at a time." She didn't add that when he was home, he often was not home. It wasn't Christopher's business. "A month passed, and I decided to go to Chulina to see if your family had seen him. Tomás went to look for him. When he returned, he was sure..."

Her eyes begged him to believe, and for a moment Christopher did.

Barnabas was dead.

He stared thoughtfully at the map, and she imagined he was trying to guess places the plane might have crashed. But then she noticed that he really wasn't seeing the map, was simply staring.

A long time passed, and her thoughts began to drift, too.

Christopher said softly, "I'm sorry about the baby, Dulcinea."

MOTH CAME that afternoon, and Christopher and Dulcinea sat with him in the living room. He was about Christopher's age and wore a shaggy beard that reminded Dulcinea of American graduate students who sometimes visited Bolivia, doing research. Moth said it would be expensive and difficult to look for the plane and there was no guarantee of success. Christopher asked him to look, anyway, and Dulcinea produced the drawing she had made of Barnabas's airplane.

Curious to see the mural his brother had painted, Christopher leaned forward to examine the sketch she'd made with some felt-tip markers he'd rounded up. She was a competent artist, and with limited supplies she'd done very well.

Even Moth, studying the representation of the mural, said, "Looks a little like Yankee Boy Basin."

Christopher thought so, too. The setting was not Andean. It was Colorado, and it might have been the high basin near Sneffels where he and Barnabas had hiked and ridden as kids. They still owned pasture land up there, where he grazed the horses in the summer.

Strange if Barnabas had chosen that place. He'd left Colorado for the last time at seventeen, angry at an air force that required perfect eyes in jet pilots, at the innumerable black vitreous bodies that made his eyes less than that and at a grandfather who wouldn't lie about it. But he'd blamed his desertion on the Gores. Jonah had never wanted his daughter, Christopher's and Barnabas's mother, to marry a Bolivian. After Roderigo's death, Barnabas had chosen to take that personally, inventing racial prejudice in his grandparents. *Of course they like* you, *Chris. You're blond.*

My tough luck, thought Christopher, staring at the picture Dulcinea had drawn and thinking of her pregnancy. My tough luck.

Moth asked Dulcinea, "Is there anything else, anything at all, that might help us find him? Any little thing he might have said? Favorite places he liked to fly?"

Sitting on a striped wing-back chair at the end of the coffee table, Dulcinea thought of the manila envelope she'd brought from Bolivia. The packet of strange aerial photographs Barnabas had taped under the tabletop in their house in La Paz. It was now in the top drawer of Christopher's mother's vanity. She opened her mouth, ready to speak.

Both men were watching her.

"Not a thing," she said. Maybe she'd tell Christopher later.

Christopher stared at her. *She knows something else.* "Dulcinea."

She lowered her eyes. Christopher would understand Barnabas's shady doings, but she didn't want to discuss them with a stranger.

After watching her bowed head for a moment, Christopher shrugged at Moth. *Later,* he thought.

Moth stood up. "I'll do what I can."

Christopher saw him out to his car, then returned to the living room, where Dulcinea still sat in the striped chair, her head against one of the wings, eyes closed. Again it struck him how white she looked, how frail. Now was not the time to press her on what she hadn't told Moth.

It was possible the meeting had upset her. Thinking about Barnabas...

Filing his emotions in a deep internal drawer, Christopher sat on the edge of the couch. "Feel like going downtown?"

Dulcinea opened her eyes. Downtown. The checking account. "I can't borrow money from you, Christopher. I'll find a job or something. Please stop trying to give me money."

He didn't reply at once. Find a job. Did this mean she planned to stay in Sneffels? That she'd given up trying to convince him to break the curse?

The victory seemed too easy, but he pushed aside the doubt. Was she serious about a job? She wouldn't find one in Sneffels in the off-season. Not to mention that she'd need to contact the Immigration and Naturalization Service for a work permit.

But if she wanted a job— "Would you like to work in my office? I could use a receptionist, someone to help with filing, that kind of thing." Christopher didn't know where the offer had come from, except that it seemed simple.

Which it wouldn't be.

Dulcinea felt too warm. Warm and a little shaky, the way she had when she'd seen that he'd set out a cup of tea for her and made a morning-sickness remedy. Of course now she knew why he'd done those things. To appease his conscience about the curse. Science over superstition.

Still, she could hardly look at his face. "I don't want you to invent a job for me. I want to pay you back the money I've borrowed."

This had to stop, thought Christopher, more than irritated—though not at her. *We were always struggling....* He said carefully, "You haven't borrowed anything. And we really need help at the office. I have a lot of Hispanic patients, and you speak Spanish."

Dulcinea searched his face. Was he sincere?

His eyes never left hers. "Yes?"

"Okay." After a pause she added, "Thank you."

"*De nada.* Thank *you.* Now let's go downtown."

SLEEP CAUGHT HIM that evening. He dozed on the couch in his office with a glass of wine beside him, and the dreams came. Screams filling the corridors. The sound of a firing squad, gunshots and then silence. He was brought into the interrogation room. There was a bucket in the middle of the floor...

When he awoke, the reading lamp was still glowing over his head, but the log in the hearth had burned low. He lay for a while in silence, shaking, listening to the clock ticking on the mantel near the moon globe.

He had cried out in his sleep. Remembering that Dulcinea was in the house, he held his breath, listening. No sound but the clock. His cry could not have reached upstairs. She was probably sleeping with the exhaustion of a woman in her first trimester.

But he had slept on the couch because he was afraid he would dream.

Death brought those dreams.

He got up, shivering as he walked out to the darkened living room and down the hall to the kitchen. He could not stop shivering. At last he returned to his study to put out the fire, then went outside to let the cold numb his senses and remind him how far he was from that prison.

When he felt half-frozen, he walked around to the mineral springs and took off his clothes and got in. He sat in the warm water in the moonless night, steam all around him, ghosts in his mind.

It was comforting to know there was someone, anyone, in the house. Nothing frightened him more than being alone with those memories with no one near.

In the pool, he hugged his arms around his naked body, over his scarred chest, and continued to shiver. In Mayorga's prison, he had learned there could be dignity in a gruesome death, because the memory of the brave lived even in a desecrated corpse. The power of human good did not die with a body. It was the survivor who was doomed to eternal cowardice.

He was.

Have to let Moth look for Barnabas, he thought, disconnected. He couldn't go himself. His practice...

Coward.

There was no curse. He didn't believe in magic or curses. But a shadow of uneasiness hovered over him. Dulcinea seemed so white, wraithlike. Probably anemic. Prenatal vitamins would help. They'd both feel better after she went to the doctor.

He sank lower in the water, trying to put her out of his mind, trying not to wonder too hard about Barnabas and the smoking engine and if his brother was really dead.

TWO DAYS LATER, he drove Dulcinea into Ridgway for a 10:30 a.m. appointment with the obstetrician there. During the drive, she was quiet and pale, and Christopher wondered if she was thinking of the stillbirth or of her dead husband or of the fact that her old lover was driving her to the doctor's office. Or maybe she was just nervous about the exam.

As he parked against a snowbank outside the building, he glanced at her. "Would you like me to sit in the waiting room with you?"

She stared with trepidation at the door of the doctor's office. "Please."

When they went inside, into a room with warm walls painted a pale golden color, Dulcinea approached the reception counter to let them know she was there. The receptionist smiled from her to Christopher. Realizing what the woman must think, that Christopher was the baby's father, Dulcinea flushed.

The receptionist handed her a clipboard with a new-patient information form on it, and Christopher touched her arm. "Let's sit down." As they took seats in an empty corner of the room, he put his head near hers and told her, "The doctor knows you're my sister-in-law. I spoke with him myself."

"Him?"

Christopher wanted to kick himself. There was only one obstetrician in Ridgway, the nearest town to Sneffels and the home of the nearest hospital. Christopher carried obstetrical insurance and delivered babies, but Tucker Trace was the only other option. Dr. Trace was a kind country doctor who'd been practicing in the area for thirty-five years. But Christopher wished he'd thought to tell Dulcinea that the obstetrician was male.

"He's an older man. He delivered me and Barnabas."

Dulcinea thought of Christopher's mother's death.

So did Christopher. But he said, "He's a good doctor. Is it all right?"

"It's fine."

She filled out the form, and Christopher told her to put Thistledown Ranch for her address. When she was called back to the office, he stepped outside and walked down the street in the snow, looking in shop windows, thinking about Dulcinea.

And the baby who'd died.

Dr. Trace would ask her about previous pregnancies. Christopher knew Dulcinea would never reveal that the stillborn child had been his. But suddenly it bothered him greatly that he hadn't asked for details himself, that they hadn't really talked about it.

I want to know, he realized. *I want to know what happened.*

He was back in the waiting room when Dulcinea emerged from the lab, where she'd had blood drawn after her meeting with the doctor. Her eyes were shining—but also suspiciously red-rimmed.

From talking about the stillbirth?

Or from thinking about the father of the child she carried now? She and Barnabas had made love not a dozen weeks before.

Christopher blotted out the thought.

When they stepped outside, the noon sun was beating down on the snow and on the windshield of his truck.

Dulcinea said, "He let me hear the baby's heartbeat!"

She sounded rapturous, and Christopher felt a quick vain hope that the experience was what had moved her to tears. The living—not the dead.

"Sounds like a washing machine, doesn't it?" He unlocked the passenger door for her.

Dulcinea smiled. That was just what the noise had resembled. Dr. Trace had used a Doppler, a hand-held ultrasound device, to pick up the heartbeat.

She climbed into the cab of the truck. Christopher slid behind the wheel, and she looked over at him, a slight frown creasing her forehead. "Christopher, do you deliver babies?"

"Some." He put the key in the ignition.

Dulcinea said something, but he couldn't hear what. He looked at her.

As though embarrassed, she dropped her gaze to her hands in her lap.

"What?"

She shook her head. Her emotions felt confused, and she didn't understand the wish in her heart—that Christopher could deliver her baby. She searched in herself for the old hatred. It would protect her.

But she could not find it, definitely not with Christopher watching her that way and asking, "How about a ride after lunch?"

Horses. Oh, heaven. She was going to ride again.

"SHE'S PRETTY," said Dulcinea when she saw the Paso filly. "What's her name?"

"Sombra de la Luna. She's a good horse." He rubbed her withers, then held the *reindas* while Dulcinea mounted. He admired how naturally she sat on the *montura*. She fingered the fine braids of the *peón,* and he thought he heard her sigh. He remembered the traditional clothes she'd worn riding in Bolivia—her vicuña poncho, her hat and low ankle boots—and felt strangely reassured seeing her dressed in the clothes they'd purchased at the hot springs, plus a heavy guide shell and old Stetson he'd lent her. This was a different country. Six years later. A different life.

After handing Dulcinea the *reindas,* he lifted the *tapaojos,* blinders, from the eyes of Rayo de Luz, the buckskin Paso gelding, and swung into the saddle.

As they walked the horses up the drive toward the highway, he watched Dulcinea school Sombra de la Luna into a smooth *paso llano.* She was smiling, her head thrown back in a way that would make anyone who saw her know her delight at the cool air on her skin, the flawless gait of her mount.

They crossed the highway and started up a graded gravel road called Eagle Creek. As the horses climbed the rise,

Dulcinea studied the valley below and the gray-and-white mountains beyond. From the higher land, it was easy to see the size of Thistledown Ranch. Easy to believe it was the biggest spread in the valley.

She and Christopher followed the road for two miles, passing several new homes but only one car. When they leveled out in a clearing under the spruce, he suggested they stop. They dismounted and tethered the horses.

The afternoon was sunny, the snow melting. Dulcinea stood near the filly, petting her. "I like her, Christopher."

"Good." He glanced over at her, and their eyes met. He was thinking of Taita and the day the horse had died.

Dulcinea suddenly flushed, certain of his thought. Voice trembling faintly, she continued talking about Sombra. "Her *paso llano* is perfect. And she's well trained."

"Ride her whenever you like." Embarrassed by his own feelings, the pleasure her words gave him, he turned to open a saddlebag. "I brought a snack for us."

He handed Dulcinea a plastic bottle of spring water and a sandwich, then reached into the bag again and found an apple. As he passed it to her, his eyes traced the dark arch of her eyebrows, her slightly parted mouth, her slender oval face. He felt far too much.

Dulcinea's heart was threatening to jump through her skin. *Stop feeling this way,* she told herself. *It's insane.*

Christopher walked some distance away to stand looking out on the valley as he ate his sandwich. Dulcinea sat on a boulder from which the snow had melted.

The silence was intense, as though it had its own meaning. Dulcinea tried to ignore Christopher, but she knew his every movement. She remembered when she had believed him the kindest man she'd ever met. She remembered when she had loved him.

The thoughts and the horses nearby were what brought her thoughts to Taita. And for a while, she let herself remember...

COLIC.

Taita had been dead when she reached the stables where she boarded him. She had been furious when she heard that he'd been allowed to roll on his back to ease his pain. The intestine had kinked, fatally, and now he was gone.

The horse that had been a gift from her father when she turned sixteen.

The priceless champion.

The sweetest animal she had ever known.

Feeling powerless, she had spoken to the vet and the owner of the stables. Then, distraught, she had returned to her dorm and called her father. Esteban was cool at the news. She knew that he, too, was angry over the loss of the valuable horse. But he wasn't angry at her; he had tried to comfort her.

When she got off the phone, Dulcinea had known whom she wanted to call, whom she wanted to see. Christopher had come to Wisconsin months before when she'd broken her arm. And since then, he'd come up occasionally on weekends. They'd ridden together, gone for walks. He was easy to talk to. Often they spoke Spanish, which she found comforting. Christopher understood her as none of her girlfriends at school could.

Dulcinea knew she loved him, but for some reason he would never behave like a boyfriend. He always greeted her with a kiss on the cheek, which was customary in South America. But otherwise, he seemed to take pains to remind her that he was a friend of her father's. The problem was, he wasn't fifty years old like her father. He was twenty-four.

And she was nineteen.

As she sat on the boulder and looked out on the Uncompahgre Valley and the mountains beyond, she remembered phoning Christopher that night. She had called him at work, at the hospital, and he had sounded worried when he heard her voice on the phone.

Now she felt a trickle of shame over her tears.

I'm working, Dulce. I really can't come.

Please.

After a few moments, he had asked, *Do you want to come to Chicago?*

The plan had been for her to stay with some nurses who lived in the apartment next to his. As it turned out, she had stayed with Christopher. And this time he was not her father's friend.

"Dulce."

His voice startled her from her reverie, and she looked up to find him standing over her. He nodded across the valley, indicating a snow-capped peak beyond the adjacent ridge. "That's Mount Sneffels. It's the highest peak in this area, but you can't see all of it from here. I'll point it out to you again next time we go to Ridgway."

"Mount Sneffels," said Dulcinea thoughtfully, remembering something from school. "*Journey to the Center of the Earth?* Wasn't the volcano in Iceland named Sneffels?"

Christopher's eyes smiled. "Good for you."

Dulcinea felt her heart twist again, and it frightened her. She didn't want to feel anything for him. But she'd forgotten how kind he was.

She'd forgotten exactly how much she'd loved him.

She noticed that his eyes had gone sober, too. He said, "Let's go home."

CHRISTOPHER ANSWERED the phone when it rang the following morning. He had been cooking pancakes, and Dulcinea was drinking tea and eating crackers at the table, fighting morning sickness.

The call was for her, from Dr. Trace's office.

Handing her the phone, Christopher wondered why the office was calling.

Dulcinea said, "Hello? Yes."

Christopher returned to the stove, trying to restrain his curiosity. But he glanced once at her face as she listened to the voice on the other end of the line, and he saw her shock. She stood up with the receiver in hand, and he saw her move into the dining room doorway as though seeking privacy.

Christopher flipped the pancakes. He was removing one from the skillet and putting it on the plate when he heard her hang up the phone.

She came over to his left side and stood there until he looked at her. Seeing her wide-eyed, desolate expression, Christopher switched off the burner and turned to her.

Dulcinea was shaking inside, filled with shame and anger. She made herself meet Christopher's brown eyes and tried not to notice that they were clear eyes, thoughtful eyes. So different from an otherwise similar pair of eyes she'd known. She asked evenly, "Could you please take me to the doctor's office today?"

"Sure." He met her gaze, which seemed both brave and vulnerable, and he knew something bad had happened. "What's wrong?"

Lowering her eyes and her voice, she told him.

CHAPTER SIX

CHRISTOPHER TRIED to steady his breath.

Dulcinea was blinking back tears. "Will it hurt the baby?"

His heart raced, his feelings explosive. "They'll give you some antibiotics so that it won't." She turned her head, hiding her face, and Christopher reached for her and pulled her against his chest. His hand on the back of her hair, he felt hot tears against his throat and was careful to hold her lightly, separating himself from his emotions—and his emotions from her.

He was so angry he couldn't talk. *Barnabas* . . .

Christopher thought of how thin Dulcinea looked. What he'd just learned made more sense than her having gone hungry in La Paz. She was sick.

Dulcinea shuddered under his touch. She wanted his respect. The desire contradicted everything she'd felt toward him for the past six years. But now she couldn't help it. He was so different from his brother.

She whispered, "I was faithful to him."

Christopher caught the words and her desperate tone. He understood her self-perception. Understood, too, what he had done six years earlier when he had violated the mores of her culture—then left her unprotected.

From Barnabas.

Christopher pulled back. Putting his hands on each side of her head, he tilted her face up so that she met his eyes. "I didn't think for a second you were unfaithful." The next words almost killed him. "To anyone." He stared down at her oval face, white and tear-streaked, the face he remembered from when she was nineteen years old and no one had ever hurt her. He said, "This is not your fault. In any way." Even if she'd known what Barnabas was up to, Christopher knew that there was little she could have done. Bolivia was a man's country. And the men in Dulcinea's life—himself, her father, Barnabas—had not treated her well.

Dulcinea stepped back from him, straightened slightly and reached for a tissue to wipe her eyes. She said with quiet dignity, "Thank you for driving me to the doctor's office. Please... forget about this. It doesn't matter."

Christopher did not answer. It mattered. He would never forget. Never forgive.

Barnabas had given her gonorrhea.

CHRISTOPHER DROVE Dulcinea to Dr. Trace's office that afternoon. She received two shots of penicillin, and then they went around the corner to the ice-cream parlor in the small Ridgway town square. Christopher watched how gingerly she sat down at the booth—sore from the shots. In other circumstances he might have teased her. Not now.

As they shared apple pie and cinnamon-swirl ice cream, Christopher wondered what she felt. If she was angry... or hurt. If she had cried that morning because she'd learned that Barnabas had been with someone else—more likely several someones. Or if she'd already known.

But he couldn't ask any of those things. So he sipped from his glass of ice water, thinking of a nameless prostitute or mistress who probably had the clap, too, and didn't know it.

He tried not to wish that his brother was truly dead.

THAT NIGHT Dulcinea dreamed of Occlo, with horns on her head made from the waxing and waning moons. Dulcinea looked down into her own arms and realized a baby was there. She saw only the face, but she knew it was a boy, and she became afraid. She knew why Occlo had come.

The beautiful figure, the glowing specter, spoke to her in the ancient language of the Incas, the secret language the Kallawaya used for healing. Dulcinea didn't know the language, and she was frightened. Holding the baby against her, she said, "Please, no...."

But when she looked down again, the child in her arms was dead.

"Dulcinea."

She jerked awake at the warm, solid, human touch. The masculine voice.

Christopher was a silhouette over her, a black shape on the edge of her bed, sinking the mattress, blocking the bright light from the bathroom doorway. He was wearing no shirt, and she could see the swell of muscle in his arms and shoulders. Taller and leaner than Barnabas...

He withdrew his hand, and she realized that it had lain on her shoulder, against the silk of her long undershirt. He said, "I was brushing my teeth. I heard you cry out."

Dulcinea swallowed. The dream. The baby.

Dead.

Christopher watched her face. The light from the bathroom cast a pale glow on one side of it, but she was looking away from him and he couldn't see her eyes. Bad dream, he thought. "Want to talk about it?"

"No." But she thought of the baby inside her. What if it was dead? Like Isabel.

Seeing her tears, hoping they weren't for Barnabas or his infidelity, Christopher bent over her, slid his arm beneath her and drew her up to a sitting position.

A sob choked out of her at his touch, at the feel of him pulling her against his body. "Shh." Her face resting on his chest, she started to hold on to him, but as soon as her fingers felt the warmth of his skin she withdrew them. Scared she might never let go.

Christopher felt her restlessness, the hands that wouldn't quite touch him. He slowed his breath. "Do you not want me to hold you?"

She lifted her head, and her eyes met his. She saw might-have-beens and what-ifs. A man she had loved. A baby who had died. Instead of answering Christopher's question, she said, "The baby's going to die. It might already be dead."

Christopher took a breath. Barnabas's baby. She wanted this baby. But perhaps it had more to do with the child—and with *their* child—than with Barnabas. He hoped so.

"I dreamed about it. I dreamed that Occlo came and killed it." Turning and slipping from his grasp, Dulcinea lay down on the bed again, retreating into herself.

"Dulcinea, pregnant women often have those kinds of dreams. You're just anxious."

She gave him a killing glare.

Christopher opened his mouth, then closed it.

Like Barnabas, thought Dulcinea. Christopher reduced the world to science and psychology. Her eyes were adjusting to the shadows, and she lifted them to see his face again, but they paused on something else, on his chest, and a choked sound came out of her.

Christopher saw her eyes widen, and his arms locked across his chest. "Don't—"

—look.

Dulcinea sat up. "What did they do to you? *What did they do to you?*"

Christopher stood up and stepped back from the bed into the shadows so she couldn't see his scars. He didn't want to talk about them. He didn't want to disturb the other never-healed scars inside his head. Instead, he focused on *her* wounds, and he was acutely sorry for saying that it was common for pregnant women to have disturbing dreams, even if it was true.

Dulcinea had been pregnant before.

And her child—*his* child—had been stillborn.

He looked at her on the bed, at the hair tumbling down her shoulders, overwhelming her small face. "Just a second, okay?"

He slipped back through the bathroom and into his own room. It was neat, the bed still made, no pictures on the walls, the only photos those of his mother and his grandparents on the dresser. He had destroyed his photos of Barnabas years earlier and never replaced them, even when his anger began to abate. He didn't own a photo of his father, who had been bitten by a parasite in a thatch-roof hut and had died of Chagas' disease when he and Barnabas were twelve.

Christopher drew a flannel shirt from a hanger in the double-door wardrobe, pulled it on and buttoned it. Then he crouched to reach under the clothes for the woven, Kallawaya-made, leather-bottomed bag on the closet floor. He found what he wanted and returned through the bathroom to Dulcinea's room.

She was sitting up in bed, and she threw him a suspicious look as he entered, her eyes sliding down to the instrument in his hand. Comprehension dawned.

Christopher smiled. "I'm not going to do this every time you have a bad dream."

Dulcinea swallowed. The shyness she might have felt was dulled by fear. As he snapped on the lamp on the bedside table, she stared at the instrument in Christopher's hand, a pocket-size radiolike box with a spiral telephone cord attached. At the end of the cord was an object like a small microphone. A Doppler. With this, Dulcinea knew, they could hear the baby's heartbeat, as she and Dr. Trace had done in his office.

Christopher thought of the curse and Dulcinea's dream—and Barnabas.

Dead?

Feeling cold, he set the Doppler on the nightstand, stood up and walked to the radiator to warm his hands.

On the bed, Dulcinea lay back and drew the covers down to her hips. From the edge of the room, Christopher saw the shape of her breasts beneath her silk long undershirt, saw the shadow of a nipple beneath the fabric. His chest went tight, and he understood the phrase "loss of objectivity."

But there was no harm in listening for her baby's heartbeat.

Barnabas's baby...

He came back to the bed.

The edge of the mattress compressed under him. Dulcinea was glad he didn't plan to listen to *her* heart. It would give her away.

She dared a glance at his eyes. He seemed to have been waiting for her to look at him, and their gazes held for a long time. He stared down at her body.

She was short of breath.

Christopher lifted the edge of her shirt. He never had these emotions or physical responses in his office, with his patients.

Barnabas is dead, he thought, trying to convince himself.

Glancing at Dulcinea, he said honestly, "It's a good thing I'm not your doctor. I get an erection just touching your skin."

Dulcinea trembled. Nonetheless, his candor eased her tension. The reminder that once the two of them had been so close, so in love, was comforting. She whispered, "It's all right."

Christopher had been watching her face. He saw her mouth and knew what she'd said, though he couldn't hear it.

Eyes on hers, he tugged the waistband of her long johns down a few inches, exposing more of her skin.

Dulcinea's blood raced toward her legs, starting a tingling below the hand he placed on her abdomen.

"Is this all right, too?" His voice sounded unnatural.

"Yes." She was hardly breathing.

Their eyes locked. His hand... It explored her belly that was barely rounded with pregnancy.

Christopher's lips felt hot, chapped, and he licked them lightly before he said, "What's your due date?"

"July twenty-seventh." Remembering what he'd said, she tried hard to keep her eyes from drifting toward the fly of his jeans. His fingers were low on her stomach, just above the line of her pubic hair, and it was hard to lie still.

But after just a second, he withdrew his hand and picked up the Doppler. His breath was ragged. *What if there's no heartbeat?*

Get a grip, Christopher. "Let's see what he's doing."

He. In her dream the baby had been a boy.

Christopher turned on the Doppler and placed the end that looked like a microphone against her skin. Moving it slightly, he listened, until a rhythmic swishing sound filled the air.

He smiled, his eyes looked into hers. "There you go."

Calm seeping over her, Dulcinea listened to her baby's heart.

The sound filled Christopher's left ear like the blood rushing in his head, and he thought of Isabel. Had Dulcinea wanted his baby this much?

Later, after they'd said good-night and he'd returned to his own room, Christopher lay on his bed in the dark still thinking of the baby Dulcinea had carried for nine months. Tonight hadn't been the time to bring it up—after he'd eased the fears left by her dream. But sometime he would ask her to tell him about the child they'd made together.

He hoped she would understand how badly he wanted to know.

He hoped she would think he had the right.

CHRISTOPHER RETURNED to work on Monday, and Dulcinea went with him. The small clinic staff welcomed her. There was just Sissy, Christopher's nurse, and Bonnie, the lab technician. Both seemed glad that Christopher had found a receptionist.

Because Bonnie was busy taking strep cultures—a sore throat was going around—Sissy explained the office procedures. Dulcinea liked the nurse at once. Though her freckled face was not classically pretty, her brown eyes were intelligent and full of humor.

"Now, when you answer the phone, just, whatever you do, *don't* say, 'Sniffles Family Practice.'"

Dulcinea laughed.

"Even though," added Sissy, "it's what we call it amongst ourselves."

"Does Chr— Does Dr. Choqueneira mind?"

"He doesn't mind anything," said Sissy. She glanced toward the waiting room, where a mother was trying to keep two children in line. Turning back to Dulcinea, she lowered her voice slightly. "He's totally nice, totally reasonable." Regretful, she said, "I'm sorry about your husband. They were twins, weren't they?"

"Not . . . identical."

Sissy nodded, and Dulcinea wondered whether she was curious if Christopher's brother had been as handsome as he was. Did the nurse know Christopher had spent a year and a half in prison? That he'd been tortured? Did Christopher confide in anyone?

Sissy changed the subject. She pointed to a hand-lettered sign taped on the counter, out of view of patients on the other side of the window. It read *Lo que puedes darme.*

Whatever you can afford, translated Dulcinea.

"That's the rule," said Sissy. "For everyone. Just look the patient in the eye when you say it, and it usually does the trick to get them to—you know—pay what they can afford. I'm trying to learn Spanish, but it's slow going." She eyed Dulcinea. "Maybe you can help?"

"Sure."

Sissy looked relieved. "Good. Dr. Choqueneira's great, but he's really a tease. I mean, he teaches me how to say things like 'Sit down. I'll buy you a drink,' and 'I'm looking for a rich husband,' and . . ."

Dulcinea laughed. Christopher could tease, but it was a side of him she hadn't seen since she arrived in Colorado.

She was glad he still possessed it.

Through the morning and afternoon, she answered the phone and tried to learn the workings of the office. A pregnant woman came in for a prenatal, and another woman brought an infant for a checkup. In the middle of the afternoon, the search-and-rescue team called to say they were bringing in a man who'd broken his leg ice climbing on Mount Sneffels. Christopher was busy all day, seeing one patient after another, and sometimes there were five or six people in the small waiting room at once. Not only that, Sneffels old-timers were constantly popping in, asking if he had an opening.

Late that afternoon, after the man with the broken leg had been sent on to the hospital in Ridgway, when the waiting room was empty at last and there was only one patient left to be seen, Christopher came into the reception area, where Dulcinea was filing patients' records in the old oak filing cabinets that had been his grandfather's. "How's it going?"

"Great." She'd enjoyed the day. She felt comfortable working for Christopher and was glad she could repay the money he'd lent her. "Thank you for letting me do this."

"You're helping me." Dulcinea had never finished college, because of him. What kind of work would she have chosen had he left her alone? Or would an arranged marriage have ended any career outside the home? He glanced toward the empty waiting room, then pulled up a chair beside Dulcinea's. He had one last patient to see, for an annual pap smear, but he knew the woman was changing clothes. "I need to go grocery shopping in Ridgway after work, and then I'm coming back into town to bring a lady her groceries. It'll take a while, so I'll drop you at home first." Trying not to hope, telling himself he had no reason to feel guilty for hoping, he said, "Unless you want to come."

His brown eyes were so clear, so alert, so attractive. . . . Dulcinea remembered all the things that had happened the day before and how kind he had been. She had always perceived him as kind—until the day he'd said, *I don't want to marry you.*

They were not lovers now. He was her brother-in-law—and her friend. She wanted to be near him, because against all reason she felt deep security around him, as though he could and would protect her from harm. She deliberately avoided the memory of the way he'd abandoned her before. Everything was different now.

"I'll come."

THE DRIVE TO RIDGWAY was quiet but companionable. It was snowing, flakes flying at the windshield in a fireworks pattern. As he drove slowly north on the highway, watching for deer on the road, Christopher asked her to read him the shopping lists, theirs and Mrs. Prosper's, which she did using the light from the glove box.

But his mind wasn't on it. He was thinking about what Barnabas had done—given her a venereal disease. And he was thinking about the past, the brother he had known.

They shopped quickly and efficiently, working together with two carts and enduring the speculative glances of Christopher's acquaintances. Then they drove back into Sneffels, all the way to the south end of town and up Rhodochrosite Street to a two-and-a-half-story Victorian, the last house in the row. It was built into the rocky hill above, its bottom floor hewn from the surrounding stone. The street itself continued to rise another half block, right up to the steeply sloping mountainside. But there were no homes beyond Mrs. Prosper's.

As he parked outside and the porch light went on, Christopher nodded to a white slope dead ahead. "That's the Jack-Be-Nimble Slide. There used to be three houses just like this one right under that chute."

"Avalanche?" Dulcinea asked.

He nodded. "These days they won't let you build in a place like that. But Mrs. Prosper's house is a hundred years old. The slide has never come this far." He shrugged, thinking of Kitty's attachment to her house. He'd once suggested she move because of the number of stairs. No dice. She'd been born in that house and had lived there with her husband. *Now stop worrying, Christopher,* she had said.

Mrs. Prosper came outside. Christopher carried the groceries, and Dulcinea followed him up to the second-floor porch, where she recognized the patient who had been at the clinic the day she'd arrived in Sneffels.

"Bless your heart," said Mrs. Prosper. "Do you two want to come in?"

Christopher said, "Sure. For a few minutes."

They sat in the front parlor, which contained many well-kept antiques. Dulcinea admired the room and accepted a cup of tea, and then she sat quietly while Mrs. Prosper showed them photos of an old mine where her father had worked, a mine Christopher's family had once owned.

They stayed for half an hour, and then Christopher said they needed to go. Dulcinea was famished, and when they were settled in his truck, he reached into the back seat and produced salads from the supermarket deli. He drove down the street to a snowy park, where they sat in the pickup and ate. Dulcinea felt more contented than she had in years, but there was a tingling heat in her veins, a constant awareness of Christopher. Sexual attraction.

It made her realize and acknowledge that accepting his friendship was *not* safe—and forgetting the past was unwise.

Christopher had hurt her badly.

And if she began to love him, he could do it again.

HE WAS HARD not to love.

The next day after work, he pulled into the hot-springs resort on the way home.

Dulcinea regarded him curiously from the passenger seat.

"Swimsuit," he said.

"Oh."

"For you."

Dulcinea was glad for the 5 p.m. darkness of January. "I can't swim."

"I know." He opened his door and got out.

A moment later, when he opened her door, Dulcinea wouldn't look at him.

"What's wrong?"

Her body was on fire, his too close. "I'm pregnant."

Christopher understood. Bathing suits and svelte bodies. He started to say that he'd always been partial to pregnant women. What came out was, "You're beautiful, Dulcinea. And being pregnant is beautiful."

He saw a rhythmic throbbing at her throat, and her eyes seemed misty. She still wouldn't meet his.

"I won't be able to find a swimsuit to fit. I'll grow out of it."

"Get a bikini." Why had his voice dropped so low? "I'll give you a T-shirt to wear over it."

She climbed out of the truck.

That night after dinner, he said, "Swimming lesson?"

Apprehensively, she agreed, and when she went upstairs to put on her swimsuit, he brought her a heavy white T-shirt with a faded blue logo reading Sneffels Search and Rescue. Ten minutes later, she met him down at the pool, glad for the T-shirt skimming her thighs. Christopher was already in the water, and a submerged light cast a greenish glow throughout the stone pool.

The air temperature was forty, so Dulcinea wasted no time getting in the shallow end, and he came over to join her, the water glistening on his shoulders, his hair wet around his face.

Dulcinea huddled on the steps, keeping her breasts below the surface, her arms locked about her knees.

Studying her, Christopher remembered children he'd taught at the hot-springs resort during the summers when he was a teenager. "The first lesson is getting used to the water."

Her eyes said, I'm afraid.

Christopher thought, So am I.

Of you.

My brother's wife.

THERE WAS NO WORD about Barnabas, though Moth's men were searching the Yungas by air for any trace of the plane.

As the month wore on, Dulcinea's morning sickness disappeared, and the antibiotics defeated Barnabas's unwelcome legacy. Her pregnancy began to show. She bought two dresses in Ridgway, both of crinkled sand-washed silk and some dress boots to go with them, and she loosened the drawstring waists of her pants and wore big tops that draped over the front.

Dr. Trace scheduled an ultrasound for the second week in February, when she would be four months pregnant. But as Dulcinea saw the time passing, her anxiety increased.

By day it was easy to call the curse superstition, to laugh it off. But at night, when shadows fell on her room and she lay alone in the ash-and-black-walnut bed, primal fears came forth, powerful in the darkness.

Unwilling to forget the matter, she buried herself in it, instead. She took Mariano Choqueneira's journal from the bookcase downstairs and read it. Like his blond descendant, Mariano Choqueneira had not been a superstitious man. He had been educated by Spanish missionaries, and he was an atheist. He had left home one day, telling his wife he was off to join the forces of Tupac Amaru II, who had been leading the mountain peoples in an attempt to restore the Inca empire. That was a lie. In truth, Mariano had wanted peace away from his wife, who was pregnant and had nagged him for riches he couldn't provide. On the way home from his travels, he had stumbled upon a moon shrine in an uninhabited region of the forest. Seeing all the riches within as his for the taking, he had stolen a golden urn.

But when he got home, he found that the moon had begun to exact payment for her treasure. . . .

Tomás had told Dulcinea the rest. For two centuries, no Choqueneira birth had escaped mishap. Either the mother died—or the child.

The curse must be real.

In the dark hours, Dulcinea lay awake praying, and her prayers were a terrified mantra. *Please let my baby be all right. Please let my baby live. Please make Christopher take back the urn.*

She was going to have to approach him again, plead with him. But she put it off. Things had been good for the past few weeks. A respite from the loneliness that had never gone away, even with Barnabas. But Christopher was like her. He enjoyed quiet, rarely even turned on the television. In the mornings he was up first and always set out some tea for her. And sometimes after work they made dinner together, conversing easily in Spanish or English. Later they went swimming.

On the night before her ultrasound, Dulcinea opened the top left drawer of the dresser in her room to take out a nightgown, and beneath her underwear she spied the manila envelope she'd brought with her from Bolivia. She should have given the photos to Christopher long ago—after Moth left that day. But she didn't want to answer his questions about Barnabas. She had brought the photos with her only because she'd hoped he would use them to find the moon shrine.

With a sense of desperation, she rested a hand on the dresser. She was four months pregnant. He didn't have much time.

Neither did she. Or her baby.

She slid the envelope from the drawer.

"CHRISTOPHER?"

He was in the solarium off the living room repotting a cactus. When he turned, he saw Dulcinea just outside the arch, and tension went through him because he hadn't heard her approach. That loss of hearing was something he practiced accepting, tried to accept, every day. It still angered him.

Dulcinea stepped into the solarium. She was wearing a white nightgown and his old blue bathrobe, and he noticed the robe swelling out slightly over her body.

That, too, he practiced accepting. Ignoring. Forgetting.

Barnabas's baby.

His own was dead.

"I keep meaning to show you these," said Dulcinea, and she held out a battered manila envelope.

Christopher stared at it warily, a chill inside him. But he reached out. As he took the envelope, he asked, "What is it?"

"They belonged to Barnabas. They're . . . some kind of aerial photos."

Christopher's heart thudded, and he opened the envelope. Barnabas's plane was still missing. Moth's associates hadn't seen the wreck from the air, and now two men were hunting on foot. Already, the bill was five figures. Could these photos provide a clue to where Barnabas had been when—if—his plane crashed?

He drew the photographs from the envelope, and when he saw what they were, he felt as though someone had wrapped a cord around his ribs and pulled tight.

Red, blue, yellow, green. Four-color multispectral aerial photos of a rain forest, with the coordinates marked. Christopher thought of the maps in his study. He didn't want to articulate any of the bizarre notions filling his mind. *What had Barnabas been doing with the photos?*

"Where did you get these?"

Dulcinea saw his intensity. She should have given him the photos earlier. Embarrassed, she said, "They were taped under a table in our house in La Paz. Barnabas must have left them before he—"

"And you didn't give them to me until now? When we've spent thousands of dollars hunting for his plane? You must have brought them with you. You've had them all this time." Christopher remembered the day Moth had come to the house. Was this what Dulcinea had withheld?

His anger made her feel like crying. "I thought he was doing something illegal." It sounded stupid now that she said it aloud. Even Christopher looked dismayed.

"Like what?" He had his own ideas. There were many legitimate reasons for taking multispectral aerial photos. Geologists, agricultural experts, archaeologists, all might use the photographs in their work. But Barnabas... Only one thing made sense. Antiquities. Maybe even... *No*. Not *that* ruin.

Her face red, Dulcinea turned away from him as she spoke. "I thought he was stealing from archaeological sites." After a silence, she admitted, "I know he did once, because... I saw something he had."

Her shame was painful to witness. As Christopher replaced the photos in the envelope, he tried to calm himself, tried to see his brother's wife without seeing the motive behind what she had just done, behind the reason she'd brought the photos with her to Colorado.

She still believed in the curse.

Taking a breath, he nodded toward the living room. "Shall we sit down, Dulcinea?"

It was as though the lights in the room had dimmed. The photos would not accomplish what she'd hoped.

They sat in the living room, Dulcinea on the Eastlake settee and Christopher in a matching chair nearby, facing her. He leaned forward, forearms across his knees, and tried to gather himself.

She was still worried about the curse. Was there any way to make her understand that the curse wasn't real?

A twinge went through him.

The doubt that had shadowed him his entire life.

The curse was not real.

"Dulcie, six years ago, I went to return the urn to the shrine."

She stared at him. Seconds passed before comprehension dawned. Then she looked so stricken that he got up and sat on the couch beside her. "The urn was hidden in a cave. I traveled for days to reach it, and the urn was there."

Dulcinea's heart banged against her ribs. Christopher had seen the urn. *Six years ago...* "Start at the beginning. Please."

"I won't start at the very beginning—" he met her eyes "—because I know you've been reading Mariano's journal. I'd hoped you were accepting it for what it is. An interesting historical document."

Dulcinea held his gaze. "Especially the part about the séance, when Mariano and his father and Emilio saw—"

She must have caught the look he was sending her, because she stopped speaking abruptly, as though afraid to continue.

Silence tolled through him. He knew how the sentence ended.

You.

Mariano Choqueneira and the others had seen him, Christopher. *His hair is the color of pale straw, and he wears the medicine bag of the Kallawaya....*

He spent a few moments quiet, regaining his composure. "When you and I..."

She lifted her head.

"The day your father found us, I asked you if you were pregnant."

Dulcinea closed her eyes, remembering the scars on his body, his deaf right ear.

"I thought I should try..." he began but could hardly continue. He was still embarrassed by his superstitious response to an unconfirmed pregnancy. Though Dulcinea *had* been pregnant. "Anyhow, I got the urn out of the cave, as I said, and when I came out myself, Mayorga and his men were there. He arrested me on an antiquities violation."

Because of me, thought Dulcinea. *My father...*

"They seized the urn. I went to prison. I've never seen the urn since. I don't know where it is. It could be in a museum in Paris or in the hands of a private collector."

Dulcinea barely registered that the urn was lost. Christopher had tried to break the curse for her, and she had married his brother. While he went to jail. He had tried to break the curse, even though...

"You didn't want to marry me," she whispered.

Christopher choked back the truth.

I lied.

Averting his gaze, he said, "This is all past. It doesn't..." He couldn't say it didn't matter. "Let's leave it in the past. The important thing is finding his body." He glanced at the manila envelope still in his hand. "These photos might help. If Barnabas was hunting for ruins—"

Beside him, Dulcinea started.

Christopher ignored it, knowing what she was thinking, pretending it hadn't occurred to him. "—the photos might give us a hint where he was looking."

Her question stabbed him. "Chris, what if he was looking for the shrine?"

Chris. She had called him that in bed. *Chris. Oh, Chris, don't stop...*

He quieted the voice in his mind. "Why would Barnabas look for the shrine? He didn't have the urn."

Dulcinea's gaze met his, and the answer was there, because they had both known the man so well. Barnabas could have been looking for the shrine to steal the rest of its treasure.

Ignoring that, Christopher said, "He knew there was no curse. And he felt as I do. That in any case it isn't worth dying for."

There was a long silence. Then Dulcinea stood up from the sofa. Not looking at him, she said, "Good night," and walked out of the living room and up the stairs.

Christopher sat watching her progress, and like a shower of hailstones it fell upon him what he had just said.

That she wasn't worth dying for.

Nor was her child.

Feeling a crashing explosion of self-hatred, he remembered when he had believed that a baby was worth dying for. That a woman was.

CHAPTER SEVEN

WHEN DULCINEA AWOKE the next morning, the first thing she remembered was what Christopher had said the night before, and her spirits felt as damp as the snow-burdened sky outside.

She bathed and dressed in gray wool leggings and a long fisherman's sweater and brushed her hair, dreading the drive to work with Christopher, dreading being near him after he'd said how little he cared for her.

She reminded herself that he had tried to break the curse once on her behalf. That he had suffered hideously for it. But when he had said that the curse wasn't worth dying for...

I would have given anything, thought Dulcinea, *to have Isabel live. The baby you gave me, Cristobal.*

Obviously, he didn't feel the same way. It was childish of her to think he might.

I can't stay here. I can't stay. There were wild feelings inside her, a need to escape before Christopher could hurt her again. She longed to return to Bolivia, never to see him again. But then how could she persuade him to do what she wanted? She had to face him. And now she was hungry. It reminded her of the indigence she had left behind.

As she at last opened her door to step out and go down to breakfast, something fell at her feet. A large white envelope had been tipped against the door, a red rose beside it.

Heart hammering, she glanced down the deserted hall. Christopher's door was shut.

She reached down and picked up the rose and the envelope, which was heavy, filled with something thick. On the front was her name in Christopher's writing. She slipped back into her room and laid the rose on top of the dresser, then opened the envelope and slid the contents from inside.

It was a simple card with daisies on the front and the words "Happy Valentine's Day." *Valentine's Day*. Dulcinea hadn't received a Valentine since college. That had been from Christopher, too.

When she opened the card, folded sheets of paper spilled out. She knelt to collect them from the hardwood, at the same time reading what he had written.

I know there will never be another horse like Taita. But if this gift brings you a moment's pleasure, it will fill my heart.

Love,
Christopher

Dulcinea knew what the papers were before she unfolded them. He had given her Sombra de la Luna.

She sat on the floor and cried.

When she went downstairs several minutes later, Christopher was in the kitchen, dressed for work in a chamois shirt and jeans, and she thought he seemed afraid to meet her eyes. She walked over to the counter where he stood filling a tea ball for her.

"*Gracias*, Cristobal."

Christopher looked at her, saw that she'd been crying. His heart gave one hard beat.

She said, "I didn't get you anything."

He touched her back, between her shoulder blades, then dropped his hand. "You gave me the only thing I wanted."

She had accepted the horse.

Unable to stop the words, he said, "I want to make you happy." But she wasn't his. *Barnabas*...

Dulcinea's pulse raced. *I don't want to love him,* she thought. *I just want him to do this one thing, the thing he won't do.* She almost said, *If you want to make me happy, you'll break the curse.* But when she saw his troubled profile, something stopped her.

Perhaps the fact that his right ear was turned toward her.

Christopher glanced at her, wondering if she thought his words were empty. *There is no curse,* he thought, trying to tell her with his eyes.

She turned away, silently disagreeing.

"May I drive you to your ultrasound tonight?" He drove her everywhere; she had no license. But after what he'd said to her the night before, he'd been afraid the only ride she would accept from him was to the airport.

"Thank you." Dulcinea felt like crying again and wasn't sure why. She moved from the counter and started for the door. "I think I'll go out and see my horse."

HER ULTRASOUND was scheduled for 7:30 p.m. at the hospital in Ridgway. That night after work, Christopher took her to dinner at a Mexican restaurant. Dulcinea needed a full bladder for the sound waves to transmit properly, so she drank lemonade with her meal while Christopher teased her about the discomfort she would feel until the exam was over and she could pee.

On the way to the hospital, he stopped at the grocery store in Ridgway and bought a videotape. "They'll make a tape of the ultrasound for you," he explained. "It's a nice thing to have."

"Thank you." Dulcinea reminded herself to take his kindness for what it was. Caring—which did not necessarily spring from love.

But the urge to lean on him was strong as they reached the hospital. Though the lobby was decorated in light blue, the walls of the corridors were starkly white. Death white. Emotionally though not physically, Dulcinea clung to what was warm and alive, Christopher walking beside her.

He accompanied her to the radiology department, where they sat together in a white waiting room. The receptionist knew him, and both the other patients in the waiting area appeared to recognize him, as well. Under their curious glances, Christopher wondered what Dulcinea felt. Did it upset her that people thought they were a couple?

Something had upset her. He tried to read in her face what it might be. She looked withdrawn. Sad.

But after a moment she asked, "Do you work in this hospital?"

"Sometimes. I have privileges here."

Did the white bother him? She supposed he was used to it. On the walls at his office were copies of his diplomas and certificates from medical school and the hospitals where he'd worked. Dulcinea knew that he'd completed his residency in Denver after getting out of prison.

Preoccupied, she was hardly aware of Christopher's denim-covered leg beside her until he put his head near hers and asked in a low voice no one else could hear, "What's on your mind?"

Dulcinea kept her eyes trained on the far wall. "Everything's white."

White.

Of course, thought Christopher, understanding too well. In the Andes, white was the color of death, of burial shrouds for babies. Quietly, he said, "The birthing room has blue wallpaper."

She lifted her head and looked at him, feeling the peace that came with friendship. He understood her. She shut her eyes in relief, then opened them again, thinking how close his were. His mouth was close, too.

Christopher wanted to kiss her, to make her forget her dread. He knew what it would be like. Mouths touching and opening, tongues meeting. *Oh, God, Dulcie...* Drawing a breath, he straightened up just as the ultrasound technician came out from the back room.

"Dulcinea Choqueneira?"

They both stirred.

When the technician noticed Christopher, her eyes widened noticeably. "Dr. Choqueneira. Hello."

Christopher smiled tensely and stood up with Dulcinea. "Hi, Jan."

The technician's eyes darted between the two of them, and she asked Dulcinea, "How about if I take some measurements, and then he can come in and watch? Oh, good. You brought a videotape."

Dulcinea's eyes darted up to Christopher's.

His gaze fleeted over her ivory skin, paler than the wool of her sweater. "Do you want me to come in?"

She nodded emphatically.

Mouth dry, he tried to smile reassuringly. It was only after she had followed the technician from the room that he remembered his brother's body had not been found. Barnabas, who had never lived on the right side of the law, was only missing.

Not necessarily dead.

And Christopher wanted nothing so much as to make love to his wife.

As Jan prepared Dulcinea for the exam, taking preliminary measurements, then coating her stomach with mineral oil so that no air would come between the transducer and her skin, she asked, "So... are you his sister?"

"In-law," said Dulcinea. "My husband passed away recently."

"Oh." The technician nodded soberly. "I'm sorry." After a brief pause, she tilted her head in the direction of the waiting room, indicating Christopher. "That's one nice man. You never hear anything bad about him, and you can't say that with all the docs. But he's incredible. Really sweet with newborns—and moms. Women whose babies he's delivered just can't say enough good about him." She eyed Dulcinea. "But you have Dr. Trace, huh? He's good, too. And actually, when it comes to gynecological things, I prefer an older doctor. You know what I mean? I mean—" again she nodded toward the waiting room "—he's pretty sexy."

Dulcinea was embarrassed, and the technician looked apologetic. "That's probably more than you wanted to hear about your brother-in-law, huh? Well, it looks like we're ready. Hey, do you want to know the baby's sex?"

Dulcinea shrugged. "Sure."

"We might not be able to see, but . . . anyway, I'll go get Dr. Choqueneira, okay?"

Jan stepped out of the room and returned moments later with Christopher.

"Okay," she said, "let's see what we've got."

There was a monitor off to Dulcinea's right. She saw an image on it, but she didn't recognize anything until the technician moved the transducer on her belly and said, "Okay, look. Here are the knees." To Christopher she remarked, "This is our new machine. Pretty good pictures, huh?"

"I'll say."

Dulcinea felt a strange jump inside her. Her eyes widened. "I think he just kicked." The baby moved again, and she watched it on the screen. It looked like an infant skeleton, but she could see the knees moving as she felt another thump inside her. Then she saw the infant's toes.

Amazed, Dulcinea glanced up at Christopher to see if he shared her reaction. His gaze was glued to the monitor. His face was white.

Her heart suddenly pounding, Dulcinea felt and watched the baby move again. And she saw and knew what Christopher must have seen, too—she was carrying a boy.

Like in her dream.

Christopher said nothing, however. His arms were across his chest, and his eyes didn't leave the screen as the technician spoke, pointing out that the baby had his thumb in his mouth.

"Look," said Jan. "See the eye?"

Dulcinea watched Christopher's lips tighten. He didn't respond, just watched the monitor. When the ultrasound was done, he thanked Jan, met Dulcinea's eyes and said in a strange constricted voice, "I'll be outside."

WHEN THEY LEFT the hospital, they could see the nearly full moon rising over Courthouse Mountain. It was the last thing Christopher wanted to see, because he couldn't forget the picture on the screen, the baby moving, sucking its thumb. As he opened the driver's door of the truck and got in beside Dulcinea, he wanted to say something about the moon. That it was roughly one-fourth the size of the earth, with one-sixth the earth's gravity. That its diameter was less than the width of the United States. That its mean distance from earth was 238,857 miles. That men had walked on the moon.

That it was a celestial object. Not divine.

But it was beautiful as it rose over the mountains on its slanted winter angle, spotlighting the snow-covered peaks. It held sway over the tide—and the tide in women's bodies. Beside Christopher was a pregnant woman, and he had seen the child in her womb. Tonight he could not think the moon mundane.

Driving south on the highway, he was glad for the times when the ball of white dipped behind the mountains, out of view. The moon felt like a chaperon, and Christopher felt as though its light was penetrating his mind and heart, laying open his thoughts and desires.

He desired his brother's wife.

Barnabas was probably dead—but it didn't feel that way.

And Christopher wanted Dulcinea, anyway.

He hadn't been with a woman for more than two years, since he'd lived in Denver. Sex hadn't been good since Dulcinea, though he wasn't optimistic enough to believe it could be the same with her again. He'd changed in prison. Sometimes it was hard to feel.

But with Dulcinea, it was too easy. And his body wanted to keep pace with his heart.

He couldn't have her.

As the highway led into the Uncompahgre Valley, she said, "Christopher, thank you for coming with me."

"You're welcome."

The moon lifted over the ridge to the east, brightening the valley, and Dulcinea ducked her head toward the windshield to peer up at its light.

Christopher pretended not to see it.

He wanted her so badly.

They neared the ranch, and he signaled, then turned down the drive, slowing as he spotted a deer near the side of the road. There were more in the meadow nearby. The snow had melted, exposing the grass, and now the animals had come to graze under the night sky.

Dulcinea was surprised when Christopher slowed the truck on the road, stopped it and turned off the engine and the lights. Rubbing her arms lightly, she turned to him, wondering if he had to close a gate, if that was why he'd stopped. But he made no move to get out. Instead, he sat silently beside her, not looking at her.

"Chris?"

Chris. It undid him. He told himself, *He's dead. He's dead.*

But he had no proof, he couldn't believe it.

Dulcinea tried to breathe evenly, tried not to ask herself why he had stopped. Tried not to wish that it was to kiss her. Clutching her feelings tightly inside, she sat up straight in the seat. She hated the moonlight making everything so bright in the cab, as though it could see inside her.

Christopher hated it, too. It illuminated her shape, and he remembered the ultrasound image of her baby. He thought of the color white and of an infant body shrouded.

Little baby, somewhere...

His heart hurt, and he turned the key in the ignition, trying to forget that the living creature he had seen on the monitor was his brother's child, not his.

LATE THAT NIGHT, Christopher sat alone in the mineral-springs pool. The vapor swirled around his head, and he thought of going down through the passage below the house to the darker space, the cave. The environment could make his thoughts no blacker.

Mayorga pacing. A guard standing ready with a lighter and a cigarette....

The urn, Dr. Choqueneira. Please tell me again about the urn. What more can you tell me about this urn? I'm not satisfied that you've told me all you know about the urn.

Christopher had told him everything. It had come out over months, and he didn't know how many times he had kissed death, narrowly avoided irreparable brain damage from the beatings.

Somewhere, a man named Bartola Mayorga still lived. He knew about the urn. He knew about the shrine.

An untouched shrine to the moon, containing all its treasures but one.

Christopher let the steam envelop him and closed his eyes. He couldn't go back. He could not.

DULCINEA SMELLED bacon and eggs frying the next morning at six when she awakened, and she followed the scent downstairs and found Christopher in the kitchen.

He smiled at her, but the smile didn't reach his eyes. "Good morning." Distantly, as though he'd shut off his feelings, he said, "I'm going to Denver today. A doctor from Telluride is filling in for me at the clinic. He can't be there until noon, so we've done some appointment juggling. I've asked Ferdy to drive you to work this afternoon. I'll pick you up."

Ferdy was the man who looked after the horses. He and his wife lived in Sneffels. Dulcinea liked Ferdy, who seemed to really care about all the animals at Thistledown Ranch. "Okay." She wanted to know why he was going to Denver, and she waited for him to tell her, but he didn't. He put on his parka, said good-bye and left for the airport.

She rode Sombra de la Luna in the corral that morning. To Ferdy's amusement, she practiced holding a champagne glass full of water, trying not to spill any, as she rode the bay filly around the ring. The champagne class was the highlight of any Paso competition. Sombra de la Luna did beautifully, and Dulcinea felt increasing rapport with her. She knew she could never lay eyes on the beautiful animal without remembering that she was a Valentine gift from Christopher. But Dulcinea could have loved Sombra de la Luna for herself alone.

She made a black-bean soup for lunch for herself and Ferdy, and afterward he drove her to the clinic. Dulcinea ached for Christopher's presence. The hours dragged, and at the clinic she often looked out the windows, hoping to see his truck arrive, hoping to see his blond hair and red parka as he got out. Missing him desperately.

Finally Sissy asked, "So...is Dr. Choqueneira coming by tonight?"

Dulcinea felt color flooding her cheeks. "To take me home."

"Mmm." Sissy whistled a few bars of a Beatles melody as she left the room. "Here, There, and Everywhere."

Dulcinea buried her hot face in her hands, knowing the truth. She was in love with Christopher. Again.

Still.

But she couldn't afford to love him unless he loved not only her but her baby. Unless he loved them enough to break the curse.

Because if he ignored her pleas and the child she was carrying died, she did not think she would ever forgive him.

AT FIVE O'CLOCK his truck pulled up outside the clinic. Dulcinea saw him through the window, and there were no patients in the waiting room, so she got up and hurried outside.

As he closed the driver door, Christopher nodded to her. She was wearing a navy blue dress and a cardigan and hiking boots—Sneffels chic—and he wanted to tell her to hold the railing as she came down the icy steps. It was snowing, bleak out, but everything inside him went warm when he saw her.

He thought of what he'd learned in Denver, and he knew he wouldn't tell her, wouldn't bring it up. Instead, meeting her on the sidewalk, he asked, "Want to go out to dinner?"

Dulcinea studied his expression, trying not to hope that she would see more than the friendship she had come to know. *Shouldn't love him* ... "Yes."

"We have to stop by Mrs. Prosper's house first. I have her groceries in the car. Let me see how things went here today, and then we'll leave."

In the truck fifteen minutes later, Dulcinea asked, "Why did you go to Denver?"

Christopher didn't answer. He didn't want to tell her about his trip to the library. He had felt amazement when he read the description of the urn, which had been acquired by a museum in Lima. It was the same urn he'd taken from the snake pit, and the date it had appeared at the museum was shortly after his arrest. But since then the artifact had been stolen in an armed robbery. Though several pieces from the theft had turned up on the black market, the urn had not. It was missing.

He turned onto Rhodochrosite Street, not answering.

"Chris?"

He tensed, then met her eyes. The feelings he'd been trying for weeks to contain leaked out. "Call me Christopher."

Dulcinea tried to imagine why he would have said that. Hurt, she murmured, "I'm sorry. A lot of people call you Chris. I didn't know—"

"It's all right," he cut her off. "I don't even know why I said it."

Be dead, Barnabas, he thought. *Be dead.*

"SOMETHING I DIDN'T SHOW you the last time you were here," said Mrs. Prosper, "is this photo of all the men who worked at the Politician Mine. This was Easter 1904. I think your great-grandfather is right here, Christopher."

Dulcinea asked, "Kitty, could I please use your bathroom?"

Christopher and Mrs. Prosper both looked up from the large framed photograph the older woman had set on the parlor table.

"Of course. Unfortunately, you'll have to go downstairs, Dulcinea. The bathroom up here is out of order."

Christopher made a mental note to look at the plumbing before he left. He wished again that he could persuade her to move. A seventy-five-year-old woman with a bad hip in a house full of stairs was a calamity waiting to happen.

Using her cane to stand, Kitty led Dulcinea from the living room and showed her to the stairs. "Now, when you reach the bottom of the steps, turn left and there it is."

"Thank you." Dulcinea started down the steps, noting the unusual stone walls, which were painted a pale blue-green. Mrs. Prosper had hung photos all along the stairwell on nails driven into the stone, and Dulcinea peered at the grainy images as she made her way down to the bathroom.

Upstairs, Mrs. Prosper rejoined Christopher on her faded velvet sofa. Glancing at him, she remarked, "She's a beautiful woman."

Christopher's stomach muscles hardened. "Yes."

"I hope she's getting along all right without your brother."

Christopher thought about the case of the clap Barnabas had given her. He made no reply but turned his attention to the photo.

Later he would always remember that faint sound, like a single leaf sliding lightly along a concrete sidewalk. The next noise was a roar, a heavy tidal sound, like being inside a wave as it broke or lying beside a train track as a locomotive went by. The room shook and began to tilt, and the lights went out. The furniture, including the couch where they sat, began to slide downward, toward the street, and in the dark Christopher heard a lamp fall, heard its base shatter. In other parts of the house, other things were falling, breaking. Glass clinked as it hit a floor. The couch continued to slide, and Christopher kicked the coffee table ahead of them as the room jarred.

Mrs. Prosper spun her head, gaping at the wall behind them, the plaster shaking down. Christopher grabbed the older woman's calves and pulled her legs up onto the couch before they could be injured by the couch hitting the coffee table, which had stopped against the front bay window.

Then the shuddering stopped, and everything was quiet and still, and there was only the faint sound of creaking.

Christopher stared out into the darkness. Ahead lay another house. The lights had been on when he arrived. Now they were out, and he heard voices. The neighbor's house was twenty feet closer than it had been minutes before, and it took him half a second to realize that the top floor of Mrs. Prosper's house had been swept off the bottom.

By an avalanche.

There was a scream in his throat that didn't give voice. He got up, afraid of the instability of the slide, afraid another would come.

Afraid of what had happened to the floor below.

CHAPTER EIGHT

THERE WAS A BALL of snow in her mouth, holding her jaws open and blocking her breath. When the ceiling came off and the snow cascaded into the bathroom, she hadn't known what was happening, what was pushing on her, falling on her with such pressure. Then she'd realized it was an avalanche, and she'd found herself using what she'd learned in the pool from Christopher. Swimming, trying to find air. She had opened her mouth to draw a breath, and snow had come in. Now there was a ball of it gagging her, and her body was being squeezed hard from all sides, so hard she couldn't move.

Dulcinea tried to breathe, but the snow in her mouth became harder, impossible to dislodge. There was a kick in her abdomen, and panic welled in her throat.

Baby.

Her left arm was near her head, her right twisted awkwardly in front of her, and her left leg hurt. It was wrenched somehow, and there was something digging into it.

She clawed with the fingers of her left hand. Could she clear a space near her mouth, her nose? Could she make a hole? The cold hurt her fingertips, and the snow was packed solid. Her mouth ached. She tried to spit out the snowball, tried to make it melt. She closed her jaws on it, as hard as she could, and it broke some.

Please, God.

Panic surged through her. Was the baby all right? *I need to breathe.*

She *was* breathing, but she felt as though she was smothering.

As she worked her jaw, the snow in her mouth crumbled some more, and she tried to spit it out. *Make it smaller.* She tensed her legs, tried to move. The snow gave a little.

In her mind, she talked to the baby. *Please hang on. We're going to get out of here. Both of us are going to get out of here.*

And she tried not to think about the dark all around her or about how much snow might be over her head. Or about the two people who had been upstairs.

"THERE WAS A SHOVEL beside the back door," said Mrs. Prosper. She had not yet risen from the couch, and Christopher knew she was afraid to move. Afraid the house would fall or collapse on itself. Afraid of another slide.

They were all reasonable fears.

Christopher walked carefully across the tilted living room to the door of the hallway. He stared down the dark corridor, into blackness. He could see nothing. The back side of the house must have been swallowed by snow.

Frantic inside, he wouldn't accept the thought that came to him again and again, like something painfully obvious. That she couldn't possibly be alive. In his mind, he could see Mariano Choqueneira's handwriting: "...what we saw, my father and Emilio and I, was a road of agony and grief...."

No, thought Christopher. *Don't let her be dead!*

AS HE HELPED Kitty out the bay window onto the avalanche of snow on which the top floor had skidded and finally come to rest, he said, "Where is the bathroom downstairs? Which part of the house?"

Mrs. Prosper gripped the outside of the building. "The... the southeast corner, against the rock."

Christopher put one leg out the window, then the other, and ducked under the sash. The power was out all up and down the block, and people were in the darkened street, their voices floating up to him.

A man standing downhill to the south, out of range of the slide, called, "Anyone else in there?"

"Yes," said Mrs. Prosper. "Downstairs."

Christopher gave her his arm as they made their way down the slide to the street. A man whose glasses shone faintly in the black night reached for the older woman, helping her the last few steps. "Are you all right, Kitty? Hello, Dr. Choqueneira."

Christopher said, "I need some help. My—" The words wouldn't come out. "There's— My sister-in-law was downstairs. Please get some probes and shovels and lights."

Trying not to think of grim statistics, that only forty to forty-five percent of people buried in avalanches survived, he turned and started up the dark slope. He looked for the bottom floor of the house, but it was completely buried.

THE SNOW WAS LESS DENSE near her head and her left arm, Dulcinea realized. In minutes, she'd been able to dig a tunnel from her left hand to her face, and then she dug more and found an air pocket, probably near the part of the ceiling overhanging the north wall.

How much snow lay above her?

She thought she felt movement in the snowpack. In the same moment she heard a sound, unreachable but close. Voices.

They were looking for her.

She drew her breath and tried to yell. "I'm right here! Help! I'm down here! Help!" But her voice was weak, cracking. They couldn't possibly hear.

Jamming the toes of her boots into the snowpack, she tried to climb upward, at the same time moving both her hands. She was sweating in her clothes, and she could feel nothing but a cold brittleness in the fingers of her left hand as she worked through the snow, feeling pieces break apart and fall down the sleeve of her sweater.

She had made a tunnel five inches in diameter, with a larger hole at the bottom, accommodating the movement of her elbow. And her legs could touch each other.

Something stabbed her right shoulder, and Dulcinea gasped, jerking in the hole she had made. The object went away. She tried to turn, but could not.

It happened again, and this time the small hard thing that had poked her did not move. She knew what it was, that they were sticking poles in the snow to find her. She tried her voice again. *"I'm down here! Help! I'm right here!"*

On the surface, Fred, one of Mrs. Prosper's neighbors, said, "I found her! She's alive. I think she's yelling at me."

Christopher was three yards away, elbow to elbow with others in the probe line. At the words, his knees felt weak. Abandoning his probe, he walked over to Fred and heard the sounds from below. He snatched up a shovel from the pile nearby, and so did the other rescuers.

HER FIRST CONTACT was Christopher's hand around hers. She knew it was his, and she heard his voice saying, "We almost have you out. Just hang on."

His hand withdrew, and then clumps of snow fell around her face as shovels cleared the area above her head.

Cool air washed her face, and the bright light of head-lamps and flashlights blinded her at first. Eventually she made out Christopher's blond hair, long and uncombed and wild, and his dark eyes and the sweat in the slight mustache on his upper lip. His hand reached down and he touched her face. "Anything feel broken?" he asked, his voice dry and strange. "Anything hurt?"

"No." Nothing but her throat, from the snow being in her mouth. Her voice still sounded raspy.

Christopher's hands dug at the snow around her. Soon she could pull her right arm free and place both hands on the rim of the hole. He slid his hands under her arms, and she dug in with her knees and heels and pushed on the snow with her own hands as he lifted her out of the hole.

Dulcinea saw other people all around and colored lights flashing on a vehicle in the street, but all she felt was Christopher pulling her against his body as they sat in the snow. His arms were tight around her, warming her through her sodden clothes; his head pressed against her wet hair, and she could feel his heart pounding.

For the first time in years, she knew what it was to matter to someone.

CHRISTOPHER'S PICKUP had been buried in the avalanche, so one of the search-and-rescue team drove them first to the clinic, where Christopher listened to the baby's heart, then to Thistledown Ranch under a full moon.

Dulcinea had been treated for shock and examined for internal injuries at the scene of the avalanche. In the back of the ambulance from the Sneffels fire station, Christopher had helped her out of her wet clothes, down to her skin, and into his pile sweater and parka and a borrowed pair of sweatpants and wool socks. After the paramedics had taken her vitals, which were fine, Christopher had checked on Mrs. Prosper and learned she was going to stay at a neighbor's for the night. He had promised to stop by the next day. When it was safe, they could try to salvage some things from her house.

Going out for dinner was no longer an attractive option, so as he let Dulcinea into the house Christopher suggested she go up to bed and he would bring her something to eat. He heated up the soup and bread she had made for lunch, fixed a salad and made her some tea.

While the soup heated, he went into his study to check the answering machine. The light was blinking and he pressed down the button for messages.

"Chris, this is Moth. Give me a call. I've got something for you."

It was the only message. Christopher picked up the receiver and dialed Moth's number in Telluride.

His friend answered. "Hi. Okay, so this isn't good, Chris."

Christopher wondered if he was going to say that Barnabas was in jail—or had been.

"Our operative went to Huajtata," said Moth, "and definitely the folks there saw a plane with a smoking engine fly over. It had a mural on it like your...like his widow drew. Also, Carlos found a ham operator in the Yungas who picked up a Mayday from your brother's plane. The plane was on fire, and he was going to try to land. According to the coordinates he gave, he was somewhere over the Boca del Diablo. A roar of static interrupted the signal, and the guy with the radio lost him."

Christopher made a sound of acknowledgment.

"We can go in there and look for the plane, but it'll cost you. So far... well, let's just say it hasn't been an easy assignment. Carlos's pack was stolen in La Paz, and we had to bring him new equipment. A Bolivian customs official planted some suspicious white powder on the guy who brought the new pack, then seized the pack. Our man got off with a five-thousand-dollar bribe. When Carlos finally set off for the Yungas, he came down with malaria and a wicked case of *turista*. He's in no shape to go into the Boca del Diablo. We'll have to send two more people."

Moth, always direct, said, "How badly do you want your brother's body?"

Christopher thought of Dulcinea. *Badly.*

But Barnabas was dead—had to be.

He asked, "Have you got anything else? Did Carlos . . . find any of his friends?"

"Yeah, I was going to get around to that," said Moth. "Another bribe to add to your bill. Apparently, Barnabas was supposed to meet someone about a month ago for some kind of deal. Antiquities was what Carlos gathered. He didn't show. His amigo's take on it was that if he didn't make this rendezvous, it was because he was dead or disappeared. There was a lot at stake, and your brother was reliable as hail in La Paz. Everyone was puzzled and disappointed, rather than pissed."

Antiquities, thought Christopher. *What were you up to, Barnabas?* "Anything else?" he asked.

"He's not in prison, and as far as we could see, he didn't leave Bolivia. He didn't land at any of the other airfields we checked. We didn't see anything when we flew over the area around Huajtata, and the pilot encountered turbulence near the Boca del Diablo and insisted on heading back. People have a real 'Twilight Zone' attitude about that place." He paused. "So, do you want us to go in and look?"

Dead, thought Christopher. Did he need more? "Let me think about it. I'll call you in a couple of days." Acting on impulse, he said, "Moth, can you check one more thing for me? If you can find out, I'd like to know what's become of someone down there. His name is Bartola Mayorga. He was with the *policía,* Department of La Cumbre."

It was Moth who had helped Dr. Jonah Gore, Christopher's grandfather, find him when he was in jail. Moth said, "You're thinking of going yourself."

"No." He would never go back. "I'm just curious."

Moth said nothing for a moment. "Sure. I'll check it out for you."

When they'd hung up, Christopher returned to the kitchen to finish putting together Dulcinea's dinner.

The plane was on fire.... Again, as he had the day she'd told him, he tried to reach out with his thoughts and feelings, as though somehow he could know if Barnabas was dead or alive.

Guilt souring his righteous anger, he wondered if his brother had intended never to be found. To leave Dulcinea always wondering—and never really free. She wouldn't relish divorce, even after abandonment by the husband who had betrayed her.

I deserted her, too.

Christopher carried everything upstairs on a tray, and when he reached Dulcinea's room he saw her sleeping on top of the coverlet. Food or sleep? he wondered.

He set the tray on the bureau, and she stirred, opening her eyes.

There was a tide of feeling in his chest. Heat, tightness. She sat up, and he propped the pillows behind her, thinking of Barnabas. She deserved to know what Moth had said.

"Hungry?" he asked.

"Thank you. You didn't have to do this."

He brought the tray to her bed and set it on top of the covers. She sat cross-legged to eat, and for a moment he studied her rounded stomach. His brother had been inside her. Made her pregnant.

The most primitive emotions overwhelmed him. Possessiveness, jealousy, anger. Knowing they were irrational didn't stop him from feeling them. She was his. He had been in love with her. Barnabas should have known.

He *did* know, thought Christopher. He knew.

For that, Christopher hated his twin. Barnabas might or might not have wanted Dulcinea for herself. He had certainly wanted her because she'd been Christopher's.

Not eating, Dulcinea peered up at him. "Aren't you having anything?"

"I thought I'd eat downstairs." *Away from you.*

But he didn't go.

Dulcinea watched him pull up the rocker and sit down. At the scene of the avalanche, he'd given her his warm clothes. He was still wearing only his jeans and a long undershirt unbuttoned at the throat, and his uncombed hair hung around his face. As he leaned forward, resting his forearms on his knees, she saw his muscles move beneath his shirt and remembered the feel of him holding her.

"I just talked to Moth. I want to tell you what he said."

Dulcinea listened silently to the story. Nothing he said surprised her.

Christopher asked, "Why have you been so sure he's dead?"

She stared at her untouched food. *I don't want to talk about this with you.* She had to. "He would have come home. He wouldn't have left me."

His mind full of objections, Christopher said only, "Did he know you were pregnant?" But he couldn't have.

"No. It happened—" She stopped.

Trying not to see the pictures in his mind, Christopher forced himself to accept what she'd said. Barnabas, whatever his transgressions, had cared enough about Dulcinea to come back to her—every two weeks or so.

Dulcinea knew what he must be thinking—that she was giving Barnabas credit he didn't deserve. She couldn't hope to make him understand how it had been. There were things one couldn't say.

Christopher was thinking the same thing. One couldn't ask a widow if her husband had loved her. Or if she had loved him.

He stood up. "I'm going to eat, then I'll go down to the vapor cave. Come and get me if you need anything."

The words thundered through her mind: *I need you to take back the urn.*

She looked at him, and he saw it in her eyes.

He said, "I can't."

AFTER HE'D EATEN soup and bread, for which he had no appetite, Christopher made his way to the stairway that led to the vapor cave and descended into the darkness. From the foot of the steps, he walked down the stone corridor until he came to the electric light switch near the "dry room." He stripped off his clothes and left them on one of the wooden shelves, then stepped out into the corridor again and moved toward the steam and dampness of the cave.

The outer door was made from thick planks of ash. Pulling it toward him, Christopher heard water dripping from the cave walls. The air was filled with steam, and the electric lamps on the wall, replicas of old miner's lamps, cast only a mellow glow over the room. Moving past an ancient wooden shower stall, he opened the door to the cave and its mineral springs. The dark cavern was glossy wet on every surface, and vapor immediately wet his face, dampened his hair.

Christopher traversed the passage to the mineral-springs room, to the hot, shallow pool cut from the limestone and lined with concrete. Around him, the walls shimmered dewy wet, bubbled with the earthen changes of the natural cavern. Stalactites grew overhead. He dipped a toe into the hot pool, stood in the water and slid his body down inside.

For some time he lay in the steam and the extreme heat trying to relax, to forget. But he ended up thinking of Dulcinea, wondering what had been between her and his brother, torturing himself with pictures of her making love with Barnabas, angry when he thought of his twin's infidelity, of the disease he'd given her.

He would have come home. He wouldn't have left me.

Christopher closed his eyes.

WHEN SHE'D FINISHED eating, Dulcinea took her tray downstairs to the kitchen. The house was silent. Under the single light that hung over the sink, she washed her dishes. Then, unable to resist the impulse, she walked down the hall to the stairway that led to the vapor cave and descended the steps. She could see lights on below, and she followed them to the dry room, where she saw his clothes crumpled on a shelf.

Christopher.

She knew it was wet in the cave, so she took off her borrowed wool socks and left them in the dry room. Feeling too warm in Christopher's big pile sweater, she stepped out into the corridor. The first heavy wooden door swung shut behind her as the warm vapor surrounded her like a mist. She heard the water running down the walls, dripping, as the steam filled her head, and she remembered that Christopher had told her she shouldn't visit the cave alone.

But he was here... somewhere.

Her bare feet felt the water on the warm stones, and she walked carefully over the slick surface to another door etched with the words "Vapor Cave." She opened the door, which had no latch, and stepped into the next room. Thick steam hung in the air, and she peered through it, up at the dark walls of the cavern and then off to her left, into the next room.

Christopher sat on the far side of the mineral bath, and Dulcinea knew he must have felt the slight draft from the doors she had opened. His body gleamed wet; she saw the familiar discoloration of scars on his chest. Eyes black, he watched her, and Dulcinea felt as though she had walked in on him bathing. Which she had.

"Hi." Honestly, she told him, "I was lonely."

Lonely.

Under the water, Christopher's penis filled, hardened. He stayed where he was, letting the dark pool hide everything below his chest. "You must be hot." *Why don't you take off your clothes?* His clothes. His sweater that he'd put on her in the ambulance. He tried to forget what he'd seen then, what he had tried not to see. She was so pretty. He'd remembered how much he had loved her, back when he was the only man who'd ever seen her naked.

Dulcinea felt a trickle of sweat slide down her back under her hair, against the pile of his sweater. Staring at him through the mist, she sat down on the wet stone ledge of the pool. As her sweatpants soaked through, she put a hand into the water. It was very hot.

Christopher said, "You shouldn't be in here." For a lot of reasons.

"I'll just stay a minute."

Too long. He imagined kissing her, helping her undress. But already her hair was damp, her face beaded with sweat. "I'll come up and go swimming with you, if you like."

Dulcinea stared at him through the mist. "I think I'll just . . . go back upstairs."

She stood and made her way toward the door, disappearing in the vapor before she reached it.

Thinking he should make sure she was all right, Christopher waited just a minute or so before getting out of the water and following. He slipped out the door and paused at the shower taps built into the cave wall. He turned on the hot and cold water and adjusted the temperature, then stood under the spray. Lonely, he thought. Dulcinea was lonely. He was lonely.

And Barnabas was dead.

SHE WAS READING Mariano Choqueneira's journal when Christopher paused in her doorway. His body sliced a dark shadow across the room, and when she saw him, she closed the book.

"May I come in?"

Dulcinea nodded. He had never asked before.

He stepped into the room, tall and muscular in his jeans and a flannel shirt unbuttoned, tails out. His pale wet hair hung loose, brushing his shoulders, and his eyes were like coal in the shadows, outside the golden glow of her reading lamp.

Lifting his eyebrows at the red journal, he said, "I'll take you to the library, if you like."

For something else to read.

Her gaze fell on her abdomen, and she rested her hands there. She closed her eyes, silently willing something to change.

He walked around the bed and sat down on the rocker. "Dulcie."

Her eyes flickered to his.

"Let me tell you about the urn." Carefully, he related what he'd discovered in Denver, that the urn had been acquired by a Peruvian museum but had since been stolen.

Listening, Dulcinea felt not despair but hope. Christopher had gone to Denver to find out about the urn. She asked, "Do you think my father knows where it is?"

Christopher sat back in the rocker, unsmiling.

She didn't repeat the question.

"I don't know," he answered at last. "I never want to see your father again."

Dulcinea's mind set off down well-trod paths. Her father...

Esteban had ordered Bartola Mayorga to pursue Christopher, preventing him from returning the urn to the shrine. And Isabel had died.

She remembered her father's pride in her, his grief when he found her with Christopher—and his cool rejection. He had cast aside the love between them, cast off his only daughter.

Dulcinea had lost *her* daughter. She would never understand his decision.

And she could see the welts on Christopher's chest.

"I never want to see him, either."

Christopher was glad to hear it. One obstacle out of the way. A father-in-law who had ordered him tortured. But Esteban was Barnabas's father-in-law, not his. The baby inside her was his brother's, too.

Jealous . . .

The chair scraped the floor lightly as he stood up. Coming around the bed to the side nearest the bathroom door, he gazed down into her schoolgirl face, her dark Spanish eyes.

He thought of how she'd looked when he'd just uncovered her face and head from the avalanche. He'd been unable to keep from holding her after helping her out of that hole. But everyone present must have known that she was more to him than a sister-in-law. More than a sister.

She must have known, too.

Her eyes hid whatever she felt now.

Tentatively, Christopher touched her hair and bent over to kiss her forehead, telling himself it would be a brotherly kiss. But she grabbed his hand and drew it to her cheek, and Christopher did what was most natural, what he had wanted to do the first time he'd seen her and ever since. He kissed her lips.

CHAPTER NINE

CHRISTOPHER'S WEIGHT sank the mattress, and her body tilted against him, her arms in silky long underwear reaching around his neck. Christopher kissed her gently, not as the throbbing in his groin begged. He hugged her as though she were as delicate as the moment. She was so slender, her breasts soft against him. He could feel her back through her shirt, and he knew how it looked when she was naked, as he had seen her earlier that night when he'd helped her change her clothes. She still looked nineteen.

And pregnant.

Barnabas had made love to her.

Dulcinea felt restless on the bed, with only the covers separating them. She hadn't kissed Christopher since they were lovers long ago, and she hadn't felt this way even then. They had both changed.

We had a child together, she thought.

His mouth parted against hers, and Dulcinea opened her mouth, too, silently begging him not to stop. She wanted to feel forever the brush of his slight mustache, his damp hair touching her skin.

Christopher deliberately relaxed, trying not to care that his brother had kissed her, too. She wasn't kissing Barnabas now.

His tongue touched her lips. Slid inside.

Dulcinea's arms tightened around his neck, and he pulled her body closer, wishing he could forget what had happened because he'd made love to her in the past. Isabel. And Barnabas, who had slept with other women and brought home a disease to Dulcinea.

But he, Christopher, was the one who had abandoned her when she needed him most.

I never want to hurt you like that again. He let his tongue caress hers for a moment more, and then he pulled back, just kissing her lightly, and then he stopped. Words came out, honest things he hadn't planned to say. ''I always respected you, Dulcinea. I never meant to hurt you. I would have married you in a second, but I was afraid.'' Trembling now, like her. ''I loved you.''

She was shaking hard, and Christopher ached. *I hurt you,* he thought. *You'd never been in love before, and I hurt you in the worst way.*

But he would have made the same choices today. All except one.

He would never have made love with her.

Dulcinea clung to the front of his unbuttoned shirt, pressed her face against his bare chest. She'd never felt a heartbeat as hard or deep as his beneath her cheek. *I've wanted to hear you say that forever. I needed to hear you say that.*

Christopher considered other things he could say. That she was sweet and alive and good and he'd thought of her on nights when the stench of his cell was so powerful and nauseating he could not sleep. And when he had heard the women scream, he had blotted her face from his mind, as though even the thought of her would somehow lead her to that place, into the hands of Mayorga. And he felt, but could not bring himself to tell her, that she had never deserved the things Barnabas had done.

She said, ''The baby's kicking me. I think he knows you.''

An intrusion.

Barnabas's baby.

Christopher didn't care if the baby knew him or not. He cared about the other baby. Searching for an appropriate response to her comment, he loosened his hold on her and asked, "What are you going to name him?"

Name him, thought Dulcinea.

She couldn't think of names.

The place beneath her breastbone seemed to grow tender, tense and hot, as horrid emotion, a black-curtain feeling, came over her. Memory. As though it was just yesterday.

There had been joy in dreaming about a name for Christopher's baby. But the joy had been diluted by fear. As she'd waited for the birth, waited to hold the child that was all she possessed of a man she couldn't stop loving, the Kallawaya had exchanged looks and whispered about the curse, and Dulcinea had grown cold and frightened.

A deep sob rose inside her.

Christopher flinched. What was wrong? What had he done? She couldn't be thinking of Barnabas.... As he held her apart from him to see her face, his left ear heard the word she choked out.

The name of his child.

Christopher stared at her, then grabbed her hard, clung to her, as though he could hold in the strangled sounds that were an echo of something in his heart. She was crying for Isabel. "Tell me," he said. "I need you to tell me."

Dulcinea heard his words with a relief that made her cry harder. *I need you to tell me.*

"She'd been dead for three days...."

Christopher didn't recognize the feelings roaring through him.

Dulcinea gasped out the words. "She didn't move inside me, and I knew she was dead, and everyone else knew, too. They'd known it would happen. I kept hoping it wasn't true, that she wasn't moving for some other reason, that when I went into labor it would be all right. That she would be alive." Her breath came in spurts. All she knew was Christopher's chest, his warm body, hard and big around her, holding tight. "I was in labor for a long time. A day and a half. She was so beautiful. She looked like she was sleeping. She was perfect...." The cries began again. She had not cried like this for a long time. Not really, for years. How could it still feel this new? This raw?

Christopher's skin was wet from her tears. Dulcinea moved to wipe her face, and then she saw his. He was looking at her with an expression like a grimace, and there were tears on his cheeks. A low, anguished cry, a sound painful to hear, came from him. He climbed over her on the bed and lay down with her and held her tight. Feeling him shake, Dulcinea knew that for the first time she was with someone who mourned Isabel's loss almost as she had. She lay in his arms, and they both wept and wished their baby back.

The baby inside her kicked, but Dulcinea said nothing about it. It wasn't Christopher's, and now all he could want was his own.

TIME SEEMED SLOW, hardly passing as they lay together in the narrow bed, their bodies shadowed by the tall headboard with its black-walnut moldings. Dulcinea didn't notice that she'd begun stroking his hair or that they kicked the covers away to lie closer, his leg between hers. She didn't notice when the shaking in both their bodies began to settle. Even then, they clung to each other. Not hard. Just to keep contact.

Christopher lay thinking, *Why did it happen?*

Dulcinea's head was on his chest, her arm draped over him, and he held on to her because she was warm and alive. He had grieved before. He had heard the screams of friends who were tortured to death and heard the sound of the shots when others were murdered. He had known his father's death and his grandfather's. But this one was different, in some ways the worst. Out of the natural order. A mistake. There was no comfort, even in Dulcinea's warm body. He had never known she was so brave or strong.

But there was nothing to say, just desolation.

As the clock ticked beside the bed, Christopher thought of Barnabas. His twin was dead, and this moment belonged only to him and Dulcinea. No one else could understand this private sorrow; only she would understand with him. Only she had given her heart to his child.

He moved and placed a pillow under her head. Letting his own head rest on the other, he met her eyes in the lamplight and swallowed, blood pouring through him. Hurt blood. Want-to-be-alive blood.

In his eyes, Dulcinea saw the anguish and the need for the only comfort they could give each other. He said nothing, but his gaze dropped to her throat, then rose to her eyes again. His hand slid to her body, along her side, and he drew her shirt up, still looking at her with grief in his eyes.

Dulcinea began to push his shirt off. The sight of his broad, muscular shoulders aroused her. She didn't see the scars, only that he was built as a man should be and that the need in his eyes was intense and deep. And that he was Christopher.

They both sat up, and he drew her shirt over her head, catching his breath at the sight of her full breasts, her dusky pink nipples tender and erect. When he saw her belly stretching the bottoms of her long underwear and remembered she was carrying his brother's child, anger and jealousy stung him, but he didn't want to stop. He held her naked to his chest, touched her breasts, then lay down with her and kissed her, but not like before.

"Christopher..."

He pulled her onto her side so that he could kiss her more easily. His hand moved down her body, between her legs, over the silk of her long johns, stroking. She cried out again.

Christopher tugged on the waistband of her pants, slid them down over her hips, then touched her. The silk of her thighs now.

She muffled her cry in the pillow. But not his name. "Chris."

He held her hard. "Yes." Then, almost inaudibly, "Call me that."

Dulcinea sank against his hand, crying out again, softly.

Christopher took off his own clothes and the rest of Dulcinea's. They lay down on the mattress, their bodies together, and he caressed her again, looking in her eyes with things he didn't say. Exploring her body, he could feel how she was different. She had borne a child. His.

A lump grew in Dulcinea's throat. Here was a peace and comfort that had eluded her for six years. She reached for his hard penis and held it and did not shudder over the scar tissue on his scrotum, because she had already known it would be there, had already known the things they'd done to him.

She said, "I love you."

Christopher rolled onto his back and pulled her on top of him, and as she slid down over him he tried not to think that she did it with the certainty of a woman who had made love more times than she could count. But he could not dismiss the heat of her abdomen, a reminder of another presence. He'd never made love with a pregnant woman before, except Dulcinea when he hadn't known she was pregnant. Knowing, it was impossible to ignore the third party. The baby was closer to her than he was, and he knew that Dulcinea possessed a mother's instinct—that her child came first.

But when her body was embracing his, it didn't matter anymore. The baby she carried was only a silent, benign presence. The act was all. This was how they had made Isabel. Him inside her...

He made love to her.

SOME TIME LATER, they still held each other in the moonlight. The smooth skin of her cheek and slender nose was against his lips, and one of his arms cradled her body close. Again, he noticed the heat of her stomach pressed to his. Pregnant.

She must really want this baby, he thought. After one stillbirth, it must be the most important thing to her.

He tried to ignore it. His mind strayed back to Isabel, to the sadness. There were things he still wanted to know. "What day was she born?"

"January fifth." On the day that would have been Isabel's sixth birthday, Dulcinea had decided to come to Sneffels, to try to save the life of the child inside her. She didn't tell Christopher. For him, the two children could not be connected. She told herself it would be all right. Hadn't he taken her to the ultrasound? Didn't he measure out raspberry leaves for her tea each morning?

He cared about the baby. He could stretch his heart to care.

The curse...

She shut it from her mind and pressed her hands to his scarred body. Christopher's arms tightened around her, and she wished she could know his thoughts. But then he was kissing her, opening her legs, touching her. She saw his eyes in the shadows, right on hers, like a silent question.

She moved her hands down to hold his erection, and he buried his face in her hair so that she wouldn't know he was crying again.

She knew.

Dulcinea clung to him tightly, wishing with all her heart that he could be her husband. She would never love another man so much.

WHEN THE ALARM CLOCK rang the next morning, Christopher shut it off and looked at her in winter's half-light. She was already alert. Watching him. She said, "I never thought I'd sleep with you again."

Memory came to him through the remnants of slumber. How they had come to be in her bed together. He wanted to wipe the gray from his mind, his mood, but he knew the pall would be with him for a very long time. He drew her close. "Thank you."

Dulcinea's mind swept over its memories of the night. Making love. Lying silent and dazed and numb in the dark. Holding each other. Talking a little. Making love again, as though that could make things better. Now she felt bruised, as though every nerve was tender, hypersensitive. She felt better than she had in a long time.

But the feeling faded, because she knew what the night had been to Christopher. A release, physical and emotional.

She knew by the way he had said those two words— Thank you—that it wouldn't happen again. The knowledge was agony. Wishing she could call back the first words she'd spoken to him that morning, which in retrospect sounded dreamy and childish, she sat up and prepared to get out of bed.

A brown arm slipped around her, pulled her back down, and she resisted, wanting to keep her dignity. They had both been grieving, and what they had done was all right. She didn't want him to apologize. He hadn't hurt her...yet.

But he said softly, "Just lie here with me. For a minute?"

Dulcinea closed her eyes, reminding herself who he was and how he treated her every day. She let his arm draw her toward him, until she lay with her bottom against his groin, her back to his chest.

He was hard, but she knew he wouldn't try to make love to her.

Christopher held her and wanted her and tried to think of something, anything, to say to her. But he could feel where the baby was growing inside her, and he knew the past was long and would take time to unravel.

The future was a nightmare.

Their love had been cursed with the death of a child, and if the baby she was carrying died, Dulcinea would not forgive him.

But it might not be the baby, said a voice he didn't want to hear. *It could be her.*

He didn't believe it, didn't want to. He didn't want to look at himself, and instead, he thought of what it had been like to make love to her again.

He cared for her too much to say any of the inadequate things that could be said, so he just held her more tightly and wished that she could know his heart. He lay with her until he knew they would be late to the clinic if they stayed in bed any longer, and then he released her and sat up and waited for her to sit up, too, and look at him. Taking her in his arms again, he said, "Thank you, my beloved." It was what he had meant all along.

THEY TREATED each other gently. Dulcinea, because she knew his grief was newer, more raw, than hers. Christopher, because he knew hers would never completely heal.

His pickup had been totaled by the avalanche, so he used the old green ranch truck to drive to work. On the way he asked, "Want to come to Grand Junction with me this weekend? We can shop for a new car. I'd like to teach you to drive."

"Okay." Dulcinea had always wanted to learn how to drive, but she'd never had a car. Christopher's offering to teach her something that would increase her independence felt like a gift. It was the kind of thing—

The kind of thing her father might have done once. She dismissed the thought. He was dead to her.

Christopher parked in the lot behind the clinic, and before she could get out of the car, he leaned across the stick shift and embraced her and kissed her again, a lover's kiss, and Dulcinea knew her fear that morning had been misplaced. He would make love to her again.

What he would not do was break the curse.

She felt disquieted as they went into the clinic together, and her mood seemed to communicate itself to him. He left at eleven for a two-hour lunch and didn't ask her to come.

First thing, Christopher drove up Rhodochrosite Street and parked outside Mrs. Prosper's next-door neighbor's house. Through the snowflakes falling on his windshield, he saw the avalanche site and remembered the long minutes Dulcinea had spent under the snow. Then, just as quickly, he recalled making love with her.

In love with her, he thought dimly, getting out of the truck.

The avalanche crew had blasted the Jack-Be-Nimble-Slide that morning to see if they could make it run any more. At the neighbor's, Christopher found a shaken Mrs. Prosper, who said, "They say it's not safe to go back in the house." He knew she was thinking of her belongings, her photographs, possessions that were memories, too. She had mementos of her keenest love, her husband, of a daughter who lived far away and of her childhood with her parents.

He sat with her on a sofa while Mrs. Kensington, her neighbor, brought him a cup of tea. The Kensingtons were in their fifties, younger than Mrs. Prosper, and Christopher could see in Kitty's eyes that she thought she was a burden to the couple.

A solution occurred to him immediately, but when he thought of what had happened the night before with Dulcinea, it was the last thing he wanted. They needed time alone together. He wanted to sleep with her every night without anyone else nearby to hear them making love. He wanted to continue the day-to-day privacy they'd had during the weeks since she'd arrived.

With a sense of personal disaster, he saw Mrs. Prosper stare bravely out the window toward the ruins of her house.

"Kitty, have you called your insurance company?"

"Ralph did," interjected Mrs. Kensington. "I think someone's coming this afternoon. Doctor, can I get you anything else?" With one foot in the kitchen, she eyed his teacup on the coffee table.

"No, thank you," said Christopher.

As Mrs. Kensington swept up his empty cup and disappeared, he turned to Kitty. "Is there anything I can do for you?" He couldn't offer the hospitality of the ranch without at least talking to Dulcinea. It was her home, too.

In a mildly embarrassed voice, Mrs. Prosper said, "Would you mind terribly driving me down to the Silver Street Hotel? My car was buried like yours."

Another disaster she didn't need.

"Kitty," said Mrs. Kensington from the kitchen doorway, "I don't want to hear another word about going to a hotel."

Christopher saw his patient's quietly agonized expression. Chagrin and relief. "Oh, Veronica, are you sure?"

When he left the Kensingtons' ten minutes later, he felt comfortable that Mrs. Prosper would be all right there for a few days, at least.

Not ready to go back to the office, he grabbed a deli sandwich to eat on the road and drove out to the hot springs. Uncomfortable echoes of the night before came to him with every breath.

She'd been dead for three days.

He'd never had a stillbirth in his practice.

Christopher parked at the hot springs and went inside, to the lingerie store.

Danielle was working. Looking surprised to see him, she said, "Hi, Chris. What can I do for you?"

He wanted to buy Dulcinea everything—silk lingerie and scented soaps and body lotions. But she might misinterpret the gesture, think it had to do with their making love.

It had to do with loving her.

That morning after they'd gotten up, he'd come into the bathroom in a hurry and found her brushing her hair. Flustered, Dulcinea had tried to stuff her hairbrush into the pocket of the cardigan she was wearing—his old pile sweater from the free box. It had taken him a moment to gather that she didn't want him to see the sorry pink brush with its bristles missing.

Too late. It had made him think of Barnabas, who had never taken a dime from his trust. A good reason to find his brother's body—Dulcinea should have her inheritance.

Thinking of the cheap pink brush and his twin's infidelity, Christopher told Danielle what he wanted.

HE WAS CALLED to a birth that night. The call came when he and Dulcinea were washing dishes together, and when he got off the phone he told her he needed to drive to the hospital in Ridgway.

A birth, thought Dulcinea. He was going to deliver someone's baby. "I guess you'll be gone all night."

"Mmm," he agreed, draining a cup of tea he'd been drinking. "Will you be all right?"

"Of course." If she married a doctor, this was what it would be like. If she married Christopher...

"I'll give you the number for my pager—and also Sissy's number. I want you to call if..." Christopher drew a breath. He was being overprotective.

It was on the tip of his tongue to ask her to sleep in his bed, so that he could join her when he got home if it was before dawn. But something stopped him—perhaps because he was on his way to help bring a baby into the world. He'd almost begged off the birth, afraid he couldn't be effective. But he knew that he could do it and that he should.

His hand reached out and touched Dulcinea's stomach. Reflecting on what she wanted him to do—and what he couldn't do—he brushed a kiss across her temple and said, "Sleep well."

After he'd gone, Dulcinea went outside to see Sombra de la Luna. She fed her some sugar cubes and brushed her while the Paso turned her head to watch her with gentle dark eyes. Dulcinea longed to go for a ride, but Christopher would be horrified. Anyhow, she didn't want to risk the filly's being hurt in the dark. Her day off from the clinic would be soon enough to ride again, though the time till then seemed like a year. When the dogs came into the barn, Dulcinea petted them and spoke to them in Spanish and felt them at her heels as she walked along the stalls, stopping to stroke the other horses. She realized she was acutely happy.

Telling herself she wouldn't keep her nightly engagement with fear—of the curse—she went back to the house and locked up, then climbed the stairs to her room to get ready for bed. On her pillow lay an unfamiliar package, a brown paper gift bag painted with golden suns, tissue paper spilling from within.

Dulcinea reached across the bed to pick it up and pulled out a package of bath salts and a new hairbrush, maple-backed with smooth bristles. There was no card, but the gift said enough. He cared.

And there was no curse.

AT THE HOSPITAL, while the mother went through the early stages of labor, Christopher left her with her husband and took her two children, ages four and six, to the pediatric ward to dig up a coloring book and a game of Candyland. Back in the maternity wing, he played with the children in an area of the birthing room that was for kids, and then he went to check on the mother. She was eight centimeters dilated, and it went very fast from there.

When he caught the newborn boy, he laid him on the mother's stomach. Giving the parents a few minutes to themselves with their miracle, he stood a short distance away before he took the child to listen to his heart.

Christopher had always loved newborns, with their wrinkled hands and feet; they reminded him of old men who casually left the burdensome social restraints of the world, who dozed off in the middle of conversations with the privilege of age. Newborns, however, were life beginning. Tonight, holding this minutes-old child, seeing his face crumple in a tiny wince, Christopher understood things he never had. He remembered a novel he had read in which a childless woman stole a baby from a supermarket, and he knew how such a thing could happen when a person wanted something so badly.

He looked at the baby in his arms, whose name was Joshua; when he gave the child his finger, Joshua grasped it. Christopher felt the pressure and stared at the newborn's blinking eyes for a long time, then gave him back to the mother to try to nurse. He told the parents and the nurses on duty, "I'll be back in a few minutes." He left the building and went outside and stood in the shadows in the cold mountain evening and cried.

HE REACHED HOME at three in the morning and found that Dulcinea had gone to sleep in her own room. From the bathroom door, he saw her hair spread on the pillow, then he got under the shower. As he was drying himself, he heard her moan in her sleep, and he went to her without bothering to put on clothes.

Dulcinea felt his arms around her, his body lying beside her. Gentle awakening from hell.

Wasn't real.

It had seemed real. She'd dreamed that the baby had stopped moving. For days...

Now the baby shifted inside her as Christopher held her, and she shuddered with relief.

But the dream lingered.

In the moonlight, she caved under the fear. Into his chest, she said, "Cristobal, please. The curse is real. You know it. Please."

He tensed but didn't move away from her.

Get through it, he thought. *Talk about it with her.*

"You can find the urn," she whispered. "You're the one who is meant to do it. This task belongs to you."

She was warm in his arms, and her baby inside her was clasped between them like a pearl in an oyster shell. He, Christopher, was the protector, holding them both.

We have to talk about this. But some things were too hard to say. So he told her, "I'm not supposed to go back to Bolivia. I have a stamp on my passport."

"You can get a new one."

"Dulcie." He gritted his teeth, his head against hers, his heart afraid of discovery.

Afraid...

The bedside alarm clock ticked softly.

He took her small hand and led it to his chest, to the worst of the fiery welts there. *Understand,* he thought. *Understand, so that I never have to say it aloud.*

There was enough light from the moon that Dulcinea could see, as well as feel, the scars on his body. She understood what he had not said, and she answered it. "You're not a coward, Cristobal."

Christopher thought of eighteen months of psychological terror and physical suffering. He recalled nights since, nights he'd endured alone at the ranch, desperate to end the movie in his head. Never ending it. Facing tomorrow, instead. He supposed he wasn't a coward.

But admitting that the curse was real . . . it went against the grain, against who he was. He didn't think he could afford the price of that admission, which was greater than his fear of death.

If there really was a curse, his failure to break it had resulted in the death of his own child.

Suddenly unable to touch her or hold her while that possibility existed, Christopher slid from under the covers and tucked them around her. "Good night, Dulcinea."

Then he returned to his own room, to dress rather than to sleep.

CHAPTER TEN

IN THE MORNING a mug containing a tea ball sat on the counter waiting for her as usual. It was the day they had talked about going to Grand Junction to buy a new car.

The skies were heavy with snow. In the cheerless morning light, Dulcinea filled the teakettle, and as she put it on Christopher came in from outside. She heard him in the pantry first. When the kitchen door opened, she gathered the courage to look up.

He was pulling his black pile sweater over his head, and as he did, the black turtleneck underneath was drawn partway with it, revealing his hard stomach. Tossing the sweater on a kitchen chair, he found her eyes.

Dulcinea said, *"Buenos días."*

"Mmm," said Christopher. *"Hola."*

They looked at each other for a time, and at last he shut the pantry door and joined her beside the stove. His eyes sought out her mouth and the hollows of her throat and the smooth line of her jaw. It had been a long night without her. Thinking. Making decisions about the two of them, for a world without the cruelty of the curse. He'd already called Moth. Now he told Dulcinea. "I've decided to go to Bolivia—"

She stared.

"—to look for my brother's plane. That way, you can claim your inheritance." *That way, we'll both know beyond doubt that you are a widow.* "The ranch can run indefinitely, with money flowing into an account for

Barnabas, and his account sharing the expenses of up-keep. But you stand to inherit a trust that would make you comfortable for the rest of your life. I want you to have it." *I want to give you what I can.*

And please, he thought, *don't ask again for what I can't give.*

Dulcinea read it in his eyes. He was going to Bolivia because of what she'd said the night before. Without meaning to, she had challenged him. She said, "This isn't what I wanted."

"It's what I want." He changed the subject. "Want to go shopping? You'll need to be able to drive while I'm gone."

Besides a new car, a replacement for his totaled pickup truck, Christopher needed supplies for his trip. During the ninety-minute drive north to Grand Junction, he dictated a shopping list to Dulcinea. Water-purification tablets, mosquito netting . . .

Bolivia. He was going back, and he was afraid.

In Grand Junction, they went first to a camping-goods store, where Christopher tried on internal-frame back-packs while Dulcinea wandered aimlessly through the aisles. When he'd found what he wanted, he searched the store until he came upon her near the sleeping bags. He already owned one, but seeing Dulcinea looking at them, he asked, "Ever been camping?"

She shook her head. "Sissy says the mountains are beautiful in summer, full of wildflowers. I've never seen a columbine. Everything here is named for them."

"It's the state flower. Would you like to go camping with me sometime?"

He was going to Bolivia. He would never take back the urn. He didn't even know where it was. Dulcinea said nothing.

"Let's get you a sleeping bag."

They found a three-season bag the pale purple-blue color of a columbine, with a good temperature rating for the mountains. Christopher checked the zipper to make sure it was compatible with his and paid for the bag with his other equipment.

They ate lunch at a natural-foods café in an alley, then strolled through the town. In one shop window, Christopher saw a tiny *chulo*, a knitted cap with ear flaps, which he recognized as having been made in Yocalla. Dulcinea saw it, too, and neither of them said anything. They were both thinking of a little baby who'd been born in the Andes—and of white burial shrouds. Both had seen many, because one did not live in the Andes and not become acquainted with death.

Christopher put his arm over her shoulders and guided her away from the shop. In the window of the next store, he saw an oversize long-sleeved black T-shirt with a sun on the front. It was displayed with a pair of black leggings. He asked Dulcinea if she liked them. She did, so they went into the boutique. Dulcinea found extra-large leggings to accommodate her changing shape, and they bought the set.

After that, Christopher had his photo taken for a new passport, and then they went to the car dealership and looked at new and used four-wheel-drive vehicles. Dulcinea liked a red Grand Cherokee with gold wheels and trim, and they took it out for a drive and eventually bought it.

After arranging for the vehicle to be delivered to Sneffels, Christopher drove to the mall. It was snowing when he parked, and at four-thirty the day was gradually making its descent into night.

He asked Dulcinea, "Tired?"

"Yes."

"Do you have the energy for one more stop?"

What did he have in mind? More supplies for his trip, undoubtedly. "I'm fine."

They went into a department store together. Christopher led the way to the infant section, and when Dulcinea saw the baby clothing she felt almost ill. She wanted to leave, but he put his arm around her and his head near hers. "Let me get some things for your baby." He bought some little blue undershirts and a small stuffed dinosaur with a rattle inside. Somehow, he wanted to make up for not being there to gather things for Isabel. A rabbit skin to wrap his baby in . . .

But as he paid for the shirts and the dinosaur at the counter, he realized that it didn't have anything to do with Isabel at all. Instead, it was admission that Dulcinea was a mother. He needed to try to love her baby.

He wasn't sure he could.

As they drove home through gently falling snow, he said, "Dulcie, I want to ask Kitty to stay with you while I'm gone."

She blurted out, "I want to come with you."

"No."

In his tone of voice, the single word, Dulcinea heard resolution. She thought about what he'd suggested and his patient who had lost her home. She hadn't been close to another woman since she'd lived in Chulina with Barnabas.

Mrs. Prosper must feel horrible. Dulcinea knew how it felt to lose one's home, as she had lost hers at nineteen. Banished.

"I guess it's all right, Christopher."

He watched the road, thinking of what he wouldn't do. Wondering if she could love him if he ignored the curse she thought had killed their baby.

Knowing in his heart that he couldn't live with himself if there was another death.

THE FOLLOWING DAY around noon, he drove to the Kensingtons' house and found the Kensingtons and Mrs. Prosper just returning from church.

After greetings, when the Kensingtons had gone out the back door to investigate snow buildup on the roof of their garage, Christopher said, "Kitty, I'd like to ask you a large favor." Carefully, he explained that he needed to travel to Bolivia, possibly for several months, to look for his brother's plane. "Dulcinea is pregnant." The words, the thought, filled him with a heart-shaking tenderness he didn't understand. It wasn't his baby, and he and Dulcinea hadn't made love or slept together since the night she'd told him about Isabel. Maybe it was just that he was leaving her—again. "Kitty, would you consider coming to Thistledown Ranch and staying with her while I'm gone?"

The older woman's blue eyes crinkled in surprise.

"I'd fix up one of the downstairs rooms for you. It'll take a few days to put it together, but after that, would you come?" He wanted to help her. And she could truly help him.

"I'd love that, Christopher. It will give me time to look for a new place to live. I'm considering one of those condominiums over on Hematite Street. Some of them are ground-level."

So she had heard the things he'd said in the past about stairs. Christopher smiled. "I should be back by the time Dulcinea's baby is born in July."

Kitty eyed him curiously but asked no questions about his relationship with Dulcinea. "I'll be glad to stay with her till then."

IN THE TIME before he left, Christopher arranged for a doctor from the ski resort in Telluride, which would soon be closing for the season, to work in the clinic. He saw his lawyer. He made copies of his passport and other documents—one to carry in his luggage, another for the money

pouch pinned inside his pants, and a third to leave with
Dulcinea. The double zippers of his pack he outfitted with
small combination locks. And he began gathering medical supplies, for his own use, for barter and for the Kallawaya.

Christopher packed topographical maps of the Boca del
Diablo, but the photos Dulcinea had brought from Bolivia he ignored, leaving them on his desk. He wasn't going
on a treasure hunt—just to find his brother.

Tantalized by an intangible future that included such
shopping excursions, he took Dulcinea to pick out furniture for the room where Mrs. Prosper would sleep. They
chose lodgepole-pine pieces, handmade by a craftsman in
Ridgway.

And at lunchtime and in the evenings, he taught Dulcinea to drive. She learned fast, and soon he took her into
Ridgway for her test. She drove the Cherokee home, and
when they reached the ranch and she'd parked and turned
off the engine, she sat silently behind the wheel for several
seconds.

Christopher said, "What is it?"

She wet her lips. "You've taught me to swim—and
helped me get my driver's license. You gave me Sombra."

Christopher stared down at his hands.

"Thank you," said Dulcinea. "That's all I wanted to
say." She opened the driver door and got out, moving with
a spiritedness and independence that reminded him of
someone he'd known long ago. After a disoriented moment, he realized that person was her—before he'd left her.

As he, too, climbed out in the snow and they both closed
the doors of the Cherokee, Dulcinea said, "I'm going to
go see Sombra. I think I want to take her for a ride."

"I'll come with you." But he heard the phone ringing
inside, and he came around the car, grabbed the keys from
her and dashed for the house.

He picked up the kitchen extension on the fourth ring, just before the answering machine went on.

It was Moth.

"Chris? Hey, I found your man, Mayorga. You'll like this...."

When he hung up the phone minutes later, Christopher sat down at the kitchen table and put his head in his hands. Mayorga had been murdered four years earlier, his head blown off by a blast from a *campesino*'s homemade rifle.

He was dead.

ON THE DAY before his departure, Christopher brought Mrs. Prosper's things over. They had rescued some photos and knicknacks and several pieces of furniture from the top floor of her house, and he put those in one of the empty spare rooms downstairs and helped her arrange it as a private sitting room. Along with the bedroom next door, it would form private quarters for her. She and Dulcinea would be together for many weeks. Christopher hoped they would get along.

Helping Kitty set up her rooms, Christopher counted the hours slipping away. The night ahead was his last in Sneffels. He wished he could be alone with Dulcinea—and he got his wish.

After a dinner that was a strange mix of celebration and sadness, the three of them enjoying fresh-baked bread and roast duckling, Kitty said she thought she'd turn in early.

Christopher went to her room with her, to make sure she had everything she needed, then returned to the dining room, where Dulcinea was putting the silver candlesticks away in the china cabinet. He helped her, feeling the distance between them but remembering the closeness.

In the dim orange-gold light from the chandelier, he saw her wavy black hair in her loose ponytail, and her slender body, pregnant, in her navy blue crinkled-silk dress. He brushed against her as she closed the door of the cabinet, and their eyes met.

Dulcinea didn't move. For days they'd lived as though that intimate night, the night they'd made love and cried for Isabel together, had not happened. Since she'd arrived in January, he had shown her nothing but kindness. She had asked for more, and now he was leaving.

She had many nights ahead in which to wish the curse was broken. Nights spent alone.

So this is regret, she thought.

Dulcinea watched his tongue slide lightly along his bottom lip. His eyes looked black, deep as the mines of Sneffels, and the dim light hid his emotions, but she sensed they were there. He said, "Shall we take a starlight ride?"

CHRISTOPHER SADDLED Sombra de la Luna and Rayo de Luz, and he and Dulcinea set out along the road Ferdy had plowed earlier that day, the gaited animals stepping in unison. Christopher's thoughts roamed. He thought about the woman beside him and the curse that divided him. He longed to make her understand, but the naked night was too cold and crisp for such a conversation. He spoke, instead, of business—the necessary business of their parting.

As Dulcinea watched an owl take flight from a stand of oaks off to the west, he told her, "I need you to do something for me." He stared briefly across the meadow at some deer, then glanced at Dulcinea. "I've taken some legal precautions. I'm not anticipating problems, but anything can happen. If I don't come back within six months and I haven't notified my attorney of a reason for the delay, my property will transfer to you."

Dulcinea's heart thudded, both with the immensity of his action and the reason for it. Not come back?

"On the way out of town in the morning, we'll stop at my lawyer's office. I'm going to give you my power of attorney. I want you to take care of this ranch while I'm gone. Ferdy will tell you what needs to be done, and then you should let him do it. He likes you. You'll get along fine." Christopher told her about the ranch, the way things happened. The hay cutting in the spring... Hank from the Livery Barn would buy the hay.... In early July there was a rodeo, and Christopher always took his own horses to the mountains and rented out the stalls in the barn.

So much responsibility, thought Dulcinea. His giving her power of attorney was a tremendous sign of trust. But when they returned to the barn and dismounted, she felt a dismal well of emptiness inside her.

As she groomed Sombra de la Luna in her stall and heard Christopher singing in Rayo's stall, she thought about his return to Bolivia. He was facing what frightened him most, so why wouldn't he try to find the urn and return it to the shrine?

"*¿Por qué?*" she murmured to Sombra, holding her face against the black mane she had just brushed.

"Dulcie?"

She started. He stood outside the stall, his eyes quietly smiling at her pose, hugging her horse.

Dulcinea flushed.

Christopher's body was liquid-hot. "Come down to the vapor cave with me?"

Her lips felt dry. "All right."

"*Buenos noches,* Sombra. *Chaucito.*" Dulcinea kissed the Paso's neck, then slipped out of the stall while Christopher stifled a grin. Nothing in his life had ever gone as well as giving her that horse.

Together they walked to the end of the barn. Christopher shut off the lights and closed the door behind them.

As their boots crunched on the snow in the yard, Dulcinea said, "I'll just go upstairs and put on my swimsuit."

Christopher thought of the things he needed to tell her. Maybe in the vapor cave, he would find a way. "I'll meet you down there."

HE KEPT A PAIR of faded red swim trunks in the towel cabinet in the dry room. He changed into them, then walked down the warm corridor, feeling the vapor fill his nostrils, warm his body. He heard a sound behind him and looked back to see Dulcinea in her usual swimming ensemble—hiding in his T-shirt. Christopher waited for her, holding open the outer door of the cave till she had walked through. Before they reached the inner door, the steam began to dampen their bodies.

Christopher said, "We won't stay long. Tell me if you feel too warm." He propped open the door to make it cooler, but still the dripping water insulated sound, intensifying the privacy of the cave. He led the way into the room with the shallow, stone-rimmed hot-springs pool and picked up a hose that had been feeding ice-cold water into the mineral springs to cool it off. "You can run this over you, too."

Dulcinea tentatively stepped over the low stone wall that rimmed the pool and put her foot in the shin-deep water. Christopher held out his hand, and she took it without looking at him. After he stepped into the pool, she put her other foot in, too. On one side of the pool, the stone wall surrounding the mineral springs had been overtaken by the encroaching cave wall, but on the other was a wide ledge of smooth stone. They walked through the shallow water and sat side by side on the ledge, enfolded in vapor. Christopher released Dulcinea's hand and leaned forward with his forearms on his knees.

For a few minutes, he listened to the calming sound of the dripping water, of the cave itself. A cool and constant draft flowed through the wet heat from the opened door, but he asked Dulcinea, "Are you all right?"

"It's nice." She felt like weeping. If she moved an inch she would be touching his body—but there were miles between them.

Feeling the same way, Christopher searched for words to span the distance. He would be leaving the next day, and he should return within a couple of months, but he was haunted by the memory of their last parting. "Dulcie."

Slowly, as though uncertain of the movement, she lifted her head and looked at him. There was a light sheen of sweat on her lips. She was beautiful with the warm mist all around her.

The only way to explain was to say what was in his heart. He peered at her through the vapor, wishing they could be completely united, without any of the obstacles that had always divided them. His voice mingled with the sound of water in the cave. "I'm just a man. This Son-With-Hair-Like-Inti person—I don't know him."

Dulcinea blinked at him, her eyes watery.

Christopher took her hand. *Don't cry.* "He's not me. I found that out in jail. I'm lucky for what I have, that I'm a doctor and live in this beautiful place. My grandfather helped me get past what happened to me. I have a good life. But this curse . . . I have to let it go. I can't make myself believe that because I failed, a little baby died. Or that your child's life is in my hands."

Dulcinea's throat constricted. In the dizzying feeling of the mist, an awful sensation went through her—that what he was saying was true, and that she, like his family, had laid a wrongful burden upon him, a burden that was not his.

His tongue touched his lips again as he looked into her eyes. It wasn't time for the other things he wanted to say to her. He needed to clear a path between them, a way for them to find each other and not be parted.

"Dulcinea, you mean more to me than anyone ever has. I'm going to be back in a few months—at the latest, by the time your baby comes.'' He couldn't go on. How could he ask anything of her in light of what she believed—that he had a destiny and would not answer it?

It's true, a part of him said. *Not know the Son-With-Hair-Like-Inti? He is you.*

Dulcinea's voice reached into him, took hold of his heart. ''I'll be waiting for you, Christopher.''

A deep shudder went through him. *This is all I've wanted,* he thought. Turning his head away, not wanting to show what he felt in his eyes, he used his free hand to rinse water over his face. Then he said, ''This is probably enough heat for you. Let's go upstairs.''

THEY SHOWERED in the outer chamber of the cave, where the taps were built into the stone wall. There were two showers, but they used just one, and under the spray he touched her, drew her against him until her rounded belly touched his rising erection. Through the falling water, he met her eyes. She raised her face, her lips...

They peeled off their wet things in the shower and hung them in the dry room, and Christopher toweled the moisture from her hair and his. From the linen cabinet, they took more towels and wore them up to the ground floor, past Mrs. Prosper's silent rooms and upstairs to Christopher's bedroom.

He turned on a lamp, and in its dim glow Dulcinea saw the woodwork and the lodgepole-pine bed, whose massive headboard and frame seemed twisted and tilted, as though it had been caught in a strong gale. It was a beautiful bed, a bed meant for more than one.

When he tucked her between the flannel sheets, they smelled like him. He switched off the lamp and joined her. Under the sheets they reached for each other, hugging tight.

Speaking low, his mouth and nose nuzzling her face, Christopher said, ''Dulcinea...sweetheart...I love you.''

He made love to her in ways he had not the last time, the night they had mourned together. Now he took care, made it all for her, and she made it all for him, kneeling over him with her breasts swaying and taking him in her mouth.

It was exciting. Sweet.

But the action brought a thought to him, a thought he'd been able to overcome the first night. He couldn't now.

She had done this with his brother.

The thought could drive him insane. Christopher blocked everything from his mind but physical sensation. He blocked her. But later, as he made love to her with his mouth, one imperative possessed him and drove him. *Forget, Dulcie. Forget. I want him out of your mind.*

He listened to her cry out, and afterward he cradled her in his arms, feeling her body that carried Barnabas's baby against him. The child's presence made him uneasy. What if he couldn't love Barnabas's son?

He thought of his own father, who had virtually abandoned him and his twin to the care of Tomás when they were growing up. There was no place for two badly behaved young boys at the university, he had said.

It still hurt.

Like finding that Dulcinea had married his brother had hurt.

Lying in the dark with her, he remembered when he had come out of prison. Smuggled away in a supply chest in the back of a Jeep, he'd been taken to a cheerless mountain church where his grandfather, Jonah, awaited him, holding documents that would get him to the United States. Christopher had weighed 140 pounds—unshaven, filthy, and missing three teeth that had been beaten from his head, with two others broken. He had wanted to see his brother. He had wondered why Barnabas wasn't there. Jonah had sat down with him at the nearest crossroads while they waited for a *camión* to take them to La Paz. His grandfather had said, "I saw your brother, Christopher. This is going to be hard for you to hear."

It had been hard to hear.

He had bought a knife in Sorata and sharpened it incessantly, the sound of the whetting stone creating a rhythm in his head. Jonah had sat patiently beside him, not minding when people looked at him oddly, as though he was a madman. He had said, "I want to go to Chulina."

Jonah had answered patiently, "We're going to Sneffels. I need to get back to the ranch, and you must come with me. I need your help."

I want to go to Chulina.

Jonah had never breathed a word that Barnabas was not in Chulina but visiting La Paz, where they were headed, and he must have said prayers that Christopher would not meet his twin on the street and run that knife through him.

"Please let me come with you."

Christopher jerked out of his thoughts, startled by Dulcinea's words. "No," he said at once. "No."

"Please."

"No." His hand touched her round abdomen, and he tried to change the way he felt about Barnabas being with her. Inside her. "You're pregnant. You could get sick."

After a bit, Dulcinea slipped out of bed and went to her room. When she returned, she climbed back into his bed and said, "I got you this. I took it to the priest and asked him to bless it. He did, even though Christopher isn't really a saint." She fastened the silver chain around his neck. *Safe travels.*

"I won't take it off." He felt the cool weight of the medal, and then he pushed back the covers and got up. "I'm going to turn on the light," he warned, then did it. Walking to his closet, he said, "I have something for you, too."

Three large white boxes, one squarish and deep, another rectangular, the third a shape in between. As Dulcinea sat up, pulling the covers to her chest, Christopher set the boxes on the bed, the square one in her lap.

She looked at him questioningly.

He climbed back into the bed beside her. "Open it."

She pried up the lid, pulled it off and saw what lay in the tissue paper inside. It was a broad-brimmed straw hat made of the fine jipijapa straw grown near Guayaquil, Ecuador. The straw was so finely woven that as she lifted the hat from the box, it felt like linen, and she knew that if she held it up to the lamp, not a pinhole of light would penetrate.

Her throat felt choked. It was a traditional Peruvian riding hat, and Dulcinea didn't need to turn it over to see that it had been made where the best hats were crafted, in Catacaos, Peru. She knew what it had cost, not only in money but in trouble to secure.

"Try it on. I had to guess your size from how my Stetson fits you."

Dulcinea set the hat on her head. The fit was perfect, firm enough not to come off when she was riding. She started to cry.

"Dulcie," said Christopher, laughing a little, delighted nonetheless. His arm around her, he stole the box from her lap and put another in its place.

Still wearing her hat, Dulcinea worked the lid off the second box. It contained black, ankle-high *chalan* boots of fine leather, the same boots worn by Mexican *charros*. They were her size.

Her eyes were full of wonder. Christopher watched her fingers, which had dug potatoes in Chulina, touch the leather, and he embraced her, raining kisses on the white skin of her back, beneath her hair. He took off her hat, set it at the foot of the bed with the shoe box and the third box, and pulled her back to the pillows.

Her eyes were still wet and she said, "I don't deserve this. I don't deserve a man to love me like this."

There was too much genuine feeling in her words for him to interpret them merely as gratitude for his gifts. She believed what she was saying.

His hand went to her hair, stroking it back from her face. Eyes on hers in the lamplight, he said, "Why don't you deserve it?"

Old shame burned through her.

The Hacienda de la Torra is no longer your home....

Did you let Cristobal do this, Dulcie? Did you like it when my brother touched you that way?

She couldn't meet Christopher's eyes. "Nothing."

He wished he could read her mind. But he could only remember the past. He'd left her. What had happened in those six years?

Christopher didn't need details. He knew her father and he knew his brother.

"You deserve every happiness," he said. "You deserve much better than you've ever gotten."

Her eyes were cast down, not seeing him.

"Dulcinea, you were nineteen." Why was it so hard to say these things? "You loved me. I had a responsibility to you—"

"I wanted to make love with you!" It burst out of her, and Dulcinea was shocked at the intensity of her own anger. She rolled away from him so that he couldn't see her face. She dragged the covers around her, almost over her head. "It was never anyone else's business. I loved you...."

She felt his arms lock around her from behind. His head pressed close to hers, and she heard his voice in her ear. "I can't hear you."

She turned toward him and looked at his face, right next to hers. "I loved you. I wanted to marry you, and you said you would have married me if my father..." Crying again, she gasped, a strangled sound. "There wasn't anything wrong with it."

Christopher smothered her against his chest. He closed his eyes without answering. At last he said the only truth he knew. "It's a gift to have you in my arms again—to have ever had you there. I belong to you." *And you belong to me.*

His hand slid down her front, holding her abdomen, holding the baby inside. *You, too,* he thought, *I must take.*

Dulcinea gradually relaxed, drowsing against him, believing in his love. She felt his face against her hair, his hands on her body, and she knew one thing—about their feelings for each other, there could be no more mistakes or misunderstanding.

When she seemed calm, Christopher gradually moved away from her to sit up and move the boxes on the bed.

Dulcinea said, "Wait!" With an embarrassed smile she sat up, too. There was a box she hadn't opened.

He lifted the rectangular box and set it out of her reach, teasing. "No. I've decided you don't deserve it."

She dived across him and snatched the box from his hands.

Smiling, Christopher lay down to watch her open the lid and remove the rest of the classical Peruvian riding attire he had assembled for her: white riding pants and shirt, white silk scarf and the alpaca poncho.

"Sorry it's not vicuña," he said.

She held the poncho against her face. "They're endangered. This is perfect. I wouldn't have wanted anything else."

She spent a long time looking at the clothes, then folded them and put them away, stacking their boxes beside the bed.

She and Christopher moved into each other's arms and made love again, remaining joined for a long time, adoring each other.

Afterward, when he'd turned out the light, Dulcinea put thoughts of the morning far from her mind and lay with her head against his chest and began to doze.

His voice stirred her, coming to her through a haze of near-sleep.

"Dulcie."

She shifted.

"I want you to know... I'll try to do something."

He stopped speaking for so long that her breath grew slow and her mind wandered.

"I'll do my best about the urn. About the curse."

Silently, she linked her fingers through his.

And in the morning, when Christopher came out of the shower, he found the packet of aerial photographs on top of his pack, a reminder of his promise.

CHAPTER ELEVEN

TWO DAYS LATER Christopher was in La Paz, and it was much as he remembered. The poverty of the outer suburbs, Indian women washing clothes in a river polluted with sewage, dirty children in the streets. Then, appearing over a rise, was the pearl of the Andes itself, in a valley five kilometers wide. At night, he knew, the city lights seemed like the reflection of stars in a clear lake. By day...

It was the most beautiful city he knew. That familiar beauty helped to ease the distress he had felt ever since he'd decided to return. On the plane from Miami to La Paz, his fear had intensified to produce physical symptoms. Sweating, upset stomach. But when he'd made it through customs, when he was on the *camión* with several other Americans and a host of Bolivians speaking Spanish and Quechua, his trepidation gave way to a warm pleasure that was almost anticipation. When he saw La Paz, his heart filled.

He had come at the tail end of the rainy season, and there was mud running in the streets. As he disembarked from the rickety bus that had brought him from the airport, the deep water in the streets almost covered the tops of his boots. He ignored it, ignored the chill in the air. He would get used to being cold and wet—and hot and wet.

Despite the rain, his senses drank in everything. Before setting out for the Yungas, he would spend a couple of days in La Paz, then visit the Charazani region, the lushly fertile land of the Kallawaya. He had brought medical supplies for Tomás to use in his practice. Gifts of money, he knew, would be less appreciated than practical necessities. The Andean subsistence economy worked best without the interference of cash. However, Christopher had heard on public radio about a new water-purification system that he knew would be a godsend to Chulina; he would pose the idea to his uncle when he got there.

In the shelter of a building near the *camión* stop, Christopher took stock of his surroundings. As military police marched past in the street with machine guns, his stomach burned in reaction, and he knew it was something he might have to deal with the whole trip, the fear that went to his bowels.

Keeping an awareness of passersby, he headed up Manco Capac, making his way in the general direction of a major hotel. He ought to go to the ENTEL center, the telecommunications office, and call Dulcinea, but first he needed to decide where to spend the night. Barnabas's house seemed the obvious choice, but he wasn't sure he could stand it.

Nonetheless he stopped at a travel office and bought a map of the city, which he used to find the street where his brother had lived—with Dulcinea.

I can at least go look.

Barnabas's house was in one of the hillside neighborhoods in La Paz, not more than a mile from where the bus had let him off. Christopher walked in the rain, feeling the difference in his lungs and his body because of the altitude. Sneffels was only about 7,500 feet above the sea—La Paz was almost 12,000.

Slogging through the afternoon rain, hoping it wouldn't turn to hail, Christopher nodded to the Aymara and Quechua women, *cholas,* in their bowler hats and full skirts, a parade of color. He noticed the businessmen in white shirts, the beggars and—to the continued agony of his stomach—the *policía.* He stared through the clouds and wished for a clear day to see the three peaks of Illimani, thousands of feet higher than anything in Colorado.

When he reached Barnabas's house, he knew it by the address and by what Dulcinea had told him to look for—a brilliant turquoise woven cloth covering one of the front windows. Christopher ran through the hail to the shelter of the doorway.

Dulcinea and Barnabas had lived here. *Barnabas*...

The front door had a traditional wooden lock, the sort Christopher hadn't seen since he'd left Bolivia. Dulcinea had given him the key and he used it. He opened the flimsy door and stepped inside, into a house that smelled as houses in La Paz often did—cold, with a faint odor of dirtiness. As his eyes swept the front room with its simple woven rug, a television and a chair that could never have been good, he was struck by two things.

One was a certain bleakness, an absence of hope, in the sparse furnishings, the careful order, the lack of decoration.

The other was that, as far as he could see, nothing had been touched since Dulcinea had left.

DULCINEA AWOKE shaking in Christopher's bed and lay disoriented as the real world replaced nightmare images in her mind. Outside his window, the light was blue. It was morning. She would have to get up soon and dress to go to the clinic.

Christopher was gone.

The dream hung on. It had been lurid. Christopher... the blood...the flies and mosquitoes.. So *real*. With an eerie sense of fear, she told herself that he could barely have reached La Paz. He couldn't be lying in some forest, where the light coming through the canopy made his skin look green. Where flies and mosquitoes and tiny bugs she couldn't identify crawled in the blood on his face.

Quelling her irrational fear, she lay against the pillow for a long time, his scent all around her. But he wasn't there.

The phone beside the bed rang and she picked it up. "Hello?"

"Hi, Dulcie."

Her heart gave one huge beat of relief at the sound of his voice. "Christopher." She hugged the covers around her and clutched the receiver as though it was him. "I just dreamed about you."

He had dreamed about Barnabas—about walking in on Barnabas and Dulcinea. An inevitable twist of his subconscious, under the circumstances. In the lobby of the five-star hotel where he'd paid for a room so he could use the phone, Christopher flashed briefly on the painful night. "I slept at the house." Not *your* house. "On the couch."

Dulcinea said, "Oh," and he wondered what she was thinking. Did she wonder how he had felt being in the house where she'd lived with his brother? Seeing Barnabas's clothes and hers in the closet together and seeing how little she had? The most puzzling thing was two *polleras,* full, gathered skirts like those worn by Aymara women in La Paz. Christopher could see that Dulcinea had never worn them, and he knew she wouldn't have bought them. A white person in Indian dress in Bolivia would be considered ridiculous. Had Barnabas meant to insult Dulcinea? The thought had made him sick.

Then he'd found the infant's christening dress hidden in a shoe box beneath a pair of cheap high-heeled sandals that had never been worn. Christopher had been looking for things of his brother's, clues to his whereabouts. Finding the dress had jarred him. He had lain on the bed and looked at the gown and seen it was handmade. He had put it against his face as though the feel and scent of it could tell secrets. Why had Dulcinea hidden it with a pair of shoes rather than put it in her drawer?

He didn't notice how long the silence on the phone had become until Dulcinea's voice broke into his thoughts. "It was a bad dream, Christopher. You were hurt, and there was blood on your face and mosquitoes and flies."

His stomach burned as it did when the police were near. He glanced about and saw a German trying to communicate with a clerk at the desk. No *policía.* And there was no reason that hearing about her dream should make him afraid. Just a dream.

"I'm fine, Dulcie. There aren't too many flies here in La Paz. Just lots of hail." He felt as though he'd been running hard. Altitude... He changed the subject. "Are things all right with Kitty?"

"Yes. It's nice having her here." They'd made it through the first day easily, getting used to each other, working together on dinner.

As Dulcinea spoke, Christopher's thoughts wandered. He remembered the images from her ultrasound. He recalled the sound of her baby's heart.

Keenly, he regretted the promise he'd made. Because he didn't know how in hell he would ever find that urn.

HE TOOK a *camión,* an open supply truck, from La Paz to Abra Pumasani, the Charazani turnoff, and from there he began walking through a downpour to *ayllu* Chulina. He had bought a black wool fedora in the city, and he wore a *chulo* under it to stay warm—practical concessions to his heritage. There were others on the road, most of them Kallawaya, too, though he recognized no one. A man about his own age wearing a cloth saddlebag, a medicine bag, passed him with a standard Andean greeting, *"Ama sua, ama llulla, ama quella."* Don't steal, don't lie, don't be lazy.

Answering, *"Qampas hinallataq."* To you likewise. Christopher fell into step beside him. He introduced himself and said that he was a doctor and a Kallawaya herbalist too, and that he was going to see his family in Chulina. The other man, Gabriel, was from Calliicho, on the way to Chulina, and they walked together, talking herbal remedies, alternating between Quechua and Machaj-Juyai, the language of colleagues, of Kallawaya healers. There were earth shrines on the road, and the men halted at them and left offerings of coca leaves for Pacha Mama and the other mountain deities and for the *achachillas,* the souls of ancestors long dead. For Christopher, such ritual was a symbolic way to show thanks for the gifts of the earth and for his own health and abilities. As for the souls of ancestors, he hoped Mariano's would find no rest.

When the rain stopped, they paused for lunch and shared *charqui* and bread, and Gabriel told him he had been visiting with a *curandero* friend in Sorata who had successfully used *Lilium candidum,* the Madonna lily, to treat snakebite. Christopher kept his tongue in his cheek as he listened to Gabriel explain that a woman had been bitten in the fields and was taken to the *curandero,* and Gabriel had seen her healed. She had chewed the lily leaves and roots with vinegar.

The plant was an astringent, demulcent, emollient, stimulant and sudorific. But Christopher had seen only two things work for snakebite: antivenin and electric shock. He took some extra vials of antivenin from his pack—one for the fer-de-lance, the other for bushmasters—and gave them to Gabriel with syringes and instructions. Gabriel thanked him politely, carefully stored the supplies and gave Christopher bundles containing the roots and leaves of the Madonna lily. Christopher thanked him, too.

As they got up and Christopher shouldered his pack again, he couldn't help pointing out that the snake might not have injected venom with the bite. With a disgusted look, Gabriel replied that he himself had seen her, and her leg was swollen to her thigh. And speaking of women, *"¿Warmayoqchu kanki?"*

Christopher thought of Dulcinea and replied that he had no wife.

When they reached Calliicho, Gabriel invited him to spend the night at his house, but Christopher declined, saying he would walk on to Chulina. They said good-night, and Christopher continued on in the falling darkness. A storm was coming, and it began to sleet as he reached Chulina. In the gray-black he saw the adobe buildings. Each Kallawaya family had three—one for cooking, another for sleeping and a third for storage. The buildings formed three sides of a courtyard, with a wall and gate in front.

It was a mile uphill to the highest terraces of the *ayllu,* where the Choqueneiras lived. But even in the darkness it was all familiar. The trees in the courtyards, the scent of wildflowers on the roadside. The inevitable smells of meat cooking and of smoke, of human and animal excrement, and of rain and mud and cold.

On his street, a man wearing a fedora stood at the edge of the road in front of the third house, smoking. It was Florentine, Christopher's old neighbor, who was married to the Chulina midwife. Christopher greeted him, and Florentine recognized him and embraced him hard. Walking with him through the mud and sleet, his neighbor said, "Your place is in good shape. Your brother used to come out every few months and check on things." He looked at Christopher in the frigid night, his breath steaming, and Christopher could see that he knew Barnabas was missing. Dead. "Did Dulcinea come and find you?"

Christopher nodded. "She's in the United States." As the ice pelted his face, he thought of Florentine's wife, Nieve, who must have helped Dulcinea during her labor with Isabel. After he saw his uncle, he would go visit the cemetery and find the marker.

It was a short walk to the Choqueneira courtyard, but Christopher only glanced in between the stone walls and continued on toward his uncle's house. Florentine said, "I'll let you see Tomás alone."

Christopher paused to say good-night to the other man. The sleet had let up some. Florentine embraced him again. "My little girl Alma loved Dulcinea. Dulcinea would take her along to look after the llamas, and she made her a little doll out of alpaca. It was cruel of your brother to take her to the city. She came over to our house to see Nieve, and she cried because she had to leave her baby's grave."

Christopher thought of a number of replies. That his brother had never understood women very well. That perhaps Barnabas had hoped to take her mind off the death. But he remembered the skirts in the closet. He hadn't been there, and he would never know his twin's motives.

Florentine said, "How is her pregnancy?"

Not a simple question. He'd forgotten what it was like to be here, where everyone knew of the curse. Where everyone believed in it.

"She's fine." Forestalling other questions, he soon told Florentine, *"Allin tuta. Paqarinkama,"* and the other man told him good-night, too. They parted, and Christopher walked on to the next courtyard.

As he reached the gate, Tomás came out. His uncle, who had received no word of his trip to Bolivia, said, *"Napaykunkin,* Cristobal. I've been waiting for you."

TOMÁS HAD DINNER ready, potatoes and a stew thickened with *quinoa.* Christopher ate eagerly, and in the light from the fireplace he studied his uncle's face. Tomás was handsome, with an erect bearing and eyes that held wisdom and gentleness. He was only fifty-two, younger than Christopher's father had been.

They hardly spoke at first. Christopher was hungry and tired from hiking all day at high altitude. And Tomás seemed pleased to see him, happy just to sit and enjoy his presence. It occurred to Christopher that he had neglected his uncle by staying away so long. But what choice had he had? He had written and occasionally sent gifts of a blood-pressure cuff or a stethoscope, though Tomás never wrote back.

After dinner, they sat together by the fire and finally they began to talk. Tomás caught him up on general news. Florentine was the new mayor; had he mentioned that? Tomás's own transportation business was healthy; he had just bought a new six-ton Toyota truck. It was in Oturo just now, serving as a tour vehicle for a dozen Swiss back-packers. Christopher told Tomás about his medical practice and about the ranch and his grandfather's death. Then conversation dropped off as he thought of what had happened after he'd left Chulina the last time for a visit at the Hacienda de la Torra.

Finally, cautiously, he said, "When I wrote you from Colorado, I said I'd been in jail. You never told Dulcinea."

His uncle's eyes flickered. With wry humor painting over sadness, he remarked, "I'm supposed to repair your love affair?"

"Of course not." Christopher flushed in the darkness.

After a moment of silence grimmer than any words either had spoken, Tomás said, "She tried to make the best of things. I wouldn't have hurt her with that news. And if Barnabas had wanted her to know, it was his place to tell her. He was her husband."

Christopher heard the mild rebuke and wondered if his uncle thought him a coward.

Because of that, he said nothing about the urn. Words were empty. Sick at heart, he considered a scenario in which he hadn't buckled to temptation, hadn't made love to Dulcinea.

Now he saw a flaw in that picture, though he couldn't expect another soul to understand. Except, perhaps, Dulcinea herself. It was a crazy way to feel. But Isabel was the only child he'd ever...

His thoughts fell away into the shadows of the room, and when Tomás invited him to stay the night, rather than go home in the dark to the house that had been empty for so long, Christopher agreed. But he said he was going for a walk first.

Watching him stand and put on his parka, his uncle spoke, and his voice betrayed a compassion Christopher had been foolish enough to think absent. "She is beside your father."

WHEN HE WENT OUTSIDE, there were hailstones everywhere on the ground. It was cold, and he zipped his parka and took his *chulo* from his pocket and donned it, then pulled up his hood as frost nipped his face. Overhead, the sky had cleared, and Christopher could see the Southern Cross, but no moon. The thin, icy air bit his nose and cheeks, and he walked with his hands in his pockets. No one was around, but he saw an ancient motor scooter parked in one courtyard, heard chickens and guinea pigs in others. Burros, pigs and sheep stood in open corrals, and Christopher felt the presence of people in their houses as he climbed the road.

It was a mile to the church. The stone bell tower and the cross appeared against the starry sky long before he reached the gate. The church was a small stone building with a thatched roof, and the yard was full of crosses and stones, none of them labeled. Christopher was glad Tomás had told him where to find Isabel.

With a glance toward the church, which a priest visited once a month, he made his way among the crosses by the light of the stars. He had brought his headlamp, but left it in his pocket. It seemed better to be part of the night.

Soon, he found the stones marking his father's grave. A tall slender cross stood among them, rooted deep in the ground. Briefly, with little emotion, Christopher remembered the day they'd buried Roderigo. He did not dwell on recollections, but peered about the ground beside the grave and found the much smaller cross.

Christopher crouched beside it. Sensing an irregularity in the wood, he touched it. Carving. He squinted at it, then took out his headlamp and shone the light on the tiny grave of his infant daughter.

One word, painfully carved, ISABEL.

Dulcinea must have done it herself, unable to bear the thought of leaving an unmarked grave and going away to the city.

It was cruel of your brother...

Christopher turned off the light and put it back in his pocket. For a long time he stayed, crouched beside the grave in the solitude of the churchyard. He spoke to the darkness and the soul of the body in the grave. "I wish I knew you. I wish I could have held you once."

He closed his eyes and rested his chin in his hands and tried not to wonder what his child's life would have been like had she lived. How Barnabas would have treated her. Or what might have happened if he, Christopher, could have married Dulcinea. And returned the urn without getting caught.

That's not why, he thought. *It can't be.*

But for two hundred years, no Choqueneira birth had escaped tragedy. Alone by this humble grave, he had to face that.

Opening his eyes, Christopher stared at the ground and whispered, "I'm sorry, little baby. I'm sorry I screwed up."

HE'D BEEN GONE for a week when Dulcinea had a good dream.

It was evening, and they were lying in a tent in a meadow among tall grass and wildflowers that were white and purple and blue. Something was happening, something out of her control, but Christopher was there. Seeing his brown eyes, she knew everything would be all right.

The phone woke her, and she blinked at the softly filtered light coming through the lace curtains. Saturday morning. She had slept later than usual.

He was still gone.

The telephone rang again and she picked it up.

It was Christopher, calling from La Paz after returning from Chulina. He would be leaving for the Yungas later that day, he said. He wouldn't be able to call her....

Dulcinea told herself that the rumors about the Boca del Diablo were superstition. Christopher was strong, and he knew the rain forest. He had traveled there with his uncle when he was studying herbalism.

When the silence lengthened, Christopher asked, "How are you, Dulcie? Is everything okay?"

"Yes." She tried to sound as though it was. In truth, she was so depressed she could hardly drag herself to work. Her only comfort was in feeling the movements of the baby, in silently talking to him. What if Christopher couldn't find the twice-stolen urn?

Or didn't try.

Thrusting away the thoughts, Dulcinea said, "Kitty is going to teach me to crochet." Things for the baby. *I can't stand it,* she thought.

Christopher recognized all her unspoken words. God, if that baby died . . . He said, "I went to see Isabel."

Dulcinea pictured the barren churchyard on the *puna.*

"I saw the christening dress, too." In the hotel lobby, Christopher thought about where he had found the dress. He wanted to ask why she'd put it there. But in his heart

he knew. The only emotions that had concerned Barnabas were his own. Christopher could imagine all manner
of insensitivity. And Dulcinea had put her grief where her
husband couldn't find it.

Christopher glanced around the lobby. The clerk was
thirty feet away down the counter. He lowered his voice.
"I'm glad we made a baby together, Dulcie. I'm glad she
was. I'm sorry I wasn't there."

Dulcinea wished he was within reach of her arms. "I feel
the same way."

CHRISTOPHER PICKED UP his pack and left the hotel, hurrying down Calle Santa Cruz to Calle Linares and the
Mercado de Hechicería, the Witches' Market. In Chulina,
Tomás had given Christopher a new medicine bag containing ceremonial cloths and four gifts for his *mesa*, his
altar. Together they had gone over the herbs wrapped in
muslin in the bag, and Christopher had added the cloth
bundles containing the Madonna-lily roots and leaves that
Gabriel had given him. But there were still a few more
things he wanted. At the Mercado de Hechicería, he could
purchase high-quality herbs from anywhere in the world.

From various vendors, he bought several imported
North American and Chinese herbs whose uses he had
studied in Colorado. He also purchased a mummified
llama fetus, which was used in many Kallawaya rituals.
The miscarried fetus represented that even the gods could
err—hence, illness. As it began to drizzle, he left the market and began looking for a taxi to take him to Villa Fá-
tima, near the stadium, to catch the Flota Yungueña. He
was walking past the ENTEL office when he saw a small
man with thick gray hair and wearing a business suit
striding purposefully down the sidewalk.

The sprinkle was turning to a shower, and the man's
head was bowed, partially hidden by his hat, but Christopher recognized him. He paused and stared, blood rush-

ing, and the passing businessman must have sensed his attention, because he glanced up. He smiled and nodded, then raised his head again and stopped.

In the cold rain they faced each other, not eight feet apart.

At last the smaller, older man said in a tone of resignation and acknowledgment, "Cristobal."

Christopher nodded. "Esteban."

The eyes of neither blinked away, and Christopher thought how old Dulcinea's father looked. He tried to summon rage for the past, but all he could feel for the other man was inexplicable pity. Esteban had turned away his only daughter, the light of his life. Pride was poor compensation for loneliness.

They stood looking at each other for a long time.

Then Esteban tipped his hat and began to walk by. Christopher watched him go, thinking of the deep betrayal of friendship on both sides. As his eyes followed the figure up the sidewalk, he wished there had been more to say. But he remembered the grave on the *puna,* and he knew there could be no forgiveness.

AFTER TALKING with Christopher, Dulcinea hung up the phone, then showered and put on the leggings and long-sleeved T-shirt he had bought for her the day they went to Grand Junction. She went downstairs and found Kitty in the kitchen putting on tea.

As usual, the older woman looked pretty in the morning, her hair in its neat French twist, her smile ready. "Good morning, Dulcinea. How are you?"

Her smile was full of affection, and Dulcinea tried to equal it. "Wonderful. I hope you slept well."

For a minute or two Dulcinea plodded through the civilities of the morning, but she was soon overcome by a desperate need for solitude, to remember Christopher's voice in her mind, to reflect on what he'd said about Isabel. Seizing the excuse of getting the mail, she pulled on her boots and guide shell, and walked down to the box by the road.

The mailbox was full, mostly with junk. The whole time Dulcinea had lived at Thistledown Ranch, Christopher had never received even one personal letter, which was why she noticed the white business-size envelope with the hand-written address, still legible among the postal stickers in-dicating the letter had been rerouted. The handwriting seemed familiar, but Dulcinea didn't identify it until she saw the return address.

The letter was from Barnabas.

A LANDSLIDE had destroyed most of the village of Huajtata the day before Christopher arrived. It was still raining, in thick hard constant drops that fell like streams from the sky, but in the torrent the survivors waded through the mud, searching for loved ones.

A priest from Korea had set up an infirmary in an un-damaged hut. His Quechua was better than his English, and he sent Christopher a look of intense gratitude when he heard the words, *"Hampiq-mi kani."* I am a doctor.

Inside the hut were three patients—a man, a woman and a child whose mother was with him. The boy had yellow fever and was dehydrated, and Christopher asked his mother to boil some water. He would prepare a *mate* of quinine-bark powder to lower the fever, with sugar and salt for rehydration. The man had a compound fracture of his femur that was rapidly becoming septic. Father Yeon had been attempting to construct a traction splint using pieces of an external frame backpack. Christopher gave the pa-tient morphine and penicillin from the supplies in his pack, then cleaned the wound, and he and the priest set the leg. The woman had a high fever, complaining of a severe headache. Examining her, Christopher suspected menin-gitis. As he again prepared to administer penicillin, he told

Yeon they must quarantine the hut, and the priest went out to spread the word.

Between treating the three patients, Christopher stepped outside into the rain to check the other villagers for injuries and flulike symptoms—other cases of meningitis. Through the downpour, he saw men walking past carrying mud-covered bodies of the dead, while women and children pawed through the mud where the landslide had occurred.

He was about to step back inside to check on the patients when he saw two figures approaching on the remains of the washed-out road. One was a black man in a sodden white shirt and muddy pants, the other a pregnant woman carrying a day pack on her chest Andean-style, walking very slowly and staring straight ahead like a sleepwalker.

It was Dulcinea.

CHAPTER TWELVE

JAIME, THE DRIVER of the *camión,* pointed ahead. "There he is, I think. Your blond husband, the doctor."

Dulcinea peered through the rain. When she saw Christopher, her heart flooded with relief. She had engineered the lie on the spur of the moment when the driver offered to let her ride in the cab of the *camión.* Jaime had been a godsend, her protector against six drunken passengers enjoying the start of Carnival, Bolivia's biggest fiesta. Now she was too dazed and numb from what she had just experienced, the truck's long slide off the road into a low ravine, to worry what Christopher would think of her story.

He stood outside a thatch-roofed hut, and she saw him speaking hurriedly to a small Asian man before he came jogging through the rain and mud in his boots and heavy canvas pants and a long undershirt that was soaked, clinging to his body. He had not shaved, and he smelled as if he'd been hiking in the rain forest for a week, but Dulcinea longed to throw herself into his arms.

She told the driver, "Jaime, *quiero presentarle a mi esposo, Cristobal.*"

Registering the lie about their relationship, Christopher offered his hand to the other man. He listened briefly to the story of the truck that had gone off the road and how Jaime had assisted Dulcinea and walked with her to the village. Christopher thanked him profusely and said he should ask the priest for something to eat and drink. There had been a disaster here, as they could see.

He corralled Dulcinea under his arm. She was dressed in a pair of sweatpants and his pile cardigan from the free box. Knowing her self-consciousness about the poverty she'd endured with Barnabas, Christopher had never told her the truth about the sweater. Seeing it on her now filled him with protectiveness. Over the cardigan, she wore a guide shell they'd bought in Sneffels. It was keeping off the rain, but already her neck bore the red welts of fly and mosquito bites. Her skin was bone white against her tangled black hair, her face drenched from the humidity that made even smiling a cause for sweat.

Alarmed that she'd come, Christopher said, "What are you doing here? There's a woman in that hut with meningitis, and there's yellow fever here, too."

It wasn't the reaction Dulcinea had hoped for. Trying not to feel like a woman chasing after a lover who didn't want her, who had once rejected her, she said, "I brought you a letter. From Barnabas. He sent it in November. It was lost in the mail."

She slipped her pack from her shoulders, and Christopher took it and slung it over his own. It was light, probably containing her sleeping bag and not much more. She was shivering, as soaked as he was, and Christopher pushed aside his curiosity about the letter to ask, "Did you have shots before you came? Did you have a yellow-fever shot?"

"Not that one. It wasn't a good idea because I'm pregnant."

A good idea would have been for her to stay in Colorado. He wanted to see this letter.

Dulcinea unzipped her guide shell and fumbled with the zipper on the inner pocket where she'd put the letter. She withdrew a folded legal-size envelope.

Although she'd said Barnabas had written the letter, Christopher still felt a jolt at seeing his brother's handwriting. The letter had been opened, undoubtedly by Dulcinea. Briefly, he studied the postmarks and stickers from the postal service. Then he handed it back to her. "Hold it for me while I set up my tent for you." His eyes tried to read hers. "You weren't hurt when the bus went off the road? Did anyone bother you?"

She shook her head. The men in the back of the truck had said obscene things to her, but Jaime carried a knife, and the others had been wary of him. She told Christopher, "I'm going to stay with you now."

There was no alternative—for the moment. The *camión* from the city of Chulumani came to this part of the Yungas only once a week in good weather. Now the roads were washed out. Christopher put his hands on the sides of her hood and looked at her face, wet with rain. She was precious to him and he was afraid for her. "I want you to stay away from the hut where I'm working. You don't want to get meningitis. I'm going to check on my patients, and then I'll pitch the tent."

"I can do it."

Christopher was skeptical.

"I watched you inspect it for holes before you left."

"We'll do it together." What was he supposed to do about his brother's plane now? He couldn't take Dulcinea into the Boca del Diablo.

Just what did Barnabas's letter say?

NEARLY AN HOUR PASSED before he had a chance to read it. He sat in the tent beside Dulcinea while she lay on his inflatable camping mattress, her head on her sweater, eyes closed, her hair plastered to her head with sweat because the heat of the day had returned. Christopher knew he should go back to the infirmary soon, but it would only take a moment to read the letter. He drew it from the envelope.

It was written on yellow legal paper in blue ink. Barnabas had addressed him in Quechua as "Brother," which was how he'd always begun his letters to Christopher.

Wayqi—
Just want to tell you not to worry anymore. I'm going to break the curse! You are the sun, and I am the dark, and we are the same coin. In other words, if you are the Son-With-Hair-Like-Inti, I am, too, because I am your twin. If this doesn't make sense, I apologize, having tied one on recently. But I have decided to save you, because you could never save me and neither could my wife, the fair Dulcinea, who needs someone to tilt windmills for her. I am inviting you to a truce. I will meet you at the Jaguar in Trinidad on our birthday this year. I will buy you a trick from my favorite whore and show you the fruits of my labor, and if you ask nicely you can enjoy a flight with Bolivia's finest.

                        Tupananchiskama...
                        Barnabas

Tupananchiskama... Until we meet...
Christopher read the letter one more time, haunted. Barnabas had alluded to Don Quixote, the madman who had set out to perform acts of chivalry in the name of a country girl he called Dulcinea. Don Quixote, who had mistaken windmills for giants and tried to slay them, wounding himself, instead. It reminded Christopher of his first foray with the urn—and Mayorga. Pointless valor.
Dulcinea, who needs someone to tilt windmills...
No, thought Christopher, looking at Dulcinea dozing beside him. She just needed respect. It was all she'd ever needed. To be loved.

He took a cigarette lighter wrapped in a plastic bag from his shirt pocket, and he burned the letter before he remembered that it was the last one he would get from his brother.

IN THE INFIRMARY, the boy's fever was up and the mother was frightened, talking about having offended the gods by not feeding the earth shrines. For her comfort, because she had just lost her husband in the landslide, Christopher offered to perform a healing ritual for the boy. It had been six years since he'd worked a Kallawaya ceremony, but eight years of training did not vanish.

He moved the boy to another hut, laying his sleeping mat some distance from the fire inside. The boy's mother brought two amulets, a small table and a guinea pig who was to be used in the ritual. On the table Christopher laid his *chusilla,* a cloth made of alpaca wool, then covered it with a richly decorated cloth, the *istalla.*

From his medicine bag he removed the few elements of his *mesa,* the ceremonial altar. They were gifts from Tomás, all but a fossil and the mummified llama fetus he had bought at the Witches' Market. As he handled the unfamiliar objects, Christopher remembered his old medicine bag, which he had left at the Hacienda de la Torra when he'd gone out to ride with Dulcinea that last day. He wished he had it back, just to see it again, to remember who he had been.

The *mesa* was to represent the balance of good and evil, and Tomás had included a balance of good and evil things. On the side of the *mesa* that was to represent evil Christopher laid a traditional rotten egg and a piece of wool woven in the wrong direction. On the opposite side he set coca leaves and the fossil. In the center he placed the llama fetus, that error of the gods—death before birth. Christopher thought of his daughter. Error—or curse?

He performed the ritual speaking in Machaj-Juyai, the language of Kallawaya healers. Toward the end of the ceremony, after the boy had breathed his illness onto the guinea pig and the unharmed animal had been released into the forest, Christopher prepared a fresh *mate*. He chanted while the boy drank it, then carried him back to the infirmary and fetched cold water from the river to bathe him.

The fever broke.

That night, the boy's mother prepared dinner for Christopher and Dulcinea and Father Yeon. Christopher ate in the infirmary. The woman with meningitis was much improved, so after he'd eaten he went to his tent to find Dulcinea, but she was down at the river washing his clothes.

They were alone by the shore. He stripped and bathed in the river, while the sun filtered through the trees and a bird somewhere in the canopy made a sound like hands clapping. Christopher was dressing in a pair of nylon rain pants and a T-shirt when he saw a man coming from the village carrying the body of a dead infant uncovered from the landslide.

Dulcinea's back was turned to the man, and Christopher's first instinct was to protect her, but her head spun around and she saw the baby. As the man carried the child to the river to wash its body, she stood up without looking at Christopher. She began to walk toward the man and followed him to the water.

The baby was altered by death, but the man knew his child and he was bathing it. Dulcinea crouched beside him, and she began to splash water on the baby, too.

Watching from a distance, Christopher saw the man start to cry. Dulcinea didn't get up, but stayed, listening, her eyes full of sorrow. Christopher yearned to take away her pain. But Isabel's death would always be part of her. If only the baby she carried was born healthy...

An acute fear he couldn't express took hold of him. Not fear for the child . . .

He stared across the water at the graceful black-haired figure crouched beside the grieving man.

I've got to find that urn.

A woman came down to the shore to join Dulcinea and the man with the dead child. She had brought a white cloth for the baby. Dulcinea watched them wrap the body, and then she got up and walked slowly back to Christopher.

SHE WAS ALONE in the tent most of the night, while Christopher stayed with the patients in the infirmary. She slept part of the time and lay awake the rest, sipping purified water from a plastic bottle Christopher had given her.

Her mind felt hyperaware, beyond fatigue, geared to survival. In Colorado it had seemed imperative to bring Christopher the letter. But when she reached the airport in La Paz, she'd remembered the dangers for a woman traveling alone in Bolivia. Now the miles in the supply truck with rain cascading down the windshield and pounding the roof of the cab were just a memory, like the truck's careening off the road. Closer were the constant sounds of the night, of animals she couldn't identify, howling like humans in pain. Closer was the landslide, the recollection of the dead baby beside the river.

Her own baby moved inside her. Drawing warmth and comfort from the movement, Dulcinea sent a silent message to her son. *I love you. Everything will be all right.*

In the middle of the seemingly endless night, she heard footsteps outside the tent, and through the mesh of the mosquito net she saw Christopher. He unzipped the fly, got in and zipped the tent again, then spent a few minutes hunting and killing mosquitoes before he turned to her.

"How are you?"

"Okay." She wished she could see his eyes better, but it was too dark.

Christopher noticed she had left her sleeping bag unzipped, not joined to his. It looked inviting and he said, "So we're married."

"Yes." Dulcinea didn't smile.

Guessing her thoughts—recollections of when they'd wanted to marry each other and he'd run away, instead—Christopher said nothing.

Dulcinea lay quietly as he zipped his sleeping bag to hers. He stripped down to a T-shirt and shorts, like she was wearing. Moving into each other's arms was easy, comforting.

"I missed you," she whispered.

"Likewise." Christopher held her close, so that her warm stomach, where the baby lay inside her, pressed into his waist. He drew up the bottom of her shirt and put his hand on her pregnant abdomen as he brought his lips to her neck. "You shouldn't have come."

She buried her face in his chest, as though hiding. "You don't think the letter is important."

"Didn't say that." In the infirmary, he'd been unable to get his mind off it. Barnabas's reference to Dulcinea, the attempt at reconciliation with him.

And the urn.

Why had his brother wanted to break the curse?

Possibilities occurred to him. One was rivalry, Barnabas's wanting to accomplish what Christopher had failed to do. Other reasons revolved around Dulcinea. She believed the curse had killed the baby she'd loved; perhaps Barnabas had wanted to make her love him by doing what it took to end the curse. Either to gain a rung above Christopher or...

Holding her, Christopher was subdued.

Barnabas *couldn't* have cared about her.

But had he been serious about breaking the curse? He couldn't have done it without the urn, and the urn had been stolen from a Lima museum in an armed robbery.

Could Barnabas have done that?

Yes.

So where was the urn now?

He knew the answer. It had to be on his brother's plane, the plane that might have exploded or burned.

"Dulcinea."

She shifted out of his arms so that she could see the dark shape of him in the night.

"I'm going to take you back to La Paz. You can fly home to Colorado."

Dulcinea thought of the dreams she'd had since he'd left Colorado. So real. The dream with the flies had come three times. "I don't want to go back. The roads are washed out. And it's Carnival. All the hotel rooms will be booked for the fiesta."

They could stay in the house she'd shared with Barnabas. But Christopher didn't point that out—or seriously contemplate it. Instead, he considered the condition of the roads, the hordes of drunken revelers. They should wait until after the fiesta to go. But what could they do until then? Yellow fever...meningitis...the landslide... Huajtata was no place for Dulcinea.

Neither was the Boca del Diablo.

"I'll figure it out in the morning." His hand settled on her breast, and his lips covered hers.

Dulcinea pressed closer to him, and she gladly let him lift up her T-shirt and slide it over her arms and head. They made love silently, and Dulcinea prayed that it felt as good to him as it did to her and that he wouldn't make her return to Colorado.

Later, when she fell asleep against his body, she dreamed of flies swarming around the blood on his face.

THEY ARGUED for two days about what to do. Thinking of her recurrent dream, intuiting a reason for it, Dulcinea hammered him with logic. If she was going to have to stay in Huajtata for a week, waiting for him or waiting for the *camión*, why shouldn't they go into the Boca del Diablo? At least there wouldn't be anyone with meningitis there. And she was healthy and strong.

Concern for her finally persuaded Christopher. There were two more cases of meningitis, and because of the condition of the roads, he and Dulcinea might be cut off from the cities for more than a week. On the third morning after her arrival, he gave Father Yeon a store of antibiotics and instructions for herbal *mates,* and he and Dulcinea set out for the Boca del Diablo. She would probably be safer in the uninhabited forest than in the landslide area, where sanitation problems had already become intense.

In the center of the Boca del Diablo was a deep ravine, which the villagers believed was the center of the mystical vortex that supposedly trapped planes and brought the deaths of scientists and curious hikers. Christopher examined his maps of the area—one handmade and purchased from a man in La Paz, the other a geological-survey map—and at last he chose a heading that should lead him and Dulcinea into the supposed vortex area.

She carried her sleeping bag in the day pack she'd brought. Christopher carried everything else. They used sap from the *ajo-ajo* tree for insect repellent. It smelled like garlic, but Dulcinea made no murmur of complaint. Yellow fever was spread by mosquitoes.

The first day's travel was slow.

There was an old road for a mile, but it petered out to a trail and then to nothing, and Christopher cut their way with a machete. He paused often to collect plants while Dulcinea rested, and every few hours they applied more *ajo-ajo* sap, which he had collected in a plastic honey bottle.

The odors were intense. Dulcinea could smell her own body, and her eyes and nose stung from the strong scent of decay in the jungle. Sweat ran off her in rivulets until the rain came, and then the cold water mingled with her perspiration. She never felt clean or dry. The rain was ceaseless, and she grew used to the sight of Christopher's wet head in front of her and the drenched clothing clinging like an elephant's skin to his body. She watched for snakes and ignored the welts from thorns on her arms and the bites of invisible insects undeterred by the *ajo-ajo*.

They stopped for lunch in a small clearing and sat on their packs eating cherimoyas and bananas, *charqui* and ground *quinoa*. When they resumed walking, Dulcinea nearly stepped on a snake, which turned out to be harmless, and they passed several ant trees swarming with inch-long *buna,* whose bite could cause excruciating pain.

That night, the forest was full of wild calls and insects that whined like power saws. The air was cold, with the whimsy of Bolivian weather, and inside the tent they zipped their sleeping bags together. Christopher drew her against him to warm them both, and they made love, losing fear in the haven of each other.

ON THE THIRD DAY they crossed the Rio Rabia, at a place where it was flowing slowly and green algae clung to the banks and the mud on the shore was thick.

Christopher tested the depth with a tent pole and found it not much more than waist-deep, so he led the way in, holding the pack on his head, and Dulcinea followed, clinging to the waistband of his pants with one hand, keeping her pack balanced on her shoulder with the other.

Overhead a bird made a ringing sound, and somewhere else in the forest a monkey called. Gray clouds filled the sky through the slot in the canopy above the river, and as they stepped into deeper water, above his waist, Christopher felt the first trickle of rain. There was a clap of thunder, and he moved more quickly across the river, making sure Dulcinea was still with him.

Behind him Dulcinea saw a black oval thing like a slug on her arm, near the hand that was holding onto Christopher's pants. If her other hand had been free, she would have tried to brush it away. Instead, she released Christopher and swished her arm back and forth in the water.

Turning in the river, Christopher saw the three-inch-long worm and took a breath. "It's all right, Dulce. You picked up a leech. I'll get it off you in just a minute."

As the rain came, assaulting the ground and the river with its force, Dulcinea stared down at the leech. She reached for a higher place on Christopher's body, near his shirt, and held on, trying to breathe slowly and evenly.

In the deafening downpour, they climbed the opposite bank, slogging through deep mud, and Dulcinea struggled not to fall. Slinging her pack over her shoulder by its strap, she followed Christopher through the veil of rain and tried not to think about the leech.

Christopher found some high ground among the trees, set down his pack and began clearing underbrush with the machete. Working, he planned. When he had pitched the tent and hung the mosquito net to provide some protection against the insects that would be drawn to the blood, he would fire up the camp stove to make her a *mate* to calm her nerves and prevent hemorrhage.

"Chris?" Her voice reached him through the rain. "It hurts."

She was staring at the leech. Christopher waited until she looked up to say, "I know. I'm going to set up the tent and get us out of the rain."

Dulcinea put down her pack and sat on Christopher's to watch him. Her stomach itched, the skin stretching with pregnancy, and she peered down at her boots, eager to empty the water. One pant leg had come loose from her socks, so she pulled up the hem.

A watery, swaying sensation went over her eyes and through her whole head. Leeches, some larger than that on her forearm, clung to her calf.

Her abdomen heaved once, and a current of feeling shot up and down her spine. As the rain soaked her hair and shoulders, she lowered her head, trying to draw an even breath. Her soaked shirttails hung limply down in front of her belly. The shirt was untucked.

Her shirt was untucked....

"Dulcie."

She looked up.

Christopher stood over her. His brown eyes fastened on hers as he grasped her hands to help her to her feet.

Her shirt was untucked.... A scream grew in her throat.

Christopher kept his eyes on hers, willing her to stay calm.

"Chris...they hurt."

"I know."

Dulcinea clung to the sight of his eyes, and softly, under the sound of the rain that was like a hundred feet stamping on a wooden floor, rain that darkened his pale hair and drew his thick eyelashes to spiky points, he began to sing to her. She recognized the language although she didn't understand it. It was Machaj-Juyai, the secret language of the Kallawaya herbalists. Christopher's eyes reached into her, and an unnatural quiet, a hypnotic calm came over her, as though she were floating away.

"No, don't faint. Stay with me, Dulcie. Stay with your baby, too. Just be present." With his left hand he lifted up her shirt and saw a leech on her stomach. One. As long as his hand. Lowering the sodden fabric, he chanted to her with his voice and his eyes and his heart.

Dulcinea could feel the leech on her stomach, and she tried again not to scream. His eyes and his voice calmed her. "Will they hurt the baby?"

"No." He took the ground cloth and tent from the pack and hastily made camp in the rain. Collecting a cook pot, his camping stove and a mosquito net, he arranged a place to work. From his medicine bag, he selected herbs—two that would calm her and stop bleeding, *hediondilla* to clean the wounds, and others to blend in an infusion for her to drink if she began to miscarry.

At last he removed both his and her boots and socks, and they went into the tent. Meeting Dulcinea's eyes, he said, "How do you feel?"

She couldn't talk, just shook her head.

"There's a big one cozying up to your tummy. As a matter of fact," he remarked with a smile, as though it was a worthy scientific novelty, "it's the biggest leech I've ever seen."

Dulcinea chewed her lip. She would be okay. Christopher wasn't worried.

He said, "I'm going to take them all off by burning them with my lighter. Then they'll let go. I'll be very careful." He gave her a *mate* in a stainless-steel camping cup. While she sipped at it, he began singing a Quechua love song and unbuttoning her shirt, revealing the leech on her abdomen.

Dulcinea began to shake hard, shuddering, unable to stop. He took the cup from her hands and held it to her lips, and she drank some more. The only sounds in the world were the rain and his voice, singing, *"Warma yanaysi suyallawachkan..."*

He took out his lighter and put his hand on her side, holding her steady. Dulcinea tried not to tremble. As he burned the leech, she saw blood running down the front of her abdomen. Her heart threatened to burst from her chest, but Christopher's voice or perhaps something else seemed to make her body feel unnaturally heavy and relaxed, even as he detached the leech. He dropped it into an empty pan and cleaned the sores it had left with a cloth dipped in an herbal infusion that produced a faint numbing sensation.

"You know, in modern medicine we no longer practice bloodletting, but leeches are still used to relieve blood congestion in certain operations. Sometimes they're the cleanest method available.... Let's get you out of those pants."

There were four leeches on her left calf. He dealt with them and then with the smaller specimen on her arm, and he looked all over her body, checking for more, and found a botfly larva embedded in her neck. He rubbed her neck with *kimsa k'ucha* leaves until the parasite came out and joined the leeches in the pan. Then he cleaned the wound and tucked Dulcinea in the sleeping bag and sat stroking her hair.

Calmer, she said, "Check yourself, Christopher."

There was a tick on the inside of his thigh but nothing worse. No leeches. He took the pan outside and emptied it in the river, and as he returned to the tent he stumbled over something sharp and metallic. A piece of aluminum. Crouching in the rain, he stared at it. Jagged, an uneven polygon...

Airplane, he thought. It must have come from an airplane.

But the nondescript piece of sheet metal kept its own secrets. Leaving it, Christopher returned to Dulcinea.

Late that night Dulcinea lay with her back to him, wide awake. Christopher had told her about the piece of metal, and it made her nervous. *Barnabas had died here.*

As Christopher nuzzled her neck in the dark, then held her closer, trying to soothe her to sleep, she whispered, "Cristobal?"

"Mmm."

Uneasily, because it meant mentioning his brother, Dulcinea asked, "Do you think Barnabas had the urn?"

Christopher didn't want to make her hope, as he was hoping, that the urn was on the plane and that the plane had not exploded or burned. After a moment he said, "Dulcinea, everything's going to be all right."

He thought of the stark little house in La Paz and of the christening dress. It took a long time to ask, uncertain minutes after painful silence. "Dulce, how did my brother behave about Isabel?"

More quiet. Just breathing. Feeling each other's hearts. Dulcinea said, "Let's not talk about him."

"I want to know."

She turned in his arms to face him in the black night. "He was my husband. I can't do what you want. I can't say things like that."

Christopher understood "that" perfectly.

"He married me when—"

She stopped speaking, and he finished the sentence in his mind. *When there was no one else.*

When he, Christopher, had left her for the wolves.

The wolves had gotten her.

THE NEXT MORNING he scouted the nearby area for more pieces of metal but found nothing, so they set out in the direction they'd been heading before.

As they moved deeper into the Boca del Diablo, the forest grew darker, and in places sunlight hardly penetrated. Toward late afternoon, rain fell with the cold of hail, and Christopher searched for a campsite. The terrain had become steep, flat areas scarce, and footing more treacherous with each step. At last he found level ground above a ravine where trees had been felled by old landslides. The forest extended as far as they could see.

Christopher set down his pack in the rain, leaving his medicine bag over his shoulder, and he began to clear some of the underbrush before he realized that the place he'd chosen was not far from an ant tree.

Drawing a breath of resignation, he slogged through mud toward his pack. He was two yards from it when the edge of the slope gave way. He sprang back, grabbing Dulcinea. The slope continued to give, and he shoved her ahead of him. She stepped on the roots of the ant tree. The ants came out, and Christopher pushed her away from the tree. "Run!"

He slashed at vines with the machete and pulled her by the hand as they ran to escape the ants. When they finally paused, he turned her toward him and searched her face. Her expression was eerie. Frozen tranquillity worn over stark fear.

He wouldn't have blamed her for going to pieces.

His pack had been swallowed by the sea of mud in the landslide that had taken away the hill on which they'd been standing. It might have taken them. Instead, gone were the antivenin and antibiotics and camp stove and tent and mosquito net and his parka and everything useful to them but Dulcinea's sleeping bag and clothes and the machete. And his Kallawaya medicine bag.

Her face wet with rain, Dulcinea asked, "Do you think we're going to die here?"

Christopher shook his head. He was drenched and getting cold, and while she had dry clothes to put on, he did not. They were in peril. They needed to go down into the ravine and look for the pack. Should he find a place for Dulcinea to rest while he searched for it? What would she do if something happened to him?

He stood in the cold, undecided, the rain chilling his skin and Dulcinea warm in his arms. "We need the pack, don't we?" she asked.

"Yes." Christopher pressed her against her shoulder, put his face to her hair. "How are you doing?"

She whispered, "Don't leave me."

"I won't. Put on your shell. You're getting soaked." As she slid her pack from her shoulders and removed her coat,

Christopher stared down into the muddy ravine and thought of the landslide at Huajtata. "We'll have to walk around this, find another way down." While she zipped her shell and pulled on the hood, he shouldered her pack and glanced up at the trees overhead.

In the branches hung part of the wing of an airplane.

Dulcinea followed his gaze and saw it, as well. She shivered in the rain. Silently, Christopher took her hand, and they started through the forest.

As he sliced vines with the machete, she focused on the trail, on the plants, on each footfall. The rain made a surreal audio and visual curtain. She was hardly aware that they were descending, only that the ground was slick and deep, her boots caked with mud. At one point, she glanced down and saw a giant insect like a cockroach on her sleeve. She gasped, making a wordless sound of misery, and Christopher turned and brushed it off her. For a moment, his hand touched her face, and she thought, *Don't leave me. Don't leave me.*

He held her whenever the path was particularly steep. She tried to make her boots fall where his had, but in some places his steps were too long. As she moved to one side, taking a less precipitous route, her foot struck something hard and rolled on the object, and she stumbled.

Christopher caught her, and they both looked down.

It was a bone. He swiped at the nearby dirt and foliage with the machete, then bent to pick it up.

Dulcinea shuddered. She stared at his hands on the bone, then up at his face, and it was on the tip of her tongue to ask what kind of bone it was, what animal it had come from. But she knew perfectly well, knew in her own bones, that it was human.

CHAPTER THIRTEEN

THE SOUND OF THE RAIN matched the cadence of Christopher's heart. It couldn't be Barnabas's humerus he held. It was unlikely even that the wing in the tree had come from his brother's plane.

Still, as he and Dulcinea descended into the ravine, he searched for signs of a downed aircraft. It would have made a scar in the canopy as it fell. But he saw only a foggy, rain-soaked jungle ravaged by natural landslides.

The night would be bitter. In Bolivia, temperatures even in the rain forest could drop below freezing at a moment's notice. And although the air was warm now, it wouldn't dry his clothing.

The land formed a bowl, funneling down into the ravine. As Christopher squinted through the rain, studying the slope, his eyes caught an irregularity in the vegetation—blocks of stone forming a wall half-covered by plants and trees. At once, he thought of the urn and the lost moon shrine. Surely the villagers of Huajtata knew of this ruin, which looked like it might be some kind of temple. It couldn't be *the* shrine. But it was worth investigating—as shelter for the night.

Still holding the bone and the machete, he caught Dulcinea's attention and nodded toward the black stone structure, which was perhaps a hundred yards below and a quarter mile laterally from where they stood. "See the ruin?"

"Yes."

"Let's check it out."

They navigated the slope, angling down to the ruin. Soon the ground leveled off and they saw the black stones set into the cliff wall. Although the structure was small, the facade in the hillside not more than fifteen feet across, the stone building blocks seemed larger than they had from a distance. They were overgrown with lush moss, and so was the statue standing guard above the vine-draped entrance, a creature whose human torso became serpentine below the waist. Its ferocious mouth and fangs reminded Christopher of the Kallawaya vampire-sorcerer deity Yawar Chchonga. But he didn't know enough about archaeology to identify the figure.

It certainly was not the moon.

Glancing about, Dulcinea shivered. "Someone's been here."

Christopher followed her gaze. Sometime before—whether months or years he couldn't judge—the nearby vegetation had been cleared. Most of the trees sprouting outside the stone structure were just saplings, and in some places nothing grew at all. Not far from the black entrance to the ruin, three aluminum poles protruded from the ground. They might, at one time, have supported an overhead tarp.

As the rain poured over him, Christopher waded through ferns to the doorway. His eyes could not penetrate the shadows, so he walked on to where the aluminum posts stood, some thirty feet from the door. His boot and shin caught something cylindrical and heavy on the ground; he stumbled forward, catching himself before he fell. For no reason, his heart raced. Some inexplicable sense of the morbid and grotesque made him cast aside the bone he held before pushing aside the lush dark green leaves of a *castilla chchillca*, good for various female ailments, to see what had tripped him.

A small generator with a rusty pulley, gathering rain and mud. Christopher straightened up.

Dulcinea stood gazing vacantly out into the forested vale below. The sheltering doorway of the ruin was only feet away, but everything in her body language said she would not go inside without him. He remembered another ruin, another day, and he wondered if she was remembering, too. When her father came... But she was getting wet. "Dulcinea, get out of the rain."

Her eyes flickered toward the vine-covered threshold. "I'm fine."

Christopher longed to get warm, but he wouldn't want to put on his wet clothes again after taking them off. Now was the time to search the area; they might find something useful.

Who had left the generator? he wondered. Archaeologists studying the ruin?

The area was wet and smelled of rot. The sound of the rain hitting metal nearby made an intense clatter; it matched the feeling of the constant drops pelting his shoulders, pouring over him. Searching out the source of the sound, he found part of an aluminum table. Further survey of the ground uncovered an old Coleman lantern, useless without fuel, a stainless-steel fork, which he picked up and pocketed, a small aluminum camping chair with broken webbing and a length of severed cable in cracked plastic housing.

The one-time residents had left in a hurry.

A disturbing thought.

Again Christopher glanced behind him, looking for Dulcinea, but a stand of young *oqoti tijra* trees hid her from view. Fascination warred with apprehension as he waded through the foliage, mud sucking at his boots, and gingerly made his way around the remains of the camp. He spotted a filthy green wine bottle, half-buried in the mire. He'd lost his water bottle with the pack....

Though the cork was in place, the bottle had been opened, part of a torn seal still showing around the neck. Christopher bent down to pick it up, and with a kind of disbelief saw a blur of motion in the grass and felt pain like a hot needle stab his hand.

Two drops of blood beaded the back of his hand. In the deep grass, a brown snake with small black-and-white spots and black stripes on each side of its diamond-shaped head slid along the ground. A fer-de-lance, the *barba amarillo,* the yellow chin. A garden-variety lethal South American pit viper, whose fangs had made the two holes on his hand from which blood was now oozing.

Heart racing, Christopher struck down with the machete, but the reptile was already gone.

"Chris?"

Dulcinea stood near the old canopy poles, rain bouncing off the hood of her parka.

"*Stay back.*" Fighting the strange aftermath of pain, the disorientation before fear, Christopher added, "There's a snake around here somewhere." It sounded like something out of a *Far Side* cartoon. The place might be crawling with snakes. He stared at his bleeding hand, trying to remember what to do first. He was carrying antivenin.

In the pack.

The pack was gone.

The pack on his shoulders was Dulcinea's.

Dulcinea could see the blood dripping from his hand. "Was it poisonous?"

"Yes." And judging by the tingling in his hand, envenomization had occurred. Peering beneath the ferns and shrubs at the muddy ground, Christopher walked slowly to where Dulcinea stood. The less he moved the better.

But he needed to move. Find the pack.

No, they couldn't.... The site of the landslide, where the pack had slid down into the ravine, was probably more than half a mile away. And the pack must have been buried.

Dulcinea said, "Tell me what to do."

"Let me think a minute." If he could think with the rain running down his face and his body, with its constant noise and the feel of the cold. He was wet, so wet.

They didn't have the pack.

They were not going to have the pack.

Focusing with effort, his mind cataloged remedies for snakebite. Each snake was different. For a South American lance-headed viper... No, to suction; fangs too long. And isolating the concentration of venom could permanently damage tissue otherwise unaffected by the bite. Antidotes... His medicine bag was still slung over his shoulder, but he needed something stronger than herbs. He needed antivenin.

Christopher stared along the slope through the clattering rain, and the mouth of the ruin beckoned. Shelter from the pouring water, from the cold.

Not yet.... He had to do something. By morning he might be unable to hike.

Silently surveying the camp, he noticed the dull metal cylinder nestled in the leaves.

A generator.

He started toward it, but Dulcinea said, "What is it? Let me do it. You shouldn't be moving."

She was right. His hand felt more tingly. Hot. Painful. But she shouldn't lift the generator. Christopher moved toward it through the rain, aware of the falling darkness. Already it was late in the day. Tonight he and Dulcinea would have no tent or mosquito net.

And he had been bitten by a fer-de-lance.

He wished he'd never stooped to pick up that bottle. The regret made him sick.

In the showering rain he approached the generator. Slowly, using the machete to push aside plants and check for snakes, he examined the aluminum cylinder. Then, with his right hand, he reached down and turned the rusty pulley. It moved.

Christopher used the same hand to try to lift the generator, but its base was wedged in the ground. Dulcinea joined him. With a grunt, she dislodged the generator from the soil. As she moved it over a few inches, away from the hole it had left, two wires encased in plastic sprung loose, waving through the air. The motion mirrored the snake's strike, and Christopher started, his heart pounding. His reaction made Dulcinea jump, too, and for a moment they both stood rigid, staring down at the inanimate object.

Both wires, for positive and negative charge, dangled from the end of the generator. In the downpour, Christopher handed the machete to Dulcinea. Crouching again, he lifted the wet cylinder. He shifted the weight to his right arm to free his snake-bitten hand and carried the generator toward the ruin. Dulcinea followed, under the gaze of the serpentine temple guardian, the statue over the door. Snakes, thought Christopher. There might be more inside the ruin, and without a light he couldn't see them.

But the water beating on his nose and eyelids and penetrating his shirt chilled him. He moved forward and paused before the low black entrance, trying again to see inside.

On each side of the mouth, the stone was rimmed by an apron of blocks butted together, and that skirt extended inside the ruin, as well, forming a ledge, a place to sit. Ducking past the moldy, pungent vines in the doorway and keeping his head down, Christopher slipped under the overhang and out of the rain. As he set down the generator, Dulcinea followed, joining him in the stone entryway. From there they could see a few feet into the darkness. No reptiles in sight, only a salamander slinking along the wet ground.

Christopher swallowed.

Dulcinea asked, "Do you think there are bats in here?"

It was a serious concern. Vampire bats preyed on cattle in Bolivia, and they could bite humans, as well, infecting them with rabies and other diseases. Stooping to keep his head from scraping the roof, Christopher peered into the impenetrable darkness, then looked out at the shadows washing the misty, rain-drenched landscape. Vines interrupted the view, and Christopher nodded at them. "Bats won't live in a cave with vertical obstructions at the opening. They have to be horizontal."

Dulcinea's mouth formed an O. "Where did you learn that?"

"I can't remember." *Can't think...* The hot shivering sensation in his hand and arm was turning to a sharp throbbing pain that Christopher knew would become excruciating. Stifling another recollection of the pack's stock of antivenin, antibiotics and morphine, he stared down at the generator, then moved to step out into the endless rain.

"Chris."

Dulcinea touched his arm, and he paused.

"Sit down. Tell me what you want, and I'll get it for you."

Her voice was steady, steadier than he was. *He* needed to be steady.

As Christopher turned to her, Dulcinea saw his pallor. She knew nothing about snake bites—had never seen one. Careful to speak into his left ear, she said, "Tell me what to do."

In the shadows he regarded the generator. It could work. It had to work. They had nothing else.

His voice shaking more than he liked, he said, "I'm going to try to get this thing going and generate a shock." He hoped the wires inside had not corroded. The generator looked good, but it had been out in the rain for a long time.

He met Dulcinea's eyes and she said again, "You should sit down."

She was right. He checked the ledge for snakes. Four feet into the ruin, all lay in blackness. How far could a snake strike?

Too far.

Nonetheless, he sat down on the damp stone, then leaned forward and touched the pulley on the generator. With lips that seemed too dry, he said, "I need a cord of some kind to fit in this groove. It has to be pretty strong and maybe four or five feet long." He nodded past the shield of vines in the doorway. "I saw a broken cable out there. It was near the table." He shuddered, shaking off a chill, wondering again why the people had left.

Machete in hand, Dulcinea turned to go.

"Be careful."

She gave him a quick look, and he felt in it everything they meant to each other. Then she slipped from the cave.

Christopher removed her pack from his shoulders. Setting it on the wet stone beside him, using it as a barrier between him and the blackness of the inner chamber, he tried to forget about the pain in his hand, the pain that was creeping up past his wrist and into his forearm. As he moved, he noticed the brightly woven fabric of his medicine bag hanging over his left shoulder.

His medicine bag. At least he could counteract the pain with coca or *amapola*. And perhaps he could slow the hemorrhaging. Dazed, Christopher stared out of the ruin at the foliage in the surrounding area. He wished antivenin grew on trees.

The black shadows at his back drew his attention again. With his right hand, he reached for the matches he kept in a plastic film canister in the pocket of his canvas shirt, but his hands shook too much to open the lid. Putting the canister back in his pocket, he thought of snakes hidden in the darkness and trembled. Blood trickled down his hand.

There was no one to help. He needed help, and there was no one. Just Dulcinea, who was pregnant with his brother's child, a Choqueneira baby. Just the rain, that sound all around him, as though he was inside a drum being played by a million tiny hands.

"Chris?"

He turned.

Dulcinea ducked into the doorway, water dripping from her hood. She held out the broken cable he'd seen before. "Is this what you meant?"

"Yes." Leaning forward, he used his right hand to move the generator until it sat between his feet.

Dulcinea crouched in front of the generator.

"Wind the wire around that wheel. Tight."

"Okay." She set down the machete and, with wet hands, wrapped the cable around the wheel as tightly as she could. At the edge of the corridor's inky darkness, still haunted by the unseen, Christopher collected the two wires extending from the generator. He watched Dulcinea finish winding the longer cable. Then, bracing his forearms on his knees, he touched the ends of the two wires to his burning left hand, over the two oozing fang marks. He thought of the irreparable damage the shock might do, and the fact that it was his left hand, always his left hand, from the time he was twelve. It still bore the scars of Mayorga's boot.

It kept on bleeding. More heavily now.

The effect of the venom. Next, nosebleeds and bleeding gums and then hemorrhage into his muscles and— "Okay, Dulce. You need to pull hard, really hard. Yank on it all at once." He clamped the generator between his boots, pressing hard to hold it. *Stupid,* he thought. *Stupid. This is all we have.*

Dulcinea looked at the wires he'd placed on his left hand. Electrical shock could hurt him—kill him—but it was all there was. She grasped the end of the cord tightly and twined it through her fingers, careful not to touch the metal end protruding from the broken housing. Clenching the cable in her fist, she braced herself for the crack of sparks and pulled with her whole body.

Christopher felt a faint twinge in his hand. Nothing more.

Not nearly enough.

The generator had corroded inside.

Dulcinea stared down at him, the cable dangling from her hand. "I'm sorry. I'll try again."

He shook his head. *Stay calm. Think....*

Hike. How far were they from the nearest shot of antivenin?

Five days at least.

That was a few days too long.

He kicked the generator, shoving it away from him with his feet.

Dulcinea's heart plunged, and for a moment they were both silent.

Her eyes caressed his blond head, his wet hair, the straight slope of his nose. His medicine bag still lay across his left shoulder. Dulcinea asked, "Have you got anything in there?"

Christopher followed her gaze. "For snakebite?" He didn't laugh but he wanted to.

Nonetheless, he slid the shoulder bag down to his lap, and Dulcinea squatted in front of him, reminding him of some primitive fertility goddess. Earthy...pregnant... "Can I help?"

Christopher shook his head, trying to think through the pain. Using his right hand, he removed the objects of his *mesa* so that he could reach the herbs. Examining the bundles his uncle had given him and the others he had collected himself at the Witches' Market and while he was walking to Huajtata, Christopher tried to remember what each cloth contained and the purpose of each herb.

His memory was excellent. Usually he didn't have to think. But now he hurt so much that he wanted to disappear into his mind as he had learned to do under Mayorga's interrogation. He felt strange all over. Starting to die from a snakebite, though it would take time. Respiratory problems. Shock.

He wanted coca, but he would wait till he knew what other herbs to use. Everything needed to interact correctly. He talked his way through the bundles of herbs, using their Kallawaya names. *"Andres waylla, helecho macho, mura mura, orégano, azucena—"* He stopped. *Azucena.* The Madonna lily.

Walking to Chulina... "Gabriel," he whispered, remembering the Kallawaya healer he had met on the road.

"What?"

She chewed the leaves and the roots with vinegar—

Vinegar?

Shit.

"Christopher, there's a snake."

He jumped up, his medicine bag and its contents spilling on the ground at his feet. He could hardly stand without swaying, but he turned to see where Dulcinea was looking—into the blackness along the floor.

A fer-de-lance was slithering away into the black. It was a larger snake than the one that had bitten him. It was a *different* snake.

Dulcinea snatched up the machete. Stepping deeper into the stone corridor, she slammed the blade across the snake's body. Its body flopped, the tail whipping at her, and she hacked at it again.

"Don't break the machete!"

The snake was dead, and Dulcinea turned on him. "You want to get bitten again?"

No.

He was light-headed. Achy. Cold and hot at once. Staring at the pieces of the snake, he thought that he'd journeyed to the underworld. This place was well named. The devil's mouth.

Outside, the rain had slowed to a drizzle. Inside, a fly bit his neck. He slapped at it, and his hand came away bloody.

Dulcinea looked at the snake's exposed flesh and felt queasy. But she used the machete to pull the pieces toward her.

Christopher said, "Throw them out of here. We don't need more bugs." Insects were buzzing in front of his face.

Mosquitoes.

The rain had stopped.

Dulcinea picked up the pieces of the snake and hurled them outside into the foliage. Then she wiped the blade of the machete on the side of her boot.

With a shaky sound like a laugh, Christopher sank onto the ledge again. The herbs and his medicine bag were at his feet. Dulcinea crouched down, laid the machete across her knees and began picking them up. She'd picked up the snake, too....

He reached out and touched a lock of her hair and held it as she put his medicine bag in his lap. On top of that she lay the bundles of herbs, one by one.

Christopher stared at the herbs. It was a long time before he remembered about the Madonna lily. Letting go of Dulcinea's hair, he picked through all the bundles until he found the one containing the roots. After that, he searched for the leaves. They were in the next bundle she set on his legs.

A *tabano,* a black horsefly, settled on his snakebite. He brushed it away, but another landed elsewhere in the blood. He tried to think. *Chew the leaves and roots with vinegar....*

Vinegar.

What else could he ...

Dulcinea searched the ground for more bundles, but there were none. She crouched beside Christopher, putting a hand on his knee. "Tell me what to do."

He knew what to do. "Outside. Where the snake bit me. There's a bottle of wine . . ."

Grasping the handle of the machete, she stood and went out, and for a hazy moment he watched her pick through the foliage, alert for snakes. His hand and body ached with each beat of his heart. The poison was spreading.

Dulcinea returned with the wine bottle, and Christopher roused himself. He tried to open the bundle containing the dried root of the Madonna lily. He couldn't manage the tie with one hand, so Dulcinea sat beside him on the ledge near the doorway and opened it for him. Christopher gave her the other, the one containing the leaves, to open, as well. The wine bottle was beside his foot.

"Do you need that opened?"

He nodded.

While he took some root and leaves and put them in his mouth, Dulcinea pulled the cork from the bottle of wine. As the bitter taste of the plants filled his mouth, she handed him the bottle, and he sniffed it.

Vinegar.

With the first thing like faith he'd felt since the landslide had carried the pack down the hill and buried it beneath tons of mud, Christopher lifted the bottle to his lips and poured some of the contents into his mouth with the bitter root and leaves. The combination was ghastly.

Dulcinea watched his profile. His face was dewy with sweat, and there were insects on his skin and his blond hair. He was shivering.

Standing, she stepped around him, picked up her pack and opened it to remove her sleeping bag.

Body trembling, Christopher put more of the root in his mouth and took another swig of vinegar, shuddering at the taste and trying to forget that darkness was falling, that here in the Southern Hemisphere winter was coming.

He trembled again, cold and hurting. Sick.

Dulcinea's sleeping bag came out of her pack in a fluffy mass, and she held it under her arm while she felt through her clothes, searching. She had brought the oversize long-sleeved T-shirt they'd bought in Grand Junction. It was dry.

Setting down the pack, she gathered the shirt and sleeping bag against her and sat beside Christopher again. As she reached up to unbutton his wet shirt, the medal she'd given him winked at her.

Christopher continued chewing, swallowing saliva and the juices of the roots and the leaves. It would take some time to work—if it worked. He should prepare something topical for the wound, too, for an antiseptic and to ease the pain.

Coca. Coca, from which came novocaine. He could put some on his wound. Later, when he was done with the Madonna lily, he would chew some coca leaves with a *lejia,* a stick made from the ashes of *quinoa* and mixed with water. The alkaline *lejia* released the alkaloids in the coca.

Pain relief. Thinking about it made him feel better.

Dulcinea eased his shirt off his shoulders, drawing a short breath when she saw that his left arm had swelled all the way to the shoulder. Carefully, she helped him out of first the right sleeve, then the left. She slid the sleeve of her dry shirt over his left hand, aware of the pain he didn't voice or show on his face, pain evidenced only in his eyes. After she'd pulled the shirt up his arm, Christopher slid his other arm inside, and she helped get the neck over his head. Fortunately, it was loose, even on him. Dulcinea spread her sleeping bag over him, trying unsuccessfully to keep it off the wet ground. Anxiously, she peered toward the interior of the ruin.

If they moved farther inside, they would be warmer when night fell. But who could walk into that blackness? They'd seen two snakes; there must be more.

"Dulce . . . help me with my hand."

She turned her attention to the task. Christopher gave her a bundle of *hediondilla* leaves and told her what to do. After Dulcinea had cleaned his wound with moist leaves, using more for a covering, she tried to plan for the night. The floor was damp, and they had no tarp, no plastic, no usable fabric. They were going to get wet.

Would it be drier farther inside?

She had matches in her coat pocket. If she could make a torch . . . She stood up. "Chris, I'm going to try to find a stick we can light to make a torch."

Chewing on the root and leaves with vinegar, he nodded. He wanted to lie down. But they should start walking. Maybe he could get Dulcinea most of the way back to Huajtata. He had no map, but he still had his compass.

As she stepped out of the ruin, haunted by the memory of another stone building and of the disaster of *that* day, Dulcinea felt the sweat trickling off her and mosquitoes biting. She had to keep Christopher dry, make him warm.

"Dulcie," said Christopher from inside.

She looked back. His nose was bleeding, and he was trying to tilt his head back.

Dulcinea hurried over to him, ducking under the vines in the doorway. "Lie down."

As he moved, blood spilling from his nose, she saw him scanning along the ledge, where neither of them could see. Looking for snakes.

The ledge was too narrow for him to lie on. Dulcinea said, "The ground. It's all right." She knelt to touch it and found it surprisingly warm, despite the dampness. "Come on."

Christopher thought of the snake she'd killed and of other snakes. In his mind, he saw a boot crushing his hand.

Not a black military boot. His father's brown work boot on a small hand....

He slid down to the ground. *Warm.* No wonder the snakes liked it here. Geothermal heat. Probably the reason for the shrine or temple or whatever it was.

He lay down, letting his feet reach into the blackness, and Dulcinea took his head in her lap. His eyes were watering, and she could see the pain in his face as he continued chewing on the root and leaves and vinegar. On the floor lay his wet shirt. She folded the sleeve and pressed it under his nose.

"It won't stop," he said. "It's the venom."

Her sleeping bag had fallen to the ground. She pulled it over him and sat stroking his hair and brushing away the mosquitoes and flies and tiny black insects humming near, landing on Christopher's face.

Memory shot through her.

The dream.

She had dreamed this.

This was the dream that had haunted her.

He's going to be okay, she told herself. *I'm here. He'll be fine....*

But he needed more than someone to watch over him. His nose would not stop bleeding, and she saw blood in his mouth, too. Small black flies continued to land on him, to buzz in a cloud around his nose and mouth. The sight and sound made her nearly frantic, but she forced herself to stay calm, to think.

Water. He should be drinking fluids. She dragged her pack from the ledge, reached into it and found her water bottle, half-empty. Fortunately, she had some water-purification tablets zipped in an inside pocket of her jacket, where Christopher had told her to put them. There should be water close by.

She said, "Try to sit up and drink something."

His eyes were shut, his face twisted in pain, but he was still trying to chew the root and leaves. He shook his head. Setting the bottle beside her, Dulcinea thought of going to look for the pack, but she was sure the mud slide had buried it.

The shirtsleeve she'd used to wipe his face was soaked with blood.

Chris, don't die....

Dulcinea moved the sleeve and tried to find another part of the shirt to use. Christopher clutched his sore arm, and she saw the bunched muscles in his neck, the strain in his face. A mosquito was biting him beside his nose, and a black fly landed in the blood on his lip. His gums bled, and that and the root and leaves in his mouth had made a brownish-black mixture. She wiped his face again, praying.

Darkness was falling. Mosquitoes whined through the dusk and landed on him. He grew more restless, and Dulcinea drew him closer to her as the night came.

Christopher couldn't stand the pain. Why were they hurting him? Mayorga was evil. Don't...

Tell me again about the shrine. Where is this shrine?

His arm... They had a snake.

Who was touching his hair? What was that sound? It was a heartbeat. Two heartbeats. *Barnabas...*

Where's my brother? I don't want them to get my brother.... He's my little brother, just fifteen minutes younger. My dad says they almost forgot another baby was coming, because I was blond....

There was a feeling against his head, a faint thumping sensation, and he remembered Dulcinea was holding him. He said, "Baby." The baby had kicked him. His baby...

He saw the cross in the darkened churchyard.

A long time passed, and he heard her voice. "Chris?"

It hurt.... Don't go back. They were taking him down the hall....

In the deepening twilight, Dulcinea watched his face respond to her voice, felt the slight movement of his head. He was cold and damp with sweat and sticky with his own blood, and she could still hear the mosquitoes whining, still feel them biting her face and hands and neck, everywhere her clothing didn't cover.

"Chris, wake up. You need to drink something."

She saw him blink. As he tried to get up, she grabbed his shoulders, but he was too big and heavy for her to support. He managed to push himself up, though, and leaned against the ledge. When Dulcinea held the water bottle to his lips, he drank, hardly opening his eyes.

"Do you need more herbs?" asked Dulcinea.

"Water."

She put the bottle to his mouth again, and when he had drunk all there was, she stuck the bottle on the ledge just outside the mouth of the ruin and hoped the rain would come and fill it.

CHRISTOPHER AWOKE with warm dampness beneath him and his face against something soft. Dulcinea's breasts under her canvas shirt.

Sunlight flooded the doorway where they lay, and he heard a bird outside in the trees making a sound like a cash register ringing up a sale. The world was emerald green, and as he moved, the pain came, and he remembered what had happened.

He was alive.

Hurt.

Feeling something slide along his back, he shuddered.

"It's just me."

Dulcinea's hand touched his chest. Gently, she eased out from under him, and Christopher sat up, nearly crying out from the pain in his arm. It was hugely swollen, stretching the sleeve of Dulcinea's T-shirt.

She studied his face. It was streaked with dried blood and dotted with insect bites, but there was color in his cheeks, and his eyes looked clearer. "How are you?"

He couldn't hear her. She'd spoken too quietly. But he knew what she'd said, and he nodded. He'd been able to sleep, unheard of for someone with an untreated snakebite.

Gabriel's remedy had worked.

ALMOST TWO HOURS after they'd awakened, they began walking back along the slope in the direction of the landslide.

Christopher chewed coca leaves until the relentless aching of his body, the screaming pain in his arm, seemed distant. He and Dulcinea found a stream, a rivulet running through the forest, and rested there, drinking from her water bottle. Christopher washed his face and his hand and applied fresh *hediondilla* leaves to the snakebite, as he had first thing that morning. His body felt stronger, more energetic.

As they set out again, he tried to judge their position by gazing down into the funnellike vale below, looking for familiar landmarks he had seen before and after the landslide.

Something glittered in the forest, a crescent of white light, dazzling in the sun, and he stopped walking and stared.

Behind him, Dulcinea paused, too, and immediately saw what must have caught his eye. Shining through a break in the trees far down in the ravine was a silver airplane tail with a swirling, cosmic sun painted on it.

Her heart jammed in her throat.

"Christopher...that's his plane."

CHAPTER FOURTEEN

CHRISTOPHER HAD KNOWN IT. The sun was just like the sun in the picture she'd drawn for Moth.

Measuring the distance down the ravine with his eyes, he saw the scars and the damage to the trees where the plane had set down. It looked like about a half mile downhill at a diagonal angle to reach the plane, and it was a vertical descent of several hundred feet.

The sky was clouding over, and Christopher pulled on Dulcinea's hand. "Let's try to go as fast as we can." And hope the rain held off.

It did not. Thunder boomed through the air, and the shower began. Dulcinea put on her shell, but the downpour drenched Christopher. He was oblivious—even to the shooting pains in his arm. He was too absorbed by the plane.

As he and Dulcinea descended into the forest and the aircraft was lost from view, he relied on his compass to guide them. The half mile stretched until he wondered if they'd overshot the plane. But it could have been the absence of conversation that made each step seem long. Neither he nor Dulcinea wanted to discuss what lay ahead.

The clearing appeared before them abruptly, the plane bigger than Christopher had anticipated.

It lay flat in the center of the clearing it had made in falling. Its back was broken, and the nearest wing seemed to have been consumed by fire. Above the saplings and shrubs that had grown around it, Christopher saw the smoky remains of the mural on the side.

It was a sad wreckage, the great airplane with its crushed nose and clipped wings. Despite the bends and twists of the metal and the signs of fire, the cockpit and most of the fuselage remained intact. Rain showered through the break in the forest canopy made by the aircraft and it hit the metal with a pinging sound.

Christopher and Dulcinea stared apprehensively at the plane. The trivial intruded on the critical as Christopher's eyes reflexively noticed one of the plants growing against the side of the plane. *Puca kkullu,* whose roots could help promote lactation... With a sense of unreality, he said, "I'm going to check out the cockpit. You stay here, okay?"

She nodded, clutching her arms around herself, numb. She didn't feel the rain wetting her skin or her hair as Christopher approached the plane and began hacking at the vines and plants in his path, making his way to the cockpit where his brother and her husband lay dead.

Dulcinea felt the heat inside her, the warmth of the baby, the extra blood. This was where Barnabas lived.

She stood in the clearing, watching Christopher and remembering his brother. Though she'd never doubted Barnabas's death, she couldn't quite believe he would be in the plane.

Christopher could. As he sliced through the brush to the door of the cockpit, he tried to quiet the feelings in his chest, a sort of fast-beating awareness. He was almost there....

The door had been blown off by the impact of the crash, and now the cockpit was open. Christopher hacked at the shrubbery growing inside. Through the leaves he saw a skeleton belted into the pilot's seat, its skull angled forward, and as he slashed a branch and it fell into the cockpit the skeleton shuddered with the impact and the skull rolled off.

His heart shook. Mosquitoes buzzed around him, landed on him. Sweat and rain ran down his skin. Mindful not to disturb the skeleton or the rags that still shrouded it, he placed the machete between his knees and used his right hand to pull away the branches he'd sliced from the cockpit, watching closely for snakes. Christopher saw the denim of Barnabas's blue jeans, stained black and eaten away, and he saw his brother's black combat boots, and his eyes walked up the corpse. He picked up the skull from the floor of the cockpit and looked at it and started crying.

The skull was Barnabas. Christopher touched his own face, the light beard covering his cheeks and jaw, and he held the skull and knew for the first time that his brother was dead.

Staring at the skull was too much like staring at a face—and as bad as seeing a corpse. Bones undressed without flesh...except the faint signs of recent decomposition. He could see his twin's teeth, grotesque in death, and he remembered them in life. *Come back,* he thought, recalling flesh and blood and laughter. Leaning against the seat, weak from hunger and the snakebite, light-headed and numb with coca, he stared dizzily at the femur showing through the ragged black denim. And he bent over and tried to embrace the skeleton of his brother's body.

CHRISTOPHER WAS a long time investigating the cockpit, and Dulcinea couldn't see him because the flora had slipped back in place behind him like a screen. He had told her to stay in the clearing, but he'd been gone too long. Perhaps another snake...

She started through the ferns and underbrush, moving toward the plane. With her hands, she pushed aside the foliage. Flies and mosquitoes buzzed around, and she smelled death.

Pulling back a branch, she saw Christopher leaning against the cockpit seat. He was sweating and shaking and crying with his eyes squeezed tightly shut. Dulcinea saw him throw himself against the seat, hugging something she knew must be his brother's bones.

Her husband's bones.

He didn't know she was there, and she stood motionless, hearing his grief.

When she touched him, he turned to her, his brown eyes sick with pain. "Go back."

She could hardly make out the words, but she knew what he'd said. "I want to see him."

"No. It's awful."

"He was my husband. Let me see him." Dulcinea tried to push Christopher out of the way, and as she did, she saw over his shoulder the skull lying on the copilot's seat. She gasped.

Christopher grabbed her, held hard. The baby kicked her several times, and they both felt it and laughed. Choking laughter. Soon Dulcinea pried Christopher loose from her and stared into the cockpit at the skeleton and the skull. Christopher tried to turn her away, but she looked again, kept looking.

Recognizing, as Christopher had, she whispered, "Oh, Barnabas."

BARNABAS HAD TRAVELED prepared.

There were supplies in the plane. The cabin, which had once seated eight or ten passengers, now held various boxes and crates. Dulcinea and Christopher examined them, working in a state of numbness, the weightless haziness of shock. In the baggage compartment, they found canned beans and a camp stove and a strong mountaineering pack and more—everything Christopher would have carried himself, including medical supplies.

As they sat on the narrow floor of the cabin eating refried beans, Dulcinea said, "Barnabas has saved our lives."

Christopher made no comment. Their lives wouldn't have been in danger if not for Barnabas. *Flying...* He felt regret. If his brother's eyes had been perfect, many things might have been different.

Barnabas....what have I been doing? I've been with your wife. My love. She's my love. She was always my love, and you took her.

He was losing his mind.

Dulcinea asked, "What are we going to do with Barnabas?"

"Take him home. Bury him." In Chulina. He couldn't leave his brother's bones in this place. Anyhow, he would have to take the mandible to match with dental records. To prove he was dead.

He's dead. He wanted his brother, and the grieving was starting again, coming in another wave.

Dulcinea had noticed his emotional state. His eyes were wild, half-mad from the loss. She knew that sometimes identical twins shared a special connection. Christopher and Barnabas were fraternal twins, but once they had been so close. Before her.

Christopher got up and went into the cockpit. He picked up the skull and sat in the copilot's seat holding it and gazing at the skeleton. He sat there remembering Barnabas and trying not to think of Dulcinea and the baby she carried. The baby was the last part of his brother. Christopher would do anything to protect that child.

The urn.

Where is it?

THE NEXT MORNING they awoke with the sun and began searching the plane for the urn. They looked in every crate and box and discovered broken pottery, bags of alpaca sweaters, a broken case of whiskey, a telescope still packed to withstand a fall, Barnabas's camera and tripod, and hundreds of pounds of coca leaves. Christopher didn't speculate on where the leaves were headed. They were legal inside Bolivia, and that was where they were.

But there was no urn.

The cargo hold had been flattened by the impact of landing, but Christopher used a crowbar to pry up the floor of the cabin and look beneath. By flashlight, he scoured the plane, keenly disappointed as he began to realize that the urn was not on board.

He had counted on its being there. The letter Dulcinea had brought him was his only lead, and it had been a red herring. Probably Barnabas had never had the urn.

The day was clouding, and Christopher knew they should start walking, should leave the mouth of the devil. For the past hours, he had thought of little but the words in Mariano's journal about the Son-With-Hair-Like-Inti. That his would be the road of agony and grief.

Nowhere was there a promise that he could find the urn and the shrine before the child Dulcinea carried was born. And in his own mother's case, it hadn't been the twins she carried who had died.

It had been her.

THERE WAS FILM in Barnabas's camera, and Christopher used the last six shots on the roll to take pictures of the plane and the cockpit as he'd found it. He and Dulcinea would leave the camera behind, but the film might prove useful in obtaining a death certificate. At least, she would have her inheritance.

After he'd unloaded the camera, Christopher prioritized items to carry in the pack, sorting through Barnabas's medical supplies and stock of antivenin, checking expiration dates. When he'd organized food stores, camp stove and fuel, he turned to Dulcinea, who'd been stuffing her sleeping bag into her pack. "I'm going to take care of Barnabas."

"Okay."

Carrying a canvas stuff sack he had found with his brother's other equipment, Christopher disappeared into the cockpit.

Through the hum of insects and the shrieking call of birds and monkeys outside, Dulcinea heard cracking sounds from the cockpit. He was breaking apart the skeleton, and she got up and went out of the plane.

She had lived with Barnabas. Conceived a child with him. Could she and Christopher live happily together after this?

Could either of them ever be happy with anyone else?

Hearing her leave, Christopher looked down at the bones he was disassembling. He put them in the sack, thinking of Dulcinea and his brother together. He couldn't forgive anyone.

He couldn't forgive himself.

Reaching across his brother's skeleton, he disconnected the humerus from the joint and carefully lifted the whole arm across the seat. As he moved it, the lower limb shook, and there was a tinkling sound on the floor of the cockpit—like the ring of truth. As Christopher held the bones of his brother's left arm, he faced a question harder than anger or jealousy.

How could Barnabas have helped loving Dulcinea?

No more than I could...

Christopher separated the humerus from the ulna and the radius and put them all in the bag before he leaned over to look for the object he knew had fallen.

HE HANDED IT to Dulcinea as they started away from the wreckage.

She closed her fingers on the wedding band. Silver from a Kallawaya jeweler in La Paz. She could read nothing in Christopher's expression.

He said, "Let's try to find that stream again and get clean."

He had hardly touched her since they'd found the plane. What was he feeling? Grief? Guilt? Or anger? Dulcinea walked silently beside him, containing her feelings. *You said you didn't want to marry me.*

But first he had tried to tell her about the curse.

They used Christopher's compass to lead them out of the ravine and back toward the Rio Rabia, where the leeches were. They needed to cross the river again, and when they reached it Christopher set down his pack on the bank. He remembered the way things had been between him and Dulcinea before they found his brother's plane. Mouth shaking from some inner wound he couldn't identify, he said, "I'll carry you."

His arm was still the size of a large tree limb. Dulcinea knew it must hurt him. "I can walk." She bent over and tucked in her pants.

Christopher picked her up and put his arm behind her knees, feeling the twenty extra pounds of blood and water and baby she was carrying.

Dulcinea shifted. "No, Christopher."

"I'm going to carry you." He held her and didn't let her body touch the water as he waded into the river.

Later, after he had carried their packs to the other side, she burned off the leech that had attached itself to his back just above the base of his spine.

FORTUNATELY, ALTHOUGH they'd lost his pack, Christopher had carried most of his money and credit cards and a copy of his passport on his body and in his medicine bag. He and Dulcinea caught a ride on a supply truck going to La Paz and sat shoulder to shoulder against crates of oranges. Christopher kept his leg through the straps of the pack that contained Barnabas's bones, vigilantly guarding the remains of his twin and often wishing he was alone so that he could look at them again, just to get used to his brother's being gone.

When the *camión* reached the city, he and Dulcinea checked into one of the world's cheapest five-star hotels and went upstairs. The room was neat and clean, and Dulcinea lay down on the bed. She felt filthy. She wore the same blue sweatpants in which she'd arrived in Huajtata, but now they were brown and stained with Christopher's blood.

Christopher watched her. It seemed like a year since they'd made love. The starkness of death made him hunger for the act that regenerated life, but it would have to wait. His throat and tongue feeling thick, he said, "We forgot to get clothes. I'll go out and buy some."

Dulcinea squinted at him. "Are you all right? Besides Barnabas?"

What was there besides Barnabas?

The urn I'll never find. And there will be another death....

Ignoring her question, he said, "I'll be back in an hour or so. Keep the door locked, okay? I'll let myself in."

He walked through the streets to the steep Calle Sagárnaga hill, where the best tourist shopping was. Many of the shops specialized in Bolivian goods—ponchos, *chulos,* vests, jackets and mufflers—but there was a good ladies' shop. He went in, and he was so filthy that the salesclerks tittered, but he explained that he'd been trekking. His credit cards erased any doubt, and he bought a long-sleeved, powder blue silk dress with smocking on the bodice for Dulcinea. The next day he would take her shopping. After seeing the Aymara skirts and the unworn highheeled sandals in her closet, he'd realized that the greatest kindness would be to let her choose her own clothing. He liked to see her feeling happy and confident in things she'd picked out herself.

In other stores, he replaced the clothing he'd lost in his pack. Then he took the film that had been in Barnabas's camera to a developer. The quality of developing would be inferior to what he could get in the States, but he wanted to leave Barnabas's body in Bolivia. Buried in the churchyard at Chulina.

Besides, he couldn't return to Colorado yet. He needed to find that urn.

Perhaps if he'd had a year to look, it would have seemed possible. But Dulcinea's baby was due in July, and it was already almost April. The quest couldn't have seemed more hopeless.

WHEN SHE HEARD the key in the door of the hotel room, Dulcinea awoke immediately. A moment later Christopher was on the bed with her, holding her, and love quickly stirred their bodies. They undressed each other and took turns in the shower, then spent the rest of the afternoon in bed, avoiding all the thorny topics that could make it hurt to be close. Each needed the other's comfort, and their love had become stronger than the pain.

They were eating dinner in the hotel restaurant that evening when the waiter brought Dulcinea a note written on a folded piece of hotel stationery. She glanced at Christopher, wondering if he was behind it. But he looked as surprised as she was. Who could be sending her a note?

She unfolded the paper.

The handwriting was her father's.

Dulcinea—
Will you please open your sweet heart and come and
sit for a moment with a man to whom you are truly
the most precious thing? All the apologies of my heart
cannot be enough, but I am prepared to make them.

Your Father

Silently, she pushed the note across the table to Christopher. She reached for her bottle of mineral water and
drank some before she looked about the dining room and
saw the small man with a heavy thatch of gray hair sitting
alone at a table by the window. He had been watching her,
and when their eyes met she saw in his not pleading but
simply the look of a person seeing a loved one for the first
time in years.

She turned away.

Didn't Christopher say that Bartola Mayorga had
known all about the urn? Had Mayorga told her father?

It was not like her father to come to her with apologies.
He was not a man who apologized, except for acciden-
tally bumping into someone. He did not apologize for de-
liberate actions.

After swiftly perusing the note, Christopher glanced
across the room at Esteban. As he had when he saw Esteban on the street, Christopher searched inside himself for
anger. He could see the shame and sorrow on Dulcinea's
face even now. But he remembered other things. Friendship and conversation. Favors...

*Could I impose upon you to look in on Dulcinea? She's
so far away now....*

Dulcinea gazed blankly at her plate. She no longer saw
the food. Instead, she saw the scars on Christopher's body.

She saw a cross in a churchyard and the face of her child.

She heard her father saying, *The Hacienda de la Torra is no longer your home.*

How could he speak of apology?

She told Christopher, "I'd like to go up to our room. Will you excuse me?"

Christopher wished he could ease her anguish. "Yes. I'll be right up."

He stood and pulled out her chair for her and didn't sit down until she had left the restaurant.

MINUTES LATER in the hotel room, Dulcinea said, "I could forgive him for what he did to me, but I can't forgive what he let them do to you. He's a sick man."

Christopher lay beside her on the bed, his eyes half-closed in memory. Esteban. Mayorga.

They were two very different men.

After Barnabas was buried, Dulcinea must return to Colorado while he searched for the urn and tried to return it to the shrine, as he had promised her. If he succeeded, he and Dulcinea would be together again.

But what if something happened to him?

Besides him and the baby she carried, Dulcinea's father was her only family.

Immersed in his thoughts, he studied the ceiling. She needed guidance, and he had only feelings. Feelings and memories of his own father and of his grandfather. Memories that had taught him the pointlessness of hatred and the grace of compassion.

"Dulcinea."

"Yes?"

"Maybe your father didn't have control. I used to believe he'd ordered Mayorga to do those things." Believing it was still easier than accepting that Dulcinea's father had believed he, Christopher, wasn't good enough for her. But love for Dulcinea made him merciful. Not convinced—but fair. "I'm not sure anymore, Dulce. When I visited your house, when we used to talk, he always defended Mayorga, calling him a patriot, a dedicated civil servant. I never knew if he really believed that—or wanted to. He was so old-fashioned it was hard to tell." He said at last, "He was blind."

And self-deceit was a kind of evil, too, thought Dulcinea. She lay silent, engrossed in memories of her childhood. She still remembered her sixteenth birthday, when her father had given her Piedro de Toque. That memory had affected her when Christopher gave her Sombra de la Luna. Her father had once treasured her. Christopher still did.

After several minutes, she felt the shifting of the mattress beside her. His hand slid to her stomach over the delicate silk of her dress. Turning onto her side, Dulcinea saw his brown eyes intent on hers.

"You have lots of time to consider what your father said, Dulcinea. Why don't you sleep on it?"

She nodded, watching his lips, wanting him.

Christopher kissed her, and she slid her arms around his neck and clung to him more tightly than he'd ever been held. But as he began to make love to her, all he could hear in his mind was the too-swift passing of time.

THEY ATE BREAKFAST together in the restaurant, and Christopher, who was facing the door, saw Esteban come in. Dulcinea's father looked right at them, as though he'd expected them to be there, and something in his face penetrated Christopher's heart.

Esteban nodded to him. Then his eyes flickered to Dulcinea, and they were full of a father's concern. Checking to see if she looked happy, if she was sitting up straight, if she seemed anemic in pregnancy.

Christopher stared down at the edge of the table and tried to forget that Esteban had come into the room.

He could not.

He's old-fashioned, thought Christopher. Traditional. Esteban had set boundaries and pointed to the writing on the wall. *This is my daughter. She is a virgin. She will marry a gentleman of Spanish descent. Look, visit, enjoy. Do not touch.*

Barnabas had been unfaithful to Dulcinea; he had given her gonorrhea. Her father had tried to protect her from such things. It was in part because of Christopher that she had come to know them.

But if I could have married her...

Though Dulcinea appeared to be studying her menu, Christopher knew she had seen her father. He leaned closer to her over the table.

She looked up, her lips slightly parted.

"Tell me what you want, Dulcinea. I'll do anything."

Her voice was inaudible to him, but he read her lips.

"I want my father."

Christopher set his napkin on the table and got up. Esteban had taken a small table near the window, near the street. A seat for a man who liked to watch people pass.

He seemed to sense Christopher coming but didn't look up until Christopher reached the table. His mouth seemed uncertain whether to smile or speak or frown. His eyes were like Dulcinea's.

"*Buenos días, señor,*" said Christopher. "Your daughter and I wondered if you would join us for breakfast this morning."

Esteban de la Torra stood up and met Christopher's eyes. He radiated a powerful presence for a small man. "Thank you. I would be honored." His eyes watered.

Christopher thought of how he had run from the ruin that day, from fear of an old friend he had ceased to trust. Abandoning the woman he loved.

This man had abandoned her, too.

Unable to make further gestures, Christopher said only the obvious. "We're sitting over here."

DULCINEA MOVED her seat so that she could sit adjacent to Christopher rather than across the table from him. When her father came to the table, she didn't meet his eyes. Her heart burned with long-ago shame and horror. He had cast her aside. He had ceased to take care of her. He had washed his hands of her because she'd made love with Christopher.

With anyone before marriage.

She knew it would take many more years of her life to get over it. He had made her feel cheap, worthless. She had told herself she was. And she had married a man who treated her that way.

Christopher sat down, and his eyes met hers. Noticing that she'd changed seats to be closer to him, he nestled his calf against hers under the table, trying to comfort.

Dulcinea made herself look at her father.

Esteban's eyes had been waiting for hers to lift. She saw he'd been crying, but his manner was very courteous and kind as he said, "You look so lovely, Dulcinea. Just like your mother. I hope you are feeling well?"

Dulcinea burst into tears.

THEY HAD PASTRIES and tea with Esteban, who said he was living at the hotel in La Paz for the present because so much of his business was here. He was dealing in gems now, and he had an office downtown. Christopher asked him where it was, knowing he would visit sometime when he was alone. Dulcinea's father told him the address, and

Christopher realized that Esteban, too, wanted to talk in private.

Dulcinea finally spoke to say that Christopher had given her a very good horse, and they talked about Sombra de la Luna and other horses. After half an hour Esteban excused himself, leaving them alone, as though he knew the brief visit had been enough for everyone.

Leaving the restaurant with Dulcinea, Christopher asked, "How was that?"

She wished she knew the words to say what he was to her. "It was good," she replied. "Thank you."

"*De nada.* I have to go pick up some photos. Would you like to come?"

THE PHOTOGRAPHS were a final memento from Barnabas. On the roll Christopher had used to take pictures of the wrecked airplane were photos his brother had shot before his death. Christopher wanted those photos. He wished he had chosen to have them developed in the United States, where the processing was better, but it was too late.

When he and Dulcinea reached the print shop and the proprietor produced the packet, he hoped that the developing would be better than he had reason to anticipate.

It was.

The intense green of the jungle reproduced on the photographic paper seemed miraculous. But the picture on top was of the skeleton in the cockpit.

Dulcinea saw Christopher's face as he examined the photo, then flipped to the next. She couldn't take away his pain, so she touched his back once, then moved away to give him more privacy with his feelings.

Christopher barely noticed. He hurried through the ghastly pictures he had shot himself to those Barnabas had taken before his death. He studied each before moving on to the next.

Barnabas's last shot showed a waterfall. Then came the stone structure of a ruin, barely visible within a green jungle. Examining the pictures, Christopher told himself that it was better to have these shots than pictures of Barnabas. This was like looking through his brother's eyes, seeing what Barnabas had found worth photographing.

A snake in a river.

A passion flower.

But then, like an arrow to his heart, there *was* a picture of Barnabas. Smile ablaze. Sweetly, brilliantly alive as he never would be again except in this two-dimensional medium.

He was holding a golden urn.

CHAPTER FIFTEEN

CHRISTOPHER STARED at the image, his eyes stinging. The photo was an interior shot with a dark backdrop, taken with a flash. Barnabas sat on a stone wall, his head back, grinning, his arm draped around a golden urn beside him. An urn molded with the face of Occlo, the moon. An urn Christopher had seen once before in his life.

Without looking at the rest, Christopher put all the photos in the envelope and checked to see if the negatives were there. Then, he smiled at the shopkeeper. "¿A como?"

The man told him how much it cost, and he paid for the developing and then he and Dulcinea left the shop and stepped out to the street. The day had grown cold. Christopher tucked the photos into an inside pocket of his parka and put his arm around Dulcinea's shoulders. Voice low, he said, "Barnabas had the urn. There's a photo. Let's go to the hotel."

Dulcinea's heart beat hard and fast. Barnabas *had* had the urn.

Their hotel room had been made up in their absence, and Christopher checked their belongings. The pack containing his brother's bones seemed undisturbed, but on the dresser sat a bouquet of flowers with a card attached.

Dulcinea eyed him questioningly.

"Not from me."

She approached the bouquet slowly, removed the card from the envelope and read it.

Thank you for the lovely gift of your company. Your Father.

After a moment she replaced the card.

"Your dad?"

"Yes."

Without comment, Christopher sat down on the bed and opened the packet of photographs. Dulcinea joined him on the edge of the mattress.

Bypassing the shots he had taken of the wrecked plane, he brought up the photo of Barnabas and the urn. *Tell me this was taken with a tripod and timer,* he silently begged his brother, *and that you showed no one else the urn.* He remembered the letter he'd burned. Barnabas had wanted to meet him in Trinidad. He would have shown him the pictures. Breaking the curse...

But he examined the photograph of Barnabas and the urn with foreboding. In the picture Barnabas stood before a black stone wall carved with an image of a circular disk. The wall was made of large blocks.

Christopher inhaled sharply. He knew what his brother had done. This explained everything—including the location of the urn.

As he studied the photo, words funneled through his mind, Mariano Choqueneira's descriptions in his journal of a shrine cut from the stone of a mountainside.

Barnabas had returned the urn to the shrine.

The wrong shrine. "He tried to break the curse, and he put it in the wrong shrine."

Dulcinea blinked at the photo, comprehending.

"The walls were cut from existing stone. Hewn from the mountain," said Christopher. "These are blocks." Why had Barnabas meddled in what wasn't his concern?

Answers occurred to him, but he would never know which was right. Had Barnabas wanted to make Dulcinea love him?

Or only to defeat me?

Christopher put his head in his hands, telling himself it was better this way. Barnabas had saved him from having to hold up a museum, which he would never have been able to do. Too afraid of Third World prisons.

Dulcinea interrupted his dismal thoughts. "Let's see the next one."

Christopher moved the photo of Barnabas and the urn and put it behind the others. The next was of Barnabas, too, red-eyed and laughing, bathing in a pool in the shrine, holding a flask in one hand, wearing the lid of the vase on his head.

Dulcinea flushed, mortified for her husband and herself.

Christopher remembered other flasks. And times his brother had passed out on the metal-frame bed in their house in Chulina. Seeing the photo of his twin drunk, he felt embarrassed. Without wanting to, he remembered Barnabas's letter—*I'll buy you a trick*... And he recalled the moment in the pantry in Colorado when Dulcinea had said she had gonorrhea.

Christopher glanced at her.

Her chin was high, her back straight. She did not look at the photo again. "How can you find that shrine? The place where he put it?"

It wouldn't be easy. Christopher slid the picture of Barnabas out of the way so he could see the one beneath it. The exterior of the shrine. Barnabas's tent. *He must have been alone.* Christopher studied the plants around the tent. Plant life was sometimes a good indicator of elevation.

Dulcinea asked, "What about those aerial photos?"

They were in the pack that had been buried in the landslide.

"Chris?"

He glanced at her, thinking of all the things he once had wondered about her and Barnabas. Wondering no more, he said something he had never uttered in his life. "He was an alcoholic."

Dulcinea lowered her eyes. Barnabas had been her husband. He was the father of the child she carried. But what Christopher said was true, and she acknowledged it with a nod.

But she had to say, "He wasn't wicked."

"No."

They were silent. Barnabas's bones lay in the pack in the corner of the room.

Dead, thought Christopher. *Won't come back.* He stared down at the photo, and he could hear his brother's voice in his mind. *I miss you,* he thought.

Dulcinea said, "It was because of me, wasn't it, that he didn't claim his part of the ranch—and his trust. He couldn't face you."

"Hmm. I don't think so." Christopher ran his tongue along his teeth before he explained. "Barnabas... When we were kids, he wanted to fly jets the way I wanted to be a doctor. But he had an eye condition that wouldn't pass muster with the air force. Our grandfather was a physician and had been in the military, and Barnabas..."

His voice trailed off, lost in old loyalty.

Dulcinea nodded, understanding without being told what Barnabas had wanted his grandfather to do, knowing also that Barnabas would have held a grudge over Jonah Gore's refusal.

Contemplating the feelings that had just silenced him, Christopher was reminded of his brother's betrayal. He tried not to envision what angered him most. But he could imagine it too clearly. The woman he loved with his brother. He had to know....

"Did he satisfy you?"

Dulcinea went still inside.

Briefly, she thought of telling him that she couldn't stand the smell of Jamaican rum, that she would always hate it. But the thought was useless. Not every memory was ugly, and Christopher wasn't asking her to say that she loved him the most. Knowing his heart, which was so entwined with his twin's, Dulcinea was sure he wanted something else.

Soberly, she answered. "He was gentle. He thought of a woman's pleasure. In some ways, he was like you."

Her words roused no jealousy in Christopher. Just a comfort he didn't understand. He hadn't expected to want to hear that his brother had tried to do at least one thing right. But the revelation was a balm on his grief. He met Dulcinea's eyes. "You were happy together sometimes?"

She stared down at the topmost photograph of Barnabas, thinking of the baby inside her, trying to remember the last time she'd been happy, trying to remember when she hadn't hated Barnabas but, instead, had felt the complicated mix of feelings that came with marriage, with being invited to see another's flaws.

There was nothing to say but the truth, a truth that would never have happened had she not married Christopher's brother, his twin. "I always missed you." After a pause she admitted, "And so did he."

THEY SPENT THAT DAY and the next getting the death certificate, then packed their belongings and leased a twenty-year-old Land Rover to drive to the Charazani region to bury Barnabas. They spent five hours on muddy roads and reached Chulina in the midst of a hailstorm. Tomás came down to Christopher's house to greet them. He asked to view Barnabas's bones and cried when he saw them.

Christopher considered telling Tomás about Barnabas's having the urn, but discussing the curse with his family had always made him uncomfortable. He couldn't face the shame of having them know he had tried to break the curse and failed.

Once, at the age of twelve, had been enough.

So he talked, instead, about his snakebite and the herbs that had saved his life, and at sunset he and Dulcinea walked up to the churchyard together to see Isabel's grave.

The cemetery was deserted, and they crouched side by side near the plot, and Dulcinea put wildflowers near the cross. Then she knelt and sat back on her heels in the dirt; Christopher squatted behind her with his arms around her and his face against her hair. Dulcinea touched one of his hands, which was against her arm, and they stayed there, feeling each other's warmth.

It was a cool evening, but not unpleasant. Crisp and clear. A pretty sunset.

Christopher said, "I think I'll bring a shovel up here tonight and start digging."

Barnabas's grave.

"Where?" asked Dulcinea. There was a space beside Christopher's father. Another beside Isabel.

Christopher stared at his child's grave, keeping his feelings to himself. His brother had hurt Dulcinea. He wouldn't hurt her, too. Thinking of the snake pit, of his father's boot on his hand, he said, "You're his widow. You decide."

Dulcinea turned, a question in her eyes. A strange vulnerability. She lowered her head, then raised it to look at him, to make sure he heard her. "I want to bury him beside our daughter."

Christopher nodded.

"He would have done his best," said Dulcinea.

To be a father to Isabel. Christopher thought of the child Dulcinea carried. He couldn't tell her what he was feeling—that *he* wanted the chance to do his best for Barnabas's baby.

He had to break the curse.

THEY BURIED Barnabas the next day, then drove back to La Paz so that Dulcinea could catch her plane in the morning.

During the drive, Christopher asked, "Would you like to see your father before you go?"

She'd already decided. "No. I might write to him from the United States. This is going to take...time. I don't quite trust him, Christopher. Though I want to."

So do I, reflected Christopher.

What would he do if he ever managed to return the urn to the shrine? Somewhere were men who'd heard the story he'd told Bartola Mayorga; Esteban might know it, too. If any of them learned that he had broken the curse—that he knew the location of the shrine—they might come after him... or the people he loved.

But if he revealed the location of the shrine to the Bolivian government, would the curse go on? The treasure would be removed from the shrine and taken to a museum.

He and Dulcinea ate in their room that night, then went to bed and made love. As she moved over him, with him inside her, he touched her thighs and her hips and bottom and finally the heat of her belly. Christopher wondered if this was one way a man came to love a child not his own. It was feeling less and less like Barnabas's baby. More like part of Dulcinea. In other words, his.

He pushed deeper inside her, in love with her, telling himself it would be okay, they would be together again. He had known agony and he'd known grief.

But there were other things on that road.

He knew because he had held them. Now he wanted to claim them for his own.

CHRISTOPHER SAW HER into the airport and stayed near as she dealt with customs officials. Then they waited together for the plane. He gave her a hug and a kiss for Mrs. Prosper and many more for herself, and while he was holding her the baby kicked. Spreading his hand on her abdomen, Christopher thought, *You, too.*

Dulcinea put her arms around his neck and her face against his throat. "Promise, you'll come back before the birth. No matter what."

Even if I fail. Christopher nodded.

"Call."

"I can't help myself." He kissed her.

THINKING OF HIS BROTHER who'd loved to fly, loved any kind of plane, Christopher watched the jet leave, and then he climbed into the rented Land Rover and drove back to La Paz, trying not to feel as though his heart had been severed.

He reached the city at three o'clock and went to Esteban's office. It was on the street where he had seen Esteban once before. Behind a window guarded by iron bars, polished gemstones gleamed.

When Christopher opened the door, a bell tinkled, and as his eyes adjusted to the darkness, he saw Esteban rise from a desk in the back of the showroom. With an expression that seemed to mingle caution and hopefulness and warmth, Dulcinea's father stepped forward. "*Buenos tardes,* Cristobal."

Returning the greeting, Christopher remembered a time it would have been accompanied by an *abrazo,* a warm embrace. Now Esteban stood back from him and indicated some comfortable overstuffed chairs arranged around a table in the rear of the office. "Will you come in?"

"Thank you." Christopher followed him back into the office and sat down. On the wall behind the chairs were photos of horses.

No pictures of Dulcinea anywhere.

Esteban said, "Madeira, was it?"

Christopher hesitated. He was not ready to accept a drink from Esteban. To trust him that far. "Your memory serves you well, but no thank you. I'm fine."

Face subdued, Esteban sat down across from him. Before Christopher could speak, he said, "I so appreciated seeing Dulcinea the other day. Thank you very much. Did she like the flowers?"

"Yes."

During the quiet that followed, Esteban sat with his hands forming a steeple in front of his forehead, as though pondering what he wished to say.

Christopher had already thought it through. His culpability, his responsibility. His part. Carefully, he began to say the words he'd rehearsed many times in his mind. They came out slowly. "I want to apologize to you for what I did six years ago. I . . ." He met Esteban's gaze, remembering feelings he'd buried. The rehearsed apology continued. "I loved her."

But he couldn't go on as he'd started.

"I loved her," he said again, the muscles in his neck almost convulsing. *God,* he thought. *I can't say any more to him.*

But he tried again. For Dulcinea.

Esteban seemed ready to interject something, but Christopher cut him off. "I shouldn't have . . . done what I did. What was in my heart . . ." Touching his own chest, he stared at Dulcinea's father and told him what he'd lacked the courage to say at twenty-four. What Esteban would not have wanted to hear. "What was in my heart was love for your daughter." He made himself say the rest. "But I abused your friendship. It brought pain to all of us."

Esteban turned his head away, then abruptly stood. *"Discúlpeme."* His back to Christopher, he moved toward a rear door and paused there.

When he turned again, Christopher saw that he'd been gathering his emotions. But his voice still shook. "And you, my friend? What happened to you?" The question was rhetorical. *"I* am sorry. I know what was done to you, and I am sorry, Cristobal. I never asked for that."

Christopher sat silent. This wasn't what he had anticipated. He didn't know what he'd expected—except the chance to apologize for his own misdeeds.

"Your brother came to me," said Esteban, "four years ago."

Christopher heard his own breath.

Dulcinea's father sat down, putting his hand under his chin. "He said that he was married to my daughter and that he was the brother of the man I had put in the hands of Bartola Mayorga." A look of pain twitched over his face. "He told me what had been done to you."

Jonah must have told Barnabas, Christopher reflected. Christopher had told his grandfather everything. Showed him everything. Jonah had been a surgeon in the Korean War. Shockproof.

Esteban watched him, his eyes penetrating. "I think it is discourteous to mingle explanation with apology for something inexcusable. The same goes for contemplating what might have been. So I will simply apologize for the way I treated you, in making known to you that you were not the prospect I wanted for my daughter. I have come to deeply regret my small-mindedness."

Christopher said nothing. He had never been ashamed of his heritage. He wouldn't apologize for it now. But he wondered about Esteban's words.

He had to know. "What would you have done if I had asked to marry her?"

The room seemed dark, the silence terrifying.

Esteban's eyes locked on his, and Christopher knew that he understood every implication of the question.

Lifting his eyebrows with an expression of resignation, the older man replied, "I don't know."

It wasn't a comfortable moment. But they both had to live with the past—and, at least distantly, with each other.

Christopher got up to leave. When Esteban stood, he held out his hand. "Thank you."

Eyebrows drawn slightly together in a troubled expression, Esteban shook his hand. Silent. Inscrutable.

Christopher said, "Goodbye."

The other man didn't answer, and at last Christopher turned his back to him. Once he would have been afraid to do that. The sensation of exposure was still there.

"Cristobal."

Christopher had almost reached the door. He turned.

Esteban hurried toward him, carrying something. Christopher recognized the weave of the faded woven cloth and the shape it had taken when filled with herbs and the contents of his *mesa*. It seemed to contain those things still. It looked as it had when he'd parted from it six years earlier.

He stepped toward Esteban, and as Dulcinea's father gave him the medicine bag, the old bag Christopher had used as an apprentice, their hands touched again. There was more friendship in the brief contact of skin than in the handshake they had just shared.

"Muchísimas gracias."

"Por nada," said Esteban. "It is yours."

Christopher put the bag over his left shoulder and held out his hand again.

Esteban disregarded the gesture. "I want to thank you, Christopher, for giving Dulcinea a horse. I know that made her happy. She seems well cared for."

They were lingering words, and Christopher sensed they were intended to draw a promise from him, that he would marry Dulcinea. That he would continue to watch over her.

The promise came. Low. "I love her."

Esteban nodded. "Good."

Their eyes held for a moment. Then Dulcinea's father, small and old, reached out and embraced Christopher. *"Vaya con Díos, mi hijo."*

My son.

FERDY MET DULCINEA at the airport in Grand Junction the next day. Kitty, he said, had wanted to come, as well, but it was her morning to work at the historical museum.

Gazing out the window of Ferdy's Ford Ranger, Dulcinea tried to adjust to the strange countryside she'd almost forgotten—long, high desert mesas, which rose to pasture and farmland and from there to the beautiful mountain valleys below the San Juans. She hadn't been away three weeks, but the snow had melted and spring had come. The grass in the pastures was emerald.

This is my home now, she thought. Zipped into a pocket of her parka was Barnabas's death certificate. It made half of Thistledown Ranch hers. She couldn't stand thinking about the other half. She wished she'd never agreed to leave Christopher's side.

To take her mind off him, Dulcinea asked Ferdy about Sombra and received a delighted, approving grin. "Oh, I expect she's itching for a ride about now."

Dulcinea clung to that thought, to seeing the horse she loved. The days would pass. She turned her eyes to the snowcapped peaks and picked out Mount Sneffels as its craggy range appeared, and then she waited for Thistle-down Ranch, her home.

ON THE FIRST DAY Dulcinea was gone, Christopher visited the La Paz offices of a petroleum company and said he was a doctor interested in plant life of the Yungas region. Would they be willing to share with him any copies they might possess of aerial photos of the Yungas?

They were accommodating, and he left the office with a packet full of photos in forty-five colors, all highlighted to show different shades of green in the vegetation. A key suggested which places were known to hide rock outcrop-pings, caves and minerals.

Christopher bought new maps and spent a week in his hotel room making notes. He studied Barnabas's photos and showed several people the pictures of the waterfall and the exterior of the ruin to see if anyone recognized it. No one did, but he remembered his twin's letter and the men-tion of Trinidad and decided to try there.

A week after Dulcinea had left La Paz, he caught a plane for the Amazon Basin and the river city of Trinidad.

There, he found a clean hotel, but he took to closing the zippers of Barnabas's pack with locks he'd bought in La Paz, and he chained the entire bag to a heavy dresser whenever he left his room. He showed the waterfall photo in taverns, explaining that he had recently lost his brother and wanted to see the places Barnabas had visited.

Nobody recognized the places in the photos.

On the night before he planned to leave, he walked sev-eral blocks to dinner, and on the way home he noticed two prostitutes outside a bar. The Jaguar.

Barnabas had wanted to meet at the Jaguar.

Christopher stood across the street for some time. A military jeep pulled up outside the bar. The prostitutes got in, and it roared away. But through the window Christopher could see other women working the room, soliciting patrons. Who had Barnabas liked?

Someone who had venereal disease. Probably, they all did.

Christopher wandered slowly back to his hotel.

In his room he sat on the bed for a while, thinking. Then he got up and opened one of the locks on his pack to remove several syringes and vials of penicillin. He put everything in a waist pack he carried in front of him to discourage pickpockets, and after that he secured his room and went down to the street and through the steamy night to the Jaguar.

SHE SPOKE TO HIM in English. "Hello. Can I help you somehow tonight?"

Christopher sat at a corner table, and the prostitute with dyed red hair and oak-colored skin was the first to approach him. She had a mole on her upper chin and a body he could easily appreciate, and her perfume smelled like raspberries. Her smile was broad and white.

Christopher smiled back. He answered her in the language she had chosen. "I don't know. Have a drink with me and we'll see. I'll buy."

She grinned. "All right."

Christopher asked her what she drank, got up and went to the bar, and bought two rum-and-Cokes. He raised his glass and she lifted hers, too.

Knowing that the look on her face would give him an answer, he dived in. *"Me llamo Christopher Choqueneira. ¿Conoces mi hermano, Barnabas?"*

She drew back slightly, then smiled a little and shrugged.

Christopher ran his tongue lightly over his teeth. "Let's go upstairs."

Her smile deepened to a grin.

HER NAME WAS LUR, and she recognized the waterfall in the photograph but not the stone building. She gave Christopher directions to the waterfall. She reacted little to the news that Barnabas was dead, and Christopher recognized the absence of feeling behind her gaze—in her case, an occupational hazard. Prison made him the same way. But his grandfather had given him reason to feel again, made sure he resumed his life, completed his residency.

And Dulcinea had given him back his heart.

"So," he told Lur at last. "My brother had gonorrhea. I have some penicillin with me. Would you like to be treated?"

Her smile was teasing. "Are you asking me to take off my clothes?"

Christopher grinned. "And if you send the other girls up, I'll do the same for them."

"Thank you, *Doctor*. And if there's anything we can do for *you* . . ."

Christopher thought about the waterfall. "You already have."

THE WATERFALL was near the village of Béni. At the village he learned the location of the ruin but was told it was a place of bad luck; no one went there.

Christopher's relief was great. *No one went there.*

A two-hour hike from the village, the ruin turned out to be an abandoned bath, the urn its only treasure. Christopher scoured the wet room with his headlamp. Water trickled from a fissure in the wall and into a pool rimmed with stone blocks. Overflow ran out a hole at the base of the rock. Though the chamber was warm, the water was cold as the moon.

The vase stood where Barnabas had left it, beside the pool. When Christopher saw it, his heart raced. The soft gold was dented, reminding him of when he'd thrown it out of the snake pit, but it was the same urn he'd seen before. He lifted the lid, looking for snakes, and inside he saw a scrap of paper. Cautiously, he reached in, grasped it and pulled it out. With the light from his lamp, Christopher read what his twin had written.

For my brother, Cristobal, whose hair is like the sun.

Christopher sank down on the edge of the pool where Barnabas had taken some of his last photographs. He sat there quietly, sweat streaming from his face, his body light and airy.

Barnabas had to have known that he'd found the wrong shrine. He'd never read Mariano's journal, but he wasn't stupid. Had he figured that returning the urn to any place consecrated to the moon would break the curse?

There was a kind of logic to that idea. It didn't convince Christopher, but what Barnabas had done made him want to cry. If his brother had sold the urn on the black market, he could have bought himself a new plane. Instead, he had tried to fix what Christopher, who had been tortured in Bartola Mayorga's prison, could not.

Christopher recalled what Esteban had said about his visit from Barnabas and suddenly wondered if he'd found the true motive behind what his twin had done. When Barnabas had learned he was in prison, he'd been upset enough to accuse Esteban de la Torra. He might have felt guilt about marrying Dulcinea.

Was trying to break the curse his way of making amends?

Christopher folded up the note and put it in a plastic bag in an inner pocket of his parka. He remembered the letter he'd burned. Not his last communication from Barnabas, after all.

Some time later, he took off his clothes and did as his brother had and got in the water. It wasn't too bad, but he could see Barnabas's face in the photograph and knew he'd been laughing at the cold. Christopher wished he could talk to him again.

He wished they were there together.

DULCINEA TRIED to keep her mind off Christopher and the curse and her fears.

She planted flowers in beds outside the house, and she and Kitty worked together on a crib quilt for the baby. It was good having the other woman at the ranch, Dulcinea decided. She finally told Mrs. Prosper about Isabel—even that she was Christopher's daughter—and Kitty listened sympathetically, unshed tears in her eyes.

They were compatible housemates, neither of them obsessively talkative, both thoughtful of the other. As the days wore on, Dulcinea began to wonder if Christopher would mind if Kitty stayed on after he got home. She would like it, and Kitty would like it because she was estranged from her only daughter and had no grandchildren.

If only the birth went right...

Christopher called in mid-April to say that he had the urn, but weeks passed before he called again, early on a Sunday morning from the hotel in La Paz where he and Dulcinea had stayed.

Lying in his bed, wanting him nearer, Dulcinea asked, "Are you...done?" Breaking the curse.

Christopher made a small sound like a laugh, trying not to think of the frustrations of the past weeks. Trying to quiet his own fears so she wouldn't feel them. "No." Af-

ter a moment he said, "I just wanted to wish you a happy
Mother's Day."

Dulcinea clutched the covers against her. "Thank you.
That's the nicest thing anyone's..." She thought of Sombra. Christopher had done all the nicest things in her life.

Briefly they caught up on news—that she had written to
her father and received a long and very kind letter in return. That she was still going into the clinic every day until noon to help do paperwork. Without Christopher in the
office, however, the work bored her. She yearned for
something else, and she knew what it was. He was on the
phone. Why not ask?

"Would you mind if I bought another horse—or two?"

At the other end of the line, Christopher tried to trans-
port himself to her world, to imagine what she was thinking. "Buy as many as you like. But you're getting kind of
big to ride."

"I'm not riding. I just work Sombra in a circle—longeing. Are you sure I can buy more?"

"Dulcie, it's your home."

"Yours, too." *Come home.*

He wanted to come home. But he was in a darker place
than she was. A place with less hope. He said, "I love you.
I have to go now."

Only when she asked him to set a time to call again did
he hear the fear in her voice. It made him feel closer to her,
and he told her again, "I really love you, Dulcinea. I'll try
to be home soon."

DULCINEA BOUGHT a Paso colt named Cuanto de Julio
and looked for a *challon* to train him. Not finding one, she
began the gentle process of starting the horse herself, until Ferdy objected because of her pregnancy. If Dulcinea
would instruct him, Ferdy said, he'd start the horse. As the
colt's training began, Dulcinea's days filled with hope.

Thistledown Ranch would be a perfect place to breed and train Peruvian Pasos. After she had the baby, she could do more of the work herself. *After she had the baby...*

She changed little inside the house, but in one of the photo albums in the parlor, she found a picture of Christopher when he was four, and she framed it and put it on the dresser in his mother's room. There was also a recent picture of him on top of a mountain with his grandfather, and she framed that one, as well, and kept it beside his bed, where she slept.

Sometimes she saw him in her dreams. Not bad dreams anymore. Just the strange dream with the tent in a field of flowers. Christopher was there. Everything would be all right, because he was there....

HE FOUND THE SHRINE on the first of July, by accident.

Since retrieving the urn from the place where Barnabas had left it, he had begun systematically checking every spot that the aerial photographs had indicated might hide a ruin. For transportation, he'd used a dirt bike, which he had bought in La Paz, and over three months he had found seven ruins, all known to the villagers who lived nearby. None was the moon shrine.

He stepped into the moon shrine while walking to a stream to get water for his camp, and his first reaction was that it was a trap set by a hunter. Hastily, he withdrew his foot, and then he saw that the top of the hole was made of stone, overgrown with moss.

His pulse beating irregularly, Christopher shrugged off his pack and set it on the ground. The urn was all it contained. He took the urn, like his medicine bag, everywhere, every minute of the day, even when he would be only yards from camp, even when he was sure there was no one about for miles. The urn had become not just the object but the symbol of his duty, and he had married himself to it.

Christopher crouched down to inspect the hole. The stone at the top of the opening was perfectly flat, and it took him just a few minutes to realize that he was touching the top of a doorway—to a structure that had been buried by a landslide.

His heart raced. Kneeling beside the hole in the afternoon shadows with the constant whine of mosquitoes around him, he knew where he was, and for a moment he just stared into the black opening. It was big enough to slide his body inside, but it reminded him uncomfortably of the snake pit where the urn was once hidden.

At last he drew his headlamp from the pocket of his parka and shone the light down in the hole. The doorway was filled with mud.

This has to be it, he thought again.

Christopher glanced at the sky. Though winter had come, it was still wet in the Yungas. Now, however, as the light faded, the sky was only faintly gray above the canopy.

Christopher took the urn from his pack and left the pack where it lay. With a faith he was glad he didn't have to explain to anyone else, he donned his headlamp, then pushed the heavy gold urn into the cavelike opening. His medicine bag over his shoulder, he crawled in after it, moving on his belly like a snake. But feeling like a man entering a woman.

AT TWO O'CLOCK on July first, Dulcinea stood in the hot sun with Ferdy as he explained, "Well, Christopher usually rents out all the stalls for the rodeo in Ridgway. We take the horses up to our pasture near Yankee Boy Basin and bring 'em down for the Fourth of July so they're safe at home during the fireworks."

As Ferdy waited for her to tell him to do what Christopher had always done, Dulcinea thought about Sombra de la Luna. That morning, when she was longeing the filly, some kids out on the road had been setting off firecrackers. It had frightened all the animals. The dogs had hidden in the barn, and Sombra had become skittish. Maybe she'd be happier up in the mountains. Ferdy would bring her home before the fireworks on the Fourth.

And Christopher was supposed to call on the fifth. Dulcinea thought of the curse—and of the white hospital with the birthing room he'd promised her was blue.

She opened her mouth to ask Ferdy to take the horses to the mountain pasture, but the words didn't come out. A wave of pleasure went through her, a strange sensation curling up her spine. The baby moved, and Ferdy noticed the slight jump under her long rayon sundress. He laughed. "There goes your boy."

The pleasant sensation stayed with her, explained only by the beautiful summer day. Dulcinea finally managed to speak. "Yes, Ferdy, please make room in the barn for the rodeo horses."

But she was thinking of the promise Christopher had made—that he would come home before her baby was born.

WHEN HE REACHED the chamber where the mud ended, where he could stand, Christopher shone his headlamp around the walls.

In the beam the dark world of the shrine glittered, and ahead of him, embedded on the wall, he saw a giant silver disk and a golden sun. As he continued to look about, faintness and fear washed over him. He had never seen a richer room. Too rich. Priceless.

The road we saw . . . was one of agony and grief.

Christopher removed his medicine bag from his shoulder and reached inside for his coca pouch. Carrying the urn and the pouch, he made his way to the wall beneath the sun and the moon. He could see where the urn belonged, because its brother urn, which showed the sun, sat opposite.

Christopher carefully set the urn in its place, and then he chewed some coca and after a time removed the wad from his mouth and set it on the shelf between the two urns, a traditional offering to the shrine.

He sank to the ground and sat there among the gold and silver, contemplating the violence of greed that had run through the blood of the Spaniards.

Have to plan...

He'd replaced the urn. Now the curse should be broken.

But at what price to himself? He didn't want to return to Sneffels with the fear that someone would pursue him, wanting to know where to find the shrine. Willing to kill for it.

Numbly, he stared at the coca he had left between the two urns. How could he know if it was safe—curse-wise—to reveal the location of the shrine to the government? To let the treasure be removed? Was he to be the shrine's protector—at the cost of his own happiness?

The intense solitude of his situation weighed on him, as being the Son-With-Hair-Like-Inti had weighed on him his whole life. No one could answer his questions except, perhaps, the deity of the shrine.

I won't bow to you, he thought, addressing Occlo, addressing all gods who might have taken his child—who hadn't stopped her from dying. *I can't believe in you.*

In the warm darkness he remembered all he had seen in the past months—his child's grave and his brother's bones and reconciliation with an enemy who was once a friend.

Most of all, Dulcinea and the love that had made him want to nurture and protect her baby—the baby she and his brother had conceived.

Love.

It was divine, and he let it guide him, as it had guided him to this place.

CHAPTER SIXTEEN

El Cuanto de Julio (Fourth of July)

THREE DAYS LATER Dulcinea sat in the old rocking chair in Christopher's mother's room, trying to sew together a baby sweater she'd made. Rocking ... and waiting.

Christopher would call the next day, but the hours till then felt long. It was the Fourth of July, and Kitty had gone to a picnic in town. Ferdy's wife had invited Dulcinea to another, a potluck at their house. But something kept her rooted to home. Maybe just that she didn't want to hear anyone ask when the baby was due ...

It can't happen again. Oh, God, where was Christopher?

Dulcinea had been upset ever since Ferdy had taken Sombra to the mountains. But he would bring the Paso home soon. It was after five already.

Her heart gave a beat of relief when she saw the truck hauling the seven-horse trailer down the driveway. Laying the sweater on top of the grandmother's-fan quilt on the bed, Dulcinea rose clumsily to her feet and went downstairs.

Ferdy was unloading Cuanto de Julio and Rayo de Luz from the trailer, while Christopher's dogs anointed the tires. As he tied the horses to the outside of the vehicle, Dulcinea approached and peered into the trailer, looking for Sombra de la Luna. She saw Tinkerbell, Christopher's quarter horse, and Mística, his Paso mare. Ferdy's Appaloosa, Kempo, was there, too.

Ferdy met her eyes.

"Where is she?" whispered Dulcinea.

"I couldn't find her. I just came down to leave the others and call my wife to say I wouldn't be home. I'm going back up to look for her."

He'd miss the Fourth of July potluck his wife had planned. As though echoing Dulcinea's reflection, a bottle-rocket whistled somewhere off to the south. The dogs raced for the barn, where she knew they would cower under the old chicken coop.

Sombra would be frightened. What if Ferdy couldn't find her?

Concealing her own fear, Dulcinea said, "No. Go on home, Ferdy. I'll—" She stopped herself in time. "We can look for her tomorrow."

Ferdy lifted his eyebrows. "You shouldn't go up there. And don't you want me to keep looking tonight?"

Dulcinea hesitated. Should she ask him to go back up to the pasture? "Where do you think she went?"

"There are a lot of trees. I don't think she got off our land—unless there's a gate open somewhere."

Don't be dead, Sombra, thought Dulcinea. If she lost the Paso, it would be worse than losing Taita. If Sombra had gotten caught in the trees or... What if the fireworks made her panic and she hurt herself?

Dulcinea knew she should ask Ferdy to go back up and look for the horse. But if he hadn't found Sombra yet... "No, you go on home."

"I'll be here when the sun rises," he promised. "Now, you call if you need anything."

THE MOMENT his truck drove out the gate, Dulcinea went inside. She wrote a note for Kitty, then assembled warm clothes, food and water. Last, she backed the Cherokee up to Christopher's smaller horse trailer and hitched it.

By 6 p.m., she was off, driving the narrow Politician Mine Road, which wound along a sheer drop-off to a deep river canyon. The scenery was spectacular. Evergreens reached for the sky along steep slopes, and wildflowers bloomed beneath rock overhangs on the roadside. As she climbed higher, past the ghost town of Bullion, the river became level with the road. They rose together, and there were low hillocks of green grass dotted with wildflowers in a quilt of colors. She saw flowers whose leaves were such a delicate white and lavender they seemed almost transparent.

Many people were up in Yankee Boy Basin for the weekend, and Dulcinea passed numerous cars before she turned up the rutted Thistledown Road that led eight miles to the pasture where Sombra de la Luna had been lost. Hers was the only vehicle. People had heeded the signs reading Private Road, and as the track worsened, Dulcinea began to wonder if she should have let Ferdy drive back up, after all. She reached the pasture without incident, but the sun had long since dropped out of sight over the mountains. The fireworks could start at any time.

Taking a flashlight and a water bottle, she climbed heavily over the pasture fence and walked carefully out into the meadow, calling for Sombra. She had walked for just twenty minutes when she heard the sound of the first fireworks from town. Peering up at the mountains to look for the colored lights in the sky, she saw the full moon rising.

THE AIRPORT VAN had let Christopher off at the driveway, and he walked up the dark road in the moonlight, carrying his pack. He could hear whistling and yelling and firecrackers from town. There would be a big Fourth of July street party, a Sneffels tradition. The firemen would try to knock each other down with spray from their hoses, and the sidewalks would be lined with tourists.

Christopher hoped Dulcinea had stayed home. Silver Street on the Fourth of July wasn't a great place for a pregnant woman.

He hadn't reached the house before he realized the Cherokee was gone. She and Kitty must be in town for the fireworks. Which of them, he wondered, had planted those delphiniums and snapdragons and bachelor buttons?

He was vulnerable, so keenly did he feel this homecoming—to a home shared with others. With his beloved.

The kitchen door was open, and Christopher let himself in, thinking to tell her she should lock it. He set down his pack in the pantry and began walking through the house, feeling like an intruder. She hadn't moved anything. But there was a book of baby names on the kitchen table, along with her prenatal vitamins, and her sweater was slung over the back of a chair.

Upstairs, he saw that she'd been sleeping in his room and that there were pictures of him there. In his mother's room, he found the baby sweater she'd been finishing. It was soft, pale blue wool with yellow cuffs, and Christopher spent a moment touching it, imagining a baby wearing it, tiny hands curled up against the cuffs.

Wishing he had a car to drive into town to look for her, he returned to his room and called Ferdy. There was no answer.

Christopher hung up. What should he do?

He could ride one of the horses into town.

An uneasiness he couldn't explain had begun to come over him, and it intensified as he went downstairs and stepped outside and saw the corrals and meadow lit by the full moon.

Was it possible she was at the hospital in labor?

He hurried to the barn, glancing about the yard. He saw the seven-horse trailer parked in its usual spot.

Where was the smaller trailer? And where were the dogs?

Puzzled, he started toward the barn. The rodeo horses should be gone. Ferdy would have brought the Thistledown horses down from the high pasture.

In the barn, Christopher heard whining and jingling tags. First Lake, then Sancho slunk out from under the vacant chicken coop. Smiling and greeting them affectionately in Spanish, Christopher crouched down to embrace them and rub their fur. They licked his face joyfully, tails wagging, until the next volley of fireworks sent Sancho scrambling back to his den. The Great Pyrenees huddled near his master.

With the dog underfoot, Christopher checked the stalls, pausing when he saw a black Paso colt with four white stockings. "Who are you? Did Dulcinea buy you?" The horse put its nose over the edge of the stall, and Christopher petted him before moving on. There was Tinkerbell and Rayo and Mística. Where was Sombra de la Luna?

Leaving the dogs in the barn, he went back to the house to call Ferdy again. This time, he got an answer. "Who did you say this is?"

"Christopher. I'm calling from Thistledown." Forestalling questions, he asked, "Ferdy, where is everyone? It looks like Dulcinea's gone somewhere with Sombra, taking the horse trailer."

"*What?*"

Minutes later Christopher hung up the phone, and it was then that he spotted the note weighted down with a glass on the kitchen counter.

Dear Kitty,
I've gone to the mountains to look for Sombra, who

is lost. I have taken a watch and will definitely come
down by midnight. . . .

Midnight? thought Christopher, picturing her navigat-
ing the Politician Mine Road by moonlight.

He packed for an emergency. Clean sheets, herbs from
the stores in the pantry. He took his own pack, still loaded
from his trip, out to the truck, then searched the house.
Surely Dulcinea had bought some things.

There were cloth diapers and a few blankets and baby
clothes in the dresser in his mother's room. Very little. A
few things in gift boxes. Had someone hosted a shower for
her?

Seeing how little there was and knowing why, Christopher pressed his mouth shut hard, trying to hold on to his
emotions. She had been so afraid.

He continued gathering things, and ten minutes later he
took everything to the truck and set out for Yankee Boy
Basin as the fireworks showered from the sky.

OH SOMBRA, thought Dulcinea, *where are you?* She'd been
walking for half an hour, and her back felt tired, but she
didn't want to leave without her horse. She whistled
through the night, and a different whistle echoed back.
Fireworks launched from the mountains to the south of
Sneffels. Crackling filled the air. Dulcinea couldn't see the
fireworks from the meadow—the surrounding mountains
were too near and too tall. She could hear them, however,
and knew they must be frightening Sombra, wherever she
was.

But what if she'd gotten colic up in the pasture?

Walking through the evergreens, Dulcinea finally
reached the fence and realized that it bordered the national forest. She walked beside it calling for her horse and

trying to ignore the rising vibration from the back of her spine, the uncomfortable feelings like menstrual cramps. She walked for another ten minutes before the sensations claimed her attention, and then alarm clanged through her, because she realized what was happening.

Casting her eyes about one last time, calling for the horse, she began walking back to the car. Thirty-six hours, she thought. Last time, it was thirty-six hours.

To the little boy inside her, she said, *Just let me get back to town.*

She quieted a forlornness inside her that she was alone this time too.

CHRISTOPHER TOOK the Politician Mine Road at a local's pace, being careful only to avoid driving off the road. Nonetheless, the winding curves seemed interminable. When he reached Thistledown Road, he had no choice but to slow down because of the ruts.

Dulcie, he thought, *your horse has more sense.*

But he wasn't frightened. Tonight the moon gave him confidence. He remembered how he'd felt as he crawled out of the shrine on his belly and saw the nearly full moon. There was a place inside him that was bruised, that remembered the wounds of childhood. But the world looked different now.

The shrine and all its treasures were in other hands, and he was free, his life his own.

As he spotted the Cherokee and the trailer parked alongside the pasture fence, Christopher breathed a sigh of relief and shut off the pickup's engine and headlights. At once he heard the fireworks shrilling into the sky. Then, *crack-crack-crack-crack-crack.* Grabbing his flashlight, Christopher climbed out of the truck and gazed across the pasture. A long distance away he saw a figure walking slowly in his direction.

Dulcinea.

Hoping her horse wasn't dead, Christopher climbed over the fence and jumped down into the meadow.

Far away, Dulcinea saw him. The moon was shining on his pale hair, and her heart clamored as she recognized the shape of the ranch truck. The cramps had intensified. She had to stop walking and breathe deeply. *A contraction*...

She trembled through it, watching Christopher. She recognized his bright red guide shell, and she knew the way he moved, that tall confident saunter. Now, though, he was running toward her in the moonlight. He caught her in his arms and held her, his body making the necessary allowances for her shape.

Dulcinea's nose filled with his scent, and she pressed her face against his neck. But that low strange force was moving up her spine, a notch at a time, like a snake rising. Backing away from Christopher, she got out the words. "I'm in labor."

She stood very still, breathing, just dealing with the contraction, and Christopher saw the strange primal glow in her eyes, the power that always seemed bigger than anything a man could summon. Silently, he waited, trying to gauge the intensity of the contraction. Hard to tell. Each woman responded differently to labor.

The contraction ended, and he looked at the illuminated digital face on his watch, then at her. He said, "Well, I'm here."

He seemed relaxed and untroubled, not tense and urgent the way Dulcinea had seen him last. He'd come back. And if he had returned...

"The curse is broken," he said. "I'll tell you everything later. Let's concentrate on getting you down off this mountain."

HER WATER BROKE before they reached the pasture fence. Dulcinea felt the tremendous rush of liquid burst over her cotton leggings beneath the oversize, flannel-lined work shirt and pile cardigan she wore. Christopher stopped walking and stared at the dripping water, then lifted his eyes to hers. They both started laughing.

The next contraction sobered them.

Dulcinea asked, "Can we get to the hospital on time?"

Christopher considered and shook his head. They were almost an hour and a half from Sneffels on a bumpy four-wheel-drive road and another half hour from the hospital. "No, we'll have to do it in this beautiful spot you two have picked. Why don't you wait here? I have to get some things from the truck."

There were mosquitoes out, so after Christopher pitched the tent and laid sleeping pads and a clean sheet on the floor, Dulcinea undressed and got inside. Following her and finding a place for her clothes, Christopher saw that she'd been wearing his old cardigan again. He'd tell her sometime. . . .

He had brought several pillows, and he propped them behind her. "Comfortable?"

"Yes." Because *you're* here.

After hanging a small battery-operated safety light from a hook on the tent ceiling and adjusting his headlamp, Christopher pulled on some rubber gloves and deliberately focused on the task ahead.

Dulcinea's voice drifted toward him. "I'm glad you're here. I never wanted another doctor."

She was crying, and he felt warm and tense and fluid at once. Eyes hot, he said, "Don't make me cry, too, all right?"

She was eight centimeters dilated, and he could feel the baby's head at station +2. "Dulcie, I can feel your baby's head." *Your baby.* Barnabas's child. He wanted it to be his, too, but he put away the thought and focused on medicine. After her next contraction, he listened to the baby's heartbeat. One hundred forty. Normal.

"Want some water, Dulce?"

"Yes, please." She shuddered, bracing herself, breathing as another contraction came. She worked her way through it and didn't notice Christopher looking at his watch. As she relaxed, he held a plastic water bottle to her lips and she drank.

He said, "I'm going to slip outside. I have some things to get ready."

Come back soon, she thought. "Okay." As he zipped the tent flap shut behind him, another contraction came. The power surged over her. It was like being in a black hole, out of control. The force took her. It was stronger than her. Her legs tensed, and she didn't know whether she was breathing or not, only that she was getting through it. *I can't do this,* she thought.

She had done it before.

Before...

In the back of her mind were black thoughts of that time. It had gone on so long, and she had known the baby was dead. She had known that when she was done she would have a dead child. She remembered little Isabel's face, her tiny nose and her eyebrows. Christopher's baby...

The tent fly unzipped.

Christopher saw her tears. "Oh, baby." He came in and zipped the tent shut behind him. "Shh. Dulcie. Do you want me to hold you?"

She shook her head, crying. Another contraction came, and the tears flowed through it. Christopher thought, *This is good.* Her mouth was loose, relaxed from crying. The rest of her would be, too. Blinking, holding on to himself, he swabbed her vagina with a warm, moist sterile cloth. He didn't want her to tear. It was her second birth. She should be fine.

He said, "I love you."

"Oh, Christopher, I needed you. And you're here." Her tears were still running, but she was utterly relaxed until the next contraction began. Then he saw her enter a state of no-mind. She went away from him, into some world that was just her and the baby. He was glad she could do that, because he had no nurse or assistant. He needed Dulcinea to be able to do it herself. He knew that she could.

"You're so brave. You're doing great." He had never loved her so much, and again he had to quiet a deep longing in his heart. Later they'd talk.

He checked her dilation again. Ten centimeters. Station +3. Fetal heart rate still 140. Dulcinea wore her anxiety in her eyes, and Christopher told her, "He's doing fine, just what he should be. Textbook-perfect." He smiled reassuringly. "You're ready to push, but I need you not to. Can you keep from pushing?"

"Yes."

Dulcinea held on through the next contraction. Then Christopher helped her up so that he could slide a fresh sheet under her. He went in and out of the tent once. In a few minutes he was kneeling in front of her. At some point, he had shed his shell, and now he was wearing just a faded blue long undershirt and blue jeans. When Dulcinea looked at him, she saw his broad shoulders and his hair tied indifferently behind him, and each time she met his brown eyes, a feeling of comfort went through her. Everything would be okay.

He said, "You can go ahead and push. If you open your knees wider, you'll give him more room."

When the next contraction came, Dulcinea pushed, knowing nothing but the force raging through her.

In the light of his headlamp, Christopher saw the child's head, and again that ripple of wanting went over him.

He wanted this baby.

This baby.

He wanted Dulcinea.

His voice unnatural, he said, "That was perfect."

With three more contractions, the head was crowning, and Christopher used his hands to gently push on the baby's head, to keep it from coming out too quickly. "Easy, Dulcie. Just relax." He touched her gently and he could sense the relaxation of her legs. He said softly, "I love you."

His voice came at her as though in a dream, and warmth rushed through Dulcinea's heart. She looked up at his eyes, and they met hers. He said it again. "I love you." Then, "Take it slow, okay? Let's bring him down a little farther. Gentle push. I think we can keep from cutting or tearing, all right? You're a good mom. You're a good mom, Dulcie. Just go slow."

The rush came over her again, powerful, blocking out everything but her baby being born into the world.

"Nice slow push. Here, Dulce."

Christopher moved her hand between her legs. She touched something velvety and warm that wasn't her. But a part of her.

"There's your baby. Relax. Take a deep breath. You're fine. Everything's fine. You're doing great."

She locked on to his voice as the next contraction swirled through her, consuming everything else in the world, seizing her entire body.

"Push gently... A little harder now."

There was an enormous release, and a small cry escaped her as the baby's head was born into Christopher's hands. Her hands were there, too, and she heard him saying, "Can you feel his head? Take a look at him, Dulce."

Propped up on the pillows, she stared down at the back of the baby's head. It was reddish-blue, with black hair, incredibly small. A creature who *looked* as though he'd come from another world, from a kinder and more innocent place. From purity.

Christopher checked for cord problems and found none. As the baby's head rotated, he wiped fluid from his face with a sterile cloth. Eyes damp, he whispered, "Hi, there," as he used a bulb syringe to suction mucus from the baby's mouth and nose. Pretty newborn... "Hold on, Dulce. Don't push this time. You're doing everything just right. You're a great mom."

She listened to his voice but didn't try to see the baby again. Trust Christopher... trust the baby... trust life... Through the tent skylight, she saw the full moon.

"Okay, a gentle push, just like before."

She pushed, and there was another release. She stung now, from the stretching and release. Feeling the baby slip out of her, Dulcinea looked down. The little boy was wincing but not quite crying. She saw Christopher examine him carefully before he slid the baby up onto her stomach, facedown.

The baby was so calm that a horrible feeling went through Dulcinea. But then she saw the small movement of a breath. Christopher covered the little body with a receiving blanket and smiled at Dulcinea and the newborn lying against her body.

He was busy for the next hour. The delivery of the placenta, cutting the cord, fixing up Dulcinea. One stitch fixed a small tear in her perineum. He gave her several drops of an herbal tincture to prevent postpartum hemorrhage—blue cohosh, shepherd's purse and motherwort. And, though Dulcinea's gonorrhea was certainly gone, he put antibiotic drops in the baby's eyes as an additional safeguard against the blindness the disease could cause in infants.

He bundled up the baby and put him in Dulcinea's arms, then took the placenta outside and used his avalanche shovel to dig a hole in the meadow among some columbines to bury it. The Kallawaya believed the afterbirth was the child's spiritual twin....

When he returned to the tent, Dulcinea was holding the baby's mouth close to her right breast. The newborn wasn't particularly interested, though his eyes were open in the dark, looking at his mother.

Dulcinea had never known such happiness. It reminded her of when Christopher had begun to love her, but there was more contentment in this new emotion. It was pure bliss.

Christopher checked her for bleeding, then examined the baby again. From his bag of supplies, he took a small blue hat, one of the things he'd found in the drawer in his mother's room. It was an old knit-cotton baby hat, and he realized it must have been one he or Barnabas had worn. He had seen it in pictures. But all he said was, "Let's keep his head warm. Snuggle that blanket around him."

There was more to do, but for a few moments, he sat close to Dulcinea, looking down at the baby's face against her breast.

Dulcinea felt him beside her, warm and strong, the sun of her world. "Do you want to hold him?"

"I thought you'd never ask."

Dulcinea watched him take the infant with more practice than she possessed. But the expression in his eyes was new and innocent, as though he was seeing something he'd never known before.

The baby peered up at him with dark eyes, and Christopher touched his tiny hand with one finger. The baby's fingers touched his. He held the child closer, in love with him. "So what's his name?"

Dulcinea's heart heaved a little. She had made herself look at names. But the name had not come to her as Isabel's had. She studied Christopher's profile as he smiled at the newborn, as he touched his cheek.

"Will you please name him?"

Christopher stilled, the matters that had been in his heart for days coming to the forefront of his mind. He met her eyes, a question in his own. "That's something the mother or father should do, Dulcinea."

Her lips were dry. She saw the way he was holding her baby, as though he was afraid someone would take the little boy from him. She remembered his voice coming to her when she was in labor. *I love you.*

"You're my best friend, Chris. I've never been closer to anyone. I want you to choose. Please."

Christopher looked down into the baby's dark eyes and thought of the long journey from which he himself had just returned. It had begun months before, with a walk to Chulina at the side of another healer—and a conversation and exchange of gifts that had later saved his life. He glanced at Dulcinea in the moonlight. "Do you like Gabriel?"

"Yes."

He drew a shallow breath. "And Esteban?"

Dulcinea nodded silently.

"Gabriel Esteban Choqueneira," said Christopher softly. Gabriel gazed up at him.

"It's beautiful," said Dulcinea. "Thank you." She wanted to hold the baby again, and Christopher gave him back to her.

"Just rub your nipple against his cheek. Remind him that you're there. He'll get the hang of it."

Dulcinea tried what Christopher suggested. She felt self-conscious with him watching her, but it was a nice feeling, too. Private. She contemplated Gabriel's tiny hands, his little fingernails. He was so beautiful. "What made you think of Gabriel?"

Christopher told her about the herbalist who had given him the root and leaves of the Madonna lily.

"I'm so glad you chose that name. I will remember the man who saved your life."

Christopher stared at her and the baby. It wasn't fair to ask her now.

He wanted to ask her, anyway.

But she wouldn't meet his eyes. Instead, she tried again to interest Gabriel in her breast. The baby's eyes opened, and his little birdlike mouth reached for her. She trained her nipple toward him. He took it clumsily, trying.

Christopher lost his train of thought. He watched the little hands, the tiny, excited movements of the baby. *I know how you feel*, he thought. *She's the best.*

"Dulcie."

She lifted her eyes from the baby's face. He had lost interest in her nipple and appeared to be comfortable with his face against her.

Christopher's gaze held Dulcinea's. "I went to see your father after I found the shrine." Dulcinea's father had helped him. He would tell her about that later. "He gave his consent."

Dulcinea jerked her head up, her heart pounding, wondering why that meaningless formality should matter. It did matter. It meant that her father had accepted Christopher—and the child who was, however indirectly, of his blood.

"I'd like to marry you."

Dulcinea met his eyes, thinking about his ear. *Hear this*, she thought. "Okay."

"Okay?"

But she just smiled down at her child.

Healed, thought Christopher.

She would never be the woman she'd been at nineteen. Neither of them would want that. But she had regained her spirit, her self-assurance. She knew her worth.

If she didn't, he would show her in every way he could.

During the night, Christopher told her about returning the urn. Asking Lur if she knew Barnabas and giving all the prostitutes shots for gonorrhea. Dulcinea teased him with confidence, and Christopher was glad she knew he was not his brother. He told her about retrieving the urn and hunting for the shrine and finding it. And about coming to the realization that his life would be in danger unless he revealed its location to the Bolivian government. In renewed faith, he had gone to her father and asked first for Dulcinea's hand, then for Esteban's help. Esteban had helped him arrange to reveal the information in a secure group setting, at the university. The treasures including the urn, would be taken to the museum in La Paz, and Christopher had promised to send the original of Mariano's journal, too. The copy he would donate to the Sneffels museum.

While they lay together, both gazing at Gabriel, Christopher said, "You bought a pretty new horse. What's his name?"

A dark recollection shot through Dulcinea. *Sombra.* Where was she?

"I'll find her for you," said Christopher. "Don't worry—it can't help. Tell me about the colt. What's his name?"

"Julio. Cuanto de Julio."

Christopher smiled. Fourth of July. "What are you going to do with him?"

"Train him. If he turns out well, I'll breed him. He comes from a good bloodline." She took a slow breath. "His sire came from Piedro de Toque."

Christopher's heart felt warm. Because of him, she had never finished college. But now... "I like your plans."

They slept with the baby between them, and Christopher got up in the night to help with the first meconium-stained diaper and to check on Dulcinea and the baby. Gabriel had gotten the hang of nursing and of making them both know when he wanted to nurse. He had a good, strong cry and registered strong complaints over the novelty of a diaper. *What do you think you're doing to me?*

In the morning Christopher woke before the sun tipped over the mountains. The world was dewy soft and quiet, and he changed Gabriel's diaper and wrapped him up and took him outside before there was any sun to hurt his eyes, when his eyes could blink open and look up at Christopher. Beside the tent was a patch of pale blue-and-white wildflowers, exotic as orchids. Christopher crouched among them and showed them to the baby. "Columbines."

He remembered that he should show them to Dulcinea, too. But when he glanced toward the door of the tent, she was already sitting up, looking out.

Meeting Christopher's eyes, she echoed the word. "Columbines."

He helped her outside and made a place for her to sit on pads and sheets among the columbines while he cleaned up the tent. He remembered something he'd forgotten the night before. He touched the front of his parka, feeling the small bulge in the inner pocket. He could give it to her now.

But as he emerged from the tent, his eyes caught a dark shape far down the pasture. A horse grazing. Sombra de la Luna lifted her head and looked innocently toward him.

"Dulcie."

Dulcinea saw the Paso and wanted to cry with relief. Her horse.

"I'll catch her in a minute." Christopher reached into his pocket for the box containing the ring her father had given him, the emerald Dulcinea had pawned in La Paz to buy a ticket to Sneffels. Esteban had seen it by accident and bought back the gem he had once presented to *his* beloved.

But the box had shifted to the bottom of Christopher's pocket. On top of it was a plastic bag, and Christopher pulled it out. The bag contained the note Barnabas had left in the urn.

Christopher looked at it, and then he looked at the newborn in Dulcinea's arms. Gabriel was watching him. Christopher read the words again. *For my brother, Cristobal, whose hair is like the sun.*

His eyes turned to the baby and the black-haired woman who held him, and he said softly, "Thank you, Barnabas. Thank you."

BRIDE'S BAY RESORT

UNLOCK THE DOOR TO GREAT ROMANCE AT BRIDE'S BAY RESORT

Join Harlequin's new across-the-lines series, set in an exclusive hotel on an island off the coast of South Carolina.

Seven of your favorite authors will bring you exciting stories about fascinating heroes and heroines discovering love at Bride's Bay Resort.

Look for these fabulous stories coming to a store near you beginning in January 1996.

Harlequin American Romance #613 in January
Matchmaking Baby by Cathy Gillen Thacker

Harlequin Presents #1794 in February
Indiscretions by Robyn Donald

Harlequin Intrigue #362 in March
Love and Lies by Dawn Stewardson

Harlequin Romance #3404 in April
Make Believe Engagement by Day Leclaire

Harlequin Temptation #588 in May
Stranger in the Night by Roseanne Williams

Harlequin Superromance #695 in June
Married to a Stranger by Connie Bennett

Harlequin Historicals #324 in July
Dulcie's Gift by Ruth Langan

Visit Bride's Bay Resort each month wherever Harlequin books are sold.

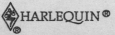

HARLEQUIN ®

BBAYG

HARLEQUIN SUPERROMANCE®

WOMEN WHO *Dare*

They take chances, make changes and follow their hearts!

HOT & BOTHERED
by Ann Evans

Alexandria Sutton is hot on the trail of
Hunter Garrett. She needs to find him; he's
determined to avoid her. Join the chase in this
funny, touching, romantic story. It's a book you
won't want to put down.
Available in July.

Be sure to watch for upcoming titles in
Harlequin Superromance's exciting series,
WOMEN WHO DARE. Each story highlights our special
heroines—strong, caring, brave and passionate women who
know their own minds and dare anything...for love.

Available wherever Harlequin books are sold.

Look us up on-line at: http://www.romance.net

WWD96-6

HARLEQUIN SUPERROMANCE®

SHOWCASE

Do you want to fall in love with a purrfect hero?
To be purrfectly entertained by a purrfectly wonderful
romance? (Or do you just love cats?)

Then don't miss

YOU AGAIN
by
Peggy Nicholson

"Tantalizing and seductively unique. Don't miss
You Again. It's purrrfect!"
—Dee Holmes, author of *His Runaway Son*

"*You Again* is delectable, delightfully different... In a
word, magnificat!"
—Anne McAllister, author of the Code of the West trilogy

"A wonderfully original, thoroughly enchanting tale that is
sure to please lovers of romance and cats alike."
—Antoinette Stockenberg, author of *Emily's Ghost*

"Suspenseful, frequently humorous, and always engaging,
You Again is impossible to put down until the final,
wonderfully satisfying page is turned."
—Kay Hooper, author of *Amanda*

HARLEQUIN SUPERROMANCE®

If you've always felt there's something special about a
man raising a family on his own...
You won't want to miss Harlequin Superromance's
touching series

FAMILY MAN

He's sexy, he's single...and he's a father!
Can any woman resist?

HIS RUNAWAY SON
by Dee Holmes

Detective Burke Wheeler's son is in trouble.
Now he's run away, and Burke and his ex-wife,
Abby, have to work together to find him. Join the
search in this exciting, emotional love story.
Available in July.

Be sure to watch for upcoming FAMILY MAN titles.
Fall in love with our sexy fathers, each determined to do
the best he can for his kids.

Look for them wherever Harlequin books are sold.

HARLEQUIN SUPERROMANCE®

Come West with us!

In Superromance's series of Western romances you can
visit a ranch—and fall in love with a rancher!

In July watch for

She Caught the Sheriff
by Anne Marie Duquette

Let us take you to the Silver Dollar Ranch,
near Tombstone, Arizona.

Rancher Wyatt Bodine is also the town sheriff. But
he's never had a case like this before! Someone's left
a hundred-year-old skeleton in Boot Hill Cemetery—
practically at the feet of visiting forensic investigator
Caro Hartlan. Needless to say, Caro offers to help the
handsome sheriff find out "who done it"—and why!

**Look for upcoming HOME ON THE RANCH
titles wherever Harlequin books are sold.**

Bestselling authors

ELAINE COFFMAN
RUTH LANGAN
and
MARY MCBRIDE

Together in one fabulous collection!

OUTLAW Brides

Available in June wherever Harlequin
books are sold.

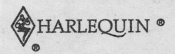